Andena the Rebel

Kin Asdi

Cover drawing: Pixie Cold. www.pixiecold.org
Editing : Ingrid Hall. www.luv2write.net

ISBN: 9082257076
ISBN-13: 978-9082257076

CONTENTS

ACKNOWLEDGMENTS

Writing this book has been an incredible adventure. It started with a crazy idea in my head, and before I knew it, I had a fantastic storyline. I have never previously experienced such passion in my story-telling, and the words flew out of my fingers.

While I was in the midst of writing the book I stumbled on the fantastic work of an artist: **Pixy Cold**. I fell in love with one of her drawings which I instantly linked to the protagonist of this book, Andena. I'm incredibly grateful that she has given permission for me to use the drawing as a base for the cover of this book. Thank you, Pixie!

What would an author be without an editor? My (copy)-editor **Ingrid Hall** has been fantastic by pointing out the flaws and holes in the story. Her editing skills are amazing; manipulating the text without changing the essence of it which is what every author wants from an editor. Thank you, Ingrid!

Last but definitely not least I would like to thank my family who have always been very supportive of me.

PROLOGUE

It was in the year 2212 that the civil war finally ended. That was because of a drastic drop in the oxygen level caused by the sudden eruption of several volcanos. The oxygen was depleted to such an extent that most of the weaponry powered by combustion engines had stopped working and many people had died. The war had lasted for 37 years, enabling the Archon military and political power-base gradually to gain the upper hand.

The rigid and strict regime imposed by this elite was despised but the remaining population of Earth nevertheless soon succumbed in order to survive.

By enforcing a curfew to protect its own members, the Archon still ruled with an iron fist. Although small rebel groups were offering pockets of resistance in an effort to undermine this oppression and establish a free society once again.

CHAPTER ONE

Andena stared into the dirty mirror situated in the bar's toilet. In spite of the fact that she knew it would ruin her efforts to look like an Archon girl, she had a strong urge to thicken the lines on her eyelids.

She shuddered when she remembered the nightmare she'd had in simply acquiring her dangly earrings. She was lucky that the slime ball had passed out before she was completely naked. Her self-brewed liquor had knocked the greasy haired man out cold just before he could lay his filthy hands on her body.

She sighed when she looked appraisingly at her silhouette aware that her figure wasn't as spectacular as Danette's, but pleased that at least the combination of bright green eyes and naturally vibrant red hair never failed to turn men's heads.

Her mission was clear: she was to get the access code

for the main door of section Gamma fifty-four and her boss, Lunn had said that the guard, who knew the code, had a soft spot for red-haired girls. It was her first assignment, a ticket to a better life and was much better than working in a bar where men continually slapped her ass or groped her breasts. She had reluctantly allowed herself to be diminished to a sex object, hoping to get the occasional tip but she rarely left work with more than a few extra credits.

Andena checked her lips and made sure her blouse and bra were straight, thereby enhancing her cleavage. The high heeled boots made her look just that bit taller, and her short skirt accentuated her toned legs. She winked at herself as she whispered, "Go get him!"

Armed with a grubby photograph of the guard she stepped out of the ladies room into the over full cafe hoping that she would be in and out without too much of a delay. It was getting late, and most of the customers were too drunk to notice her slipping past them, and it was with a sense of relief that she stepped into the cold night.

The air was remarkably fresh, and she rejoiced in its richness. Inhaling the concentrated levels of oxygen made her feel a little light-headed. Andena knew that she would be much faster and could run a lot longer than the average security guard based at the Archon quarters. Her apartment was at level eight-hundred-ninety-eight. The buildings had been sealed from the outside atmosphere to provide the necessary oxygen levels because the air in the higher regions did not contain enough oxygen to sustain life.

In the early days the levels had been up to twenty percent, but nowadays they had dropped to nineteen point two percent because all of the nearby volcanoes had suddenly erupted. Mount Merapi and Mount Ontake had claimed thousands of lives, and the high-levels of pollution meant that it was unsafe.

Andena had been born when the level was around nineteen point three five and as such, her body had adjusted to the low levels. When she was five, cars with a combustion engine were rendered useless because they weren't able to start due to the lack of oxygen. That was the moment that all chemical processes which consumed oxygen had been placed under strict rules and regulations. It was also when the hype had started: growing your own plankton to get more oxygen in your living quarters that often resulted in slippery staircases which were covered in a slimy, green substance which emitted a foul stench.

She was grateful for the fact that she had remembered to take her jacket with her because the evening had cooled the air considerably and having to seduce a guy while she felt cold didn't appeal to Andena. The streets were empty at this time of night, and she knew that she needed to hurry if she was to stand any chance of evading the curfew cameras. Two more turns and she would be at the gate of Gamma fifty-four. The heels of her boots reverberated loudly against the walls of the narrow lanes, and she decided to take them off after realising that walking on her tiptoes made the muscles in her calves ache. She shivered for a short moment as she continued barefoot but resigned herself to the fact that it was only going to be necessary for a short distance.

Peeking around the corner, she recognised the young guard from the photo who was pacing back and forward in front of the dark door. Andena thought that he looked even cuter in real life and was impressed by his sharp, chiselled features. His broad shoulders, well-developed chest and strong arms were clearly visible through his tight fitting suit. The bulge in his trousers and the heavily toned muscles on his legs made her body tingle with desire.

She stepped quietly into her boots which were still warm and slipped her jacket off. She knew that he would be distracted by the see-through fabric of her lace bra and blouse. Taking a deep breath, she stepped into the concealed area wiggling her hips just a little more that she normally would. The guard looked up and instantly flicked his helmet light on, finding himself drawn to her breasts which stood out in the light. Caught off guard, she cursed silently but managed to retain her smile, and said in her sultriest voice, "Hi, I think I'm lost. Can you help me please?"

She watched as his face turned first into a smile and then disbelief as she walked closer to him. The extra lighting gave the young man a perfect view of Andena's body and she smiled as she noticed his eyes widening. Gulping, he said in an unsteady voice, "I'm afraid I can't help you."

She knew that he was going to need a little more persuasion and moved closer all the while pushing her chest slowly forward making sure he had a clear view of her attributes. While she was holding her jacket behind her back, she shook her chest making her breasts jiggle, as she purred, "I really would love to push those against you."

Looking up into her eyes, he said hoarsely, "You mean right here?"

She caressed the fingers of the hand holding the rifle and whispered, "I need to be back before curfew, but there is plenty of time for some fun."

He tentatively moved his free hand to her breasts, and she moaned softly as she let him touch them. She nipped at his earlobe with her lips as she whispered, "Let's go inside."

He nodded nervously and turned to the keypad next to the door. He was too blinded by lust to notice Andena studying the movements that he made with his hand as he punched in the code. She was surprised by how simple the code was: nine five four four five nine. She instantly understood the logic behind it all: nine for the 'g' of Gamma and fifty-four for the section number and the order of the last three numbers was a mirror of the first three.

As soon as they were inside the building Andena hugged the man from behind, and started to caress his chest. "I like men who massage my ass," she purred. He longed to turn around, but she hissed. "No! Stay as you are now."

The guard moved his arms awkwardly backwards and travelled down to the small of her back. She bit him softly on his neck and purred in his ear, "Oh yes. That's my boy."

Lunn was sitting behind his desk and irritably straightening his desktop mat. He was annoyed that he had allowed Danette to use his desk when he was out. She always managed to turn the desk into a mess. Logging onto the system, he checked his messages. Danette had left him a short note informing him that assembling the androids was slow work. She still had three androids to finish and wanted to know if he knew of any tricks that would help speed up the process. He smiled as he read the note and shook his head slightly because he thought that her project was ludicrous. He had only gone along with it because the company providing the gear was funding the whole mission.

Lunn was more interested in the message that his technician had left informing him that not only had the latest batch been successfully launched but they were now at their precise location. Everything was still on schedule, and they would complete the ring within six weeks provided they were able to prevent their closest rival from discovering their secret. He leaned back and moved his hands behind his head letting this message sink in. Within two months he would have the ultimate weapon, and there was no doubt in his mind that he would have cause to use it in the very near future.

So far, everything was going according to plan. The preparations for the new headquarters were nearly complete, and there was no reason why they wouldn't be able to move the systems at the scheduled date. Satisfied that everything was under control, Lunn closed his eyes and thought about his plans for the evening.

He was startled by an enthusiastic female voice which sounded just a little too close for comfort. "Mr. Lunn, I have the code!"

He knew it could only be one of the three people who had access to his office today. His highly sophisticated security system had never let him down, and he was pleased that she had managed to enter his office without any problems. Opening his eyes, he saw the beautiful red-haired woman standing in front of his desk. Her bright green eyes glinted and made her sweet smile seem utterly disarming. He had studied her stunning body before: she was slim with pert breasts, full hips, and legs that went on forever. Her full, sensual lips which were painted dark red made her extremely desirable. He felt his groin stir, and as he moved forward, he smiled broadly. He felt ashamed of the fact that he was unable to remember her name, but he quickly started his database to look it up and said, "I'm very pleased that your mission went as planned."

Finding her page he continued, "Why don't you sit down Andena and tell me what you've been doing."

Andena said, "Thank you, Mr. Lunn."

Lunn always shadowed a new recruit on his or her first mission, and he was pleasantly surprised by the amount of preparation that she had put into it. The task wasn't that easy, but he thought she was a natural talent. She had remained unfazed even when the guard had unexpectedly turned his helmet light on. Lunn wanted to hear her version of events, and was curious as to what she would leave out.

He chuckled and said with a dark bronze voice, "You can call me Lunn when we are alone. Anyway, Andena, do start at the beginning."

He loved the way she blushed and wondered if he could get her in his bed someday.

Andena told him her version of events and finished by saying, "After I had given him the reward he was longing for, he was more than happy to give me directions to the nearest lift."

She looked at Lunn hoping he would approve of her approach to the task, and she felt relieved when he started to laugh. He boomed, "I guess he never even realised that he had been compromised."

Andena thought about it for a few moments and

murmured, "I surely hope not."

He got up from his chair and walked towards her. He put his hand on her shoulder and said sincerely, "I must admit you have excelled in the way you have completed your task, and I'm more than happy to welcome you to our group."

Resisting the urge to leap out of her seat and hug him, Andena breathed, "Oh that's fantastic! Thank you, Lunn! I'm so happy."

She was startled when she heard Danette's voice boom into the room, "Well well, Lunn. Congratulations on enrolling a new member into our ever-growing group."

Lunn chuckled as he moved back to his seat. He addressed Andena again, "Yes, I'm pleased that you decided to join us. We need more people if we are going to win this war."

Danette purred, "But I thought you were already in full control."

Andena was shocked by the provocative manner in which Danette paraded towards Lunn. She could see the lust building in his eyes when she zipped her jacket open slowly. The thin fabric of her blouse revealed her breasts which were in danger of spilling out of her low-cut bra. It had been a long time since another woman had managed to make Andena feel so uncomfortable. Danette straddled Lunn, behaving to all intents and purposes as if she were alone with him which made Andena's jaw drop.

Danette tried to push her body closer to Lunn, but he gently guided her off his lap and didn't seem remotely troubled by his state of arousal. "Later Danette. Let me finish with our lovely Andena."

If looks could kill Andena would have died on the spot. Danette made no attempt at hiding her displeasure as she huffed, "Why is this little slut more important than me?"

Lunn chuckled and said, "She is as important as you, because she managed to get the access code to Sector Gamma fifty-four."

Andena was very pleased with the way in which Lunn stood up for her. Her distaste for Danette was immense, which was a shame, given how she would have liked to make new friends. Danette looked with disbelief at Andena and asked, "What did she do to get that asshole to tell her the code?"

Andena took the opportunity to answer, saying with a comfortable certainty, "He didn't say anything. He simply forgot to cover his hand when he entered the code."

Lunn said, "That was indeed a smart trick. Now, I really would like you to come back tomorrow because I'll have another assignment for you. Make sure you get a good night's sleep."

It took every last ounce of willpower that she possessed for Andena to remain calm. However, her voice was warm as she responded, "Thank you, Mr. Lunn. Shall I be here at the same time as before?"

His smile met his eyes as he said, "Yes, that's fine. Good night, I'm looking forward to seeing you tomorrow."

As Andena walked away, she was certain that she heard Danette snort. She slowed her pace making sure she could overhear the conversation. Lunn asked with a calm voice, "What is the matter, Danette?"

She heard Danette exclaim, "Don't even think about fucking that bitch!"

Andena thought about what she had heard and smirked. Yes, Lunn was one sexy guy. Of course, she would, if she got the chance. What woman in her right mind, wouldn't? Tapping her finger to her lips, she broke into a huge smile as she began to plan her revenge on Danette.

CHAPTER TWO

Lunn knew he had to be careful not to upset Danette too much. Even though she acknowledged him as the leader, she was his right-hand woman, and she had proven to be very loyal. The discovery of their mutual hunger for sex was unexpected. It had happened on a mission that had gone pear-shaped and they had to dash into a cupboard where there was hardly space for them to hide. They were in there for several hours and when they finally made it out of the cupboard they tumbled onto the sofa and spent a long time satisfying their pent-up physical desires. They both used sex as a means to unwind: something which Lunn craved on a daily basis. They had established a routine whereby Danette would come most evenings into his office to enjoy his company in numerous ways. Lunn's face broke into a smile as he remembered the time spent in that cupboard, and was visibly shocked when Danette slapped him without warning across the face.

She scowled, "Were you thinking about that red-haired slut again?"

She moved her hand to slap his cheek again but this time, he grabbed her wrist and pulled her onto his lap. He held an arm around her middle and said with a dark voice, "Miss Cupboard needs to calm down a bit."

Danette groaned, "Oh Lunn, stop calling me that name. I hate it!"

"Come on Danette; it used to calm you down and bring a smile to your pretty face."

She blew some air out forcefully and said, "Yes Lunn, we had a great time then."

Lunn was taken aback by her answer and asked, "What is different? I thought last night was mind-blowing."

"Hmm, it was okay."

He shook his head in disbelief and mumbled, "It was okay?"

Danette got up from his lap and straightened her skirt. She turned to him and said, "It's rather off-putting when you call me different names when you come."

Lunn raised his eyebrow.

He had learned very early in his life never to call out a name when he had sex with a woman for precisely this reason. He knew she was playing a game and for now he was happy to go along with it. It was clear that she was attempting to manoeuvre him carefully into one of her dainty little traps. He decided to play along, and said evenly, "I don't believe that I said someone else's name."

She had unbuttoned her blouse revealing her voluptuous cleavage, and she murmured, "You nearly passed out when I gave you that blow-job and it was then that you whispered her name."

He had to admit that Danette was incredibly skilled in the art of deception. There was little doubt in his mind though that she was making this up. He mimicked her soft tone and asked, "Whose name did I call out?"

"The slut who just left."

Lunn sighed because he was convinced that she didn't know her name and asked, "What is her name, Danette?"

Her smile was cunning when she said, "Andena. You practically chanted her name after you came that hard."

Lunn knew he had lost the game, and he said glumly, "Oh dear. That's why you don't like her."

Knowing that she had won her little game, she crawled onto his lap again and purred, "Yes, and I have a perfect solution to our problem."

Lunn couldn't help that he adored Danette's body. He had been ready for action the moment she had walked into his office. He smiled and asked, "And what would that be?"

"Tell her that you're sorry and let her go."

Lunn was shocked by that answer. Andena was a natural talent, and it would be such a waste to let her go just like that. He chuckled and said firmly, "No."

Danette's smile disappeared in an instant and growled, "I don't like her."

"I know, but we need people like her. Don't forget that we have lost Pedro and Hunta."

Danette snarled, and Lunn continued with his charm offensive. "I need to send her out into the field. I have taken all reasonable precautions this time around and I am prepared. I need to find out what the fuck is going on out there; and she is my best chance of doing that."

Danette knew that Lunn had overruled her; the only consolation was the fact that she didn't expect Andena to survive the mission. Those fields were a mystery to everybody. No-one seemed to have a clue as to what was happening behind that thick gorse. Even flying drones over the field hadn't revealed anything. The only thing that was clear was that anyone who got too close never returned. The strangest part of it all was that those particular fields were the only ones in the area not to be guarded by the Archon and the fields had appeared overnight.

Danette sighed and conceded, "All right. But."

Lunn was very pleased that she had given in, and he asked with a smile, "What my lady?"

She huffed before saying venomously, "If I ever find out that you had sex with the slut, she will have to go."

He laughed and grabbed her hips to pull her closer. As he caressed her firm bottom, he murmured, "The only one I want right now is you."

She bit him softly in his neck. "I take that as a yes?"

Lunn moved his hands to her breasts evoking a soft gasp from her. He tried to distract her from her line of questioning, but she grabbed his wrists and said firmly, "Lunn, I want an answer. Do we have a deal?"

He thought about it, and while he knew that Andena had the hots for him. He also knew that he could control himself if he really wanted to and so he confirmed, "All right, all right. But I tell you: it ain't gonna happen."

Danette started to kiss him passionately, and he had the urge to rip the clothes off her gorgeous body. Her smile was mesmerising when she climbed off his lap. She patted his chest and said with a funny smile. "Behave little boy. Mama is going to sleep now."

Lunn couldn't believe his eyes when Danette started to button up her blouse. She picked her jacket from the floor and put it on. With a devilish smile, she slowly zipped it close. Lunn was so shocked that he was speechless as he watched her dress. Her heels sounded snappy on the wooden floor, and she wiggled her hips in a sexy manner as she deliberately walked next to the rugs. She winked at him when she was at the door and said happily, "Night night."

He heard her giggling in the hall, and he was dumbfounded: the bitch had left him just like that, and he knew exactly why. He got up from his chair and mumbled to himself, "Fucking bitch! I'll get you for this."

It was going to take a freezing cold shower to cool himself down.

Andena checked her watch again and was frustrated to see it was still way too early to go to Lunn's quarters. Because she had time on her hands in which to think, Andena began to question whether she could justifiably walk into his office dressed like she was. Her ultra-short latex skirt barely covered her bottom, and her lace crop top only just covered the see-through bra. The thong was just a small triangle of fabric on a few strings. She looked appraisingly at herself in the mirror, and she recalled Danette's words, "Why is this little slut more important than me?"

She sighed and muttered to herself, "Look at you! You little slut!"

She realised that maybe it hadn't been the smartest of moves to turn up at the office like that and hastily disposed of her flimsy clothes. She decided to go for her favourite and most comfortable outfit. If Lunn really wanted her, it shouldn't matter what she was wearing.

As she stepped out into the cold afternoon, she was

pleased she had chosen her leggings and her carbon boots. Her sports top together with her long sweater protected her from the biting wind. Every minute she neared his office, she became increasingly anxious as to whether or not she could live up to Lunn's expectations. Not knowing what he had planned for her made her fidgety: a fact which she hated. As she walked tentatively into his office, she was surprised at just how bad he looked.

"Oh my God Lunn, what happened to you?" she exclaimed.

The dark rings around his eyes were prominent, and he hadn't bothered to shave with the result that his chin was now covered with a dark, grey stubble. He chuckled softly and said, "I had a rough night. I couldn't sleep."

She said, "Oh, Okay. You look horrible."

He grunted.

Raising her eyebrows, Andena had difficulty believing what he had just said. To be fair, she didn't quite know what to make of him right now, but one thing was for sure, she was incredibly grateful for that fact that she had changed into comfortable clothing. In fact, she had to stifle a giggle as she imagined standing in front of him right now in her sexy playmate outfit. Lunn sighed, and as he got up from his desk, he said gruffly, "Come with me."

He walked towards a door, and when they were in the next room, Andena was taken aback by the sheer amount of weaponry that had been stacked high on the many shelves. She knew that her next mission would be a lot more dangerous than the last. Lunn looked at her face which had changed from happy to concerned, and he asked with a hoarse voice, "What do you know about the fenced fields outside the city?"

"Not much. They say that anyone that gets too close

disappears."

"Hmm."

She looked at him wondering why he didn't immediately elaborate any further and then the precise nature of her next mission sunk in. "Don't tell me you want me to go there!"

Lunn sighed and countered, "Yes, but I have more intelligence now. There is every reason to believe that you will survive."

Her eyes grew bigger as she whispered, "I'm not the first one, you have sent there, am I?"

He walked to a shelf containing several different kinds of machetes, and he conceded, "No, you're not. I want you to try one of these."

Still flustered by the shocking revelation, she stepped towards the shelf and warily eyed the knives. She picked one up and felt the surprisingly heavy weight of it before searching for a narrower specimen. There was one which might be just what she was looking for and when she took it in her hand it felt comfortable enough: not too heavy or too light. As she moved the knife in several figures of eight, she remembered that her carbon boots had special knife pockets at the sides. She carefully slid the machete into the pocket and to her delight it was a perfect fit.

Lunn watched her with a bemused expression on his face. "Have you never used a machete before?"

She had heard of that specific kind of knife, and she asked incredulously, "You think there's a jungle out there?"

"Something like that."

She saw the guilty look flash across his eyes, and she knew that he was withholding information. Straightening her back, she demanded, "Lunn, you owe it to me to tell me the truth."

Leaning against one of the shelves he looked down. "I have previously sent two people into those fields. The first one went there unprepared because, at that point, we had no way of knowing that anything was wrong. It was around five days before we realised that he was missing."

"How come it took you so long to realise that he was missing?" she asked.

Lunn chortled and shook his head before he answered, "Pedro was a person who loved nature and he often went out on field trips and stayed away for long periods. So when he didn't show up, we assumed that he was still out there having a good time. As soon as we heard rumours that other people who had also gone out into the fields hadn't returned, we began to fear the worst."

Andena shivered and asked, "If you knew it was dangerous why did you risk someone else's life?"

"Because we needed to know what those fields are and why they are dangerous. So when I send Hunta she was warned. She was a strong woman and incredibly fast. We had set up a video feed but because of the strong electromagnetic field which radiates from the fence we barely managed to sustain an audio link."

Andena was not interested in the technical difficulties they had encountered, and she asked impatiently, "What happened to Hunta?"

He stared at her for a few seconds, before replying, "After she had managed to pull back the gorse, she peeked in and started to scream. Stunned, we heard her scream that she was coming back, but then her leg was grabbed by a thick grey tentacle. It seemed that her calf had been badly wounded and then without explanation she began to calm down. She told us that everything was cool, but she sounded high: as if she were on drugs. We weren't able to engage in any form of sensible conversation with her after that point. A few moments later we lost contact, and the audio signal died out completely."

Andena shivered and said, "So we can assume she was pulled into the field."

Lunn looked down and said glumly, "Yes. I shouldn't have let her go alone."

She asked, "So, are you accompanying me?"

Lunn shook his head slowly, "I only have one carbon suit which is way too small for me, and I need to make sure that the curfew cameras don't detect you."

"You have a carbon suit?"

"Not yet, but it will be here soon. I had it made especially for you."

Andena was taken aback by what Lunn just had said. She had paid a small fortune for her carbon boots. They were practically indestructible and would protect the person wearing them from any sharp objects. She gasped when she figured out how much a tailored body suit must have cost him. Now it was her turn to look down as she whispered, "You have a lot of faith in me. Why are you so sure that I will succeed?"

She watched him come closer and looked up into his eyes as he gently tilted her chin with his hand. "I know you're strong, and I've seen you at your Martial Art classes. There are not many people who are at one with their body. I envy you Andena. Every move you make is graceful, efficient and precise. Only a highly trained soldier would have been able to do what you have just done with that machete."

Andena opened her mouth to speak, but in the end, couldn't think of anything appropriate to say. A soft knock at the door broke the spell: and Andena was left shaken for it felt as if he had penetrated her very soul.

One of the guards stood in the doorway with a package in her hand. Glancing curiously around, Lunn took it from her before instructing Andena to get undressed but leave her underwear on.

Andena panicked because she hadn't bothered to change her underwear. There was no way that she wanted Lunn seeing her in her flimsy, see-through undies!

Noticing her hesitation, he said with a smirk, "I think I've seen more women in their underwear than you have seen men in their briefs. So what is the big deal Andena? I promise I won't say anything, besides you will need my help to get this suit on."

Andena sighed, before eventually conceding defeat and murmuring, "All right."

CHAPTER THREE

Lunn was sitting behind his desk closely monitoring the curfew cameras. It had been necessary to alter the recording settings of two more cameras before he was able to turn his attention to the lovely Andena. He was impressed by how easy it was to wipe all footage of Andena passing the cameras. For the past few months, security had been tight, and curfews were routinely enforced. Anyone carrying so much equipment would certainly have come under scrutiny from the authorities.

He'd had difficulty keeping his earlier promise when he realised that Andena was wearing the skimpiest possible underwear. He'd realised just why she had been so reluctant to get undressed in front of him. However, this did give her a major advantage in the sense that the carbon suit now fitted her like a second skin, making her look incredibly sexy. He smiled as he remembered the embarrassed look on her face when he zipped the suit closed. He had been incredibly disappointed by the fact that she'd quickly hidden her gorgeous body by immediately putting her clothes back on. Lost in his thoughts, he was, therefore, startled when her voice rung in his ear, "Lunn; I'm about to reach the next curfew camera."

He was grateful for the fact that he was still able to use the frequency range for the communication devices. The Archon were now monitoring nearly all the ranges except this narrow band. The only problem was that the range was very close to that of the electromagnetic emissions of the fields. The closer you were to the fields the worse the connection became. He pushed the button and responded, "All clear Andena. How is the suit working for you?"

Her voice had a certain melodic tune that he loved, and he was pleased with her answer, "It's fantastic Lunn! I don't even feel that I'm wearing it."

"Good. It fits you like a glove as if it was your own skin."

Her laugh was short, and she scolded, "Well I hope that you enjoyed the view because next time I'll be dressing myself."

He looked at the screen and saw she had made good progress. He reckoned that she needed another five minutes to pass the last curfew camera. The field was an additional ten minutes after that. He chuckled and said, "Too bad Andena. By the way, the ETA is about fifteen minutes."

A red light flickered on his screen signalling trouble, and he hissed into the microphone, "You've got company. There's an alley just a few yards to your left."

Andena didn't answer straight away, but Lunn could

hear her breathing which was fluctuating a bit. After a few moments she said, "Just two boys playing, they didn't see me."

He checked the time, and he knew there was, at least, a full hour before the twilight, would turn into darkness. Andena commented, "I've just passed the last camera."

"Okay, you should be able to see the field after the next turn."

Andena felt much safer now that she was wearing the carbon suit. Sharp objects wouldn't be able to puncture the fabric that easily and she was amazed at how snug the suit fitted her. It was as if Lunn knew her precise measurements and she was very pleased that she was wearing the flimsy underwear. A proper bra would have felt uncomfortable, and she also knew that a snug fitting carbon suit would protect her much better than a loose fitting one. The suit would disperse an attack much better. She gasped when she turned the corner at the last building. The size of the field looked far more impressive than she had imagined. The fact that the road ended right at the massively high fence seemed strange. She said, "I have visual contact with the target."

She heard Lunn snicker. "Roger that."

Andena walked a bit slower looking for any signs of unusual growth at the side of the tarmac. The closer she came to the fence the faster her heart beat. She jumped when Lunn suddenly asked, "Do you see anything out of the ordinary?"

The dry land was covered with the usual patches of yellow-brown grass. The grass was a bit greener where it grew underneath the occasional tree. She answered Lunn as placidly as possible, "Nothing looks out of the ordinary."

He didn't need to know that she was as nervous as hell. His response became distorted by the electromagnetic field, "Good. Now make sure you're not too close."

Andena wouldn't dream of going any closer than necessary and snorted, "Don't worry about that."

She took the measuring device from her belt and walked until she was eighteen feet away from the field. She was pleased that she could finally remove the heavy anchor pins from her belt. Lunn had shown her how to drive them swiftly and without any effort into the soil. They felt sturdy and the specific angle, in which they were placed in the soil, gave them the extra support that they needed. She had double checked the knots of the ropes and the anchor points before she sat down in the middle of the road.

As she was connecting the ropes to her belt an extremely loud hissing noise behind the gorse made her jump. Andena shrieked and grabbed the emergency cord that would release the hooks of her belt in an instant. Fortunately, the hissing died down quickly and it sounded like something in the field had released a built-up pressure.

Lunn asked, "Are you okay Andena?"

She slowly exhaled before replying in a trembling voice, "Yes, I guess so. What was that sound?"

"I don't know, but we need to press on. It will get dark soon."

She knew that she couldn't dither any longer and took the telescope rod from her belt. Within a minute, the rod was fully extended, and she carefully mounted the razor sharp knife at the end of it. She got up and made sure that the emergency cord was hanging free. Moving the rod, as a fisherman would, she inched it towards the gorse, before saying in a strained voice, "I'm about to cut a hole in the gorse."

Lunn asked, "Did you prepare the camera? I don't see any video feed."

She was just a few inches away from the gorse, and she exclaimed, "Shit!"

"What?"

"I forgot the camera!"

Lunn shouted in disbelief, "What? You left the camera here?"

She carefully placed the rod on the road and said calmly, "No silly, I just didn't prepare the camera rod."

He growled, "There's only one silly person, and that is the one who forgot to extend the camera rod."

Andena knew that Lunn was as nervous as she was and couldn't help giggling when she pushed the button at the base of the camera rod. She was pleased she had tried the equipment before and directed the camera just before the gorse. The camera rod had a self-extending mechanism which became fully operational within a matter of seconds. She activated the camera and heard Lunn grunt approvingly. "Camera feed looks good. Now remember Andena, try to keep the hole you cut as small as possible."

With sweaty palms, she picked up the rod with the knife again and moved a step closer to the gorse. She knew that making a cut which she had no way of controlling was the hardest part of her mission. She pushed the knife slowly into the fabric and was reassured by the lack of resistance. She slowly moved the knife down until there was an opening of three inches before quickly retracting the knife and pushing the camera through the cut. She could feel herself becoming increasingly tense as Lunn gasped. "Do you have a clear picture?" she asked.

His voice sounded tortured, "Crystal clear, can you turn the camera clockwise?"

She obeyed his request by slowly turning the rod until she heard him exclaim, "Oh my God! Andena, get the fuck out of there!"

Just at that moment, she felt that the camera being pulled from her hands almost causing her to lose her balance. Before she realised what was happening, two tentacles had shot through the hole. Luckily she had the sense to reach for her machete the moment she lost the camera because she was pulled down by the sheer force of the two, thick tentacles which snaked around her legs, pulling them together and preventing her from getting up. She felt the sharp thorns trying to push into her legs, but the fine carbon mesh was strong enough to withhold the pressure.

The fact that the tentacles were trying to penetrate her skin was her saviour and with a guttural grunt, using the machete, she managed to slice through both of the vines at one attempt. It was with an enormous sense of relief that she was able to free her legs. She watched as the damaged tentacles slowly began to retreat and knew that it was time to run away as fast as possible because something else was attempting to squirm through the small hole. She pulled at the emergency cord, but to her dismay, nothing happened!

She tried once more, but the belt was still locked! She knew she didn't have time to fiddle with the belt, and she started to run away hoping that the anchors would pop out if they were pulled out the right way.

With all her strength she began running from the tentacles and at the moment, the ropes were pulling at the anchors she heard a loud popping sound. Andena cheered when both anchors shot out of their holes, but forced herself to keep on running. She winced as one of the anchors banged against her back, but in fact, it wasn't too painful. She saw the humour in the situation when she heard the metal anchors, bouncing with loud clanging sounds against the tarmac as she raced to safety. She would have preferred a silent retreat, but she would be happy so long as she was safe. She only stopped running when she turned into the road away from the field, and it was only at that point, that she heard Lunn frantically calling her name. Breathing heavily, she managed to whisper, "Lunn.... I'm.... Fine."

She thought she heard him whimpering as he breathed, "Thank God! I was afraid I had lost you too, on that bloody field! Just take it easy now and come to my office at your leisure."

She was still resting her hands on her thighs waiting to get her breath back to normal. Sighing with relief, she said, "Okay, I'll see you later."

As she pulled herself upright, she tugged absent-mindedly at the emergency cord and to her utter surprise, her belt dropped down on the street. Feeling confused, she shook her head and wondered why the bloody thing hadn't dislodged when it was needed. However, she was more than pleased to be able to dump the heavy weighted belt into the nearest bin. She was surprised by how quickly she regained her breath which was great because she wanted to leave this place as soon as possible. She felt well enough to make the journey and started to jog in the direction of Lunn's quarters. To her amazement, she noticed that her whole body was tingling, presumably from the realisation that she had survived this treacherous mission. Andena was astonished by how quickly she got into her jogging stride. It was as if her body craved a fast-paced run. The closer she got to Lunn quarters the more she realised that she was looking forward to seeing him. There was a burning ache inside of her, and she longed to wrap her legs tightly around his waist. She was puzzled by the fact that she seemed to be getting hornier by the second. It wasn't uncommon for her to become aroused by exciting thoughts. However, nothing had made her this randy before! In the end, she was so fired up that she no longer cared – So long as she got to have Lunn. The thought of him crawling all over her body made her moan out loud with desire.

Lunn slammed back into his chair after he was sure that Andena had managed to escape. He had closed his eyes because they felt gritty after he had been looking so intensely at the monitors for such a long time.

He shivered involuntarily as the images Andena had taken in the field, flooded back into his mind. He had never seen such a ghastly scene before. He had counted sixteen strange looking plants. The plant was around eight feet in height, and at the top sat an enormous, purple ball. He thought that the plants looked like huge lollipops, only with thicker sticks. The most disturbing fact was that each trunk had, at least, three human bodies intertwined in its vines. Their faces were flawless, and they all wore euphoric smiles. To all intents and purposes, they seemed the embodiment of happiness and contentment. Their eyes were closed: suggesting that they were sleeping peacefully, and their bodies looked as if they frequently worked out. It disturbed him that the ghoulish sight should also seem not just sensual but exceptionally beautiful.

The last clear picture Lunn saw before a vine had pulled the camera away was Hunta's body. Her naked body was intertwined with vines which held her tightly against the trunk. It was as if she was a part of the plant and her curves fitted perfectly into the wavy forms. Her arms were positioned above her head which made her body align with the vines. Next to her was a man who was positioned in the same way. He too looked blissful. Lunn had managed to create a sharp still of Hunta and to his amazement, she seemed to look much younger. Hunta had been in her early forties when she disappeared: now she didn't look a day older than thirty.

Then it dawned on Lunn, that far from being from Earth, these plants must be alien! He stood up and started to pace nervously around the room realising that it all made sense. It explained why nobody had ever seen the fields built. The aliens must have superior techniques to enable them to hide and build the fields. But still it didn't answer his burning questions: why were those fields here and were those plants alien? If those plants were truly alien, then something must have happened between the aliens and the Archon, which he, and many others, had missed. Either they have an agreement with the aliens and kept it silent, or the aliens had taken over and were oppressing the Archon.

He quickly thought back to when the first of those fields had appeared, which was roughly four months ago. He needed to find Arnost, the leader of the Archon, hoping he would give him some answers. He was shaken from his thoughts by the sound of a familiar voice calling his name.

"Lunn! Where are you?"

Andena rushed into his office with a huge grin on her

face, and she ran straight into his arms. She kissed him while she put her arms around his torso.

Lunn was completely taken aback by her sudden affection for him, but he let it be for now. It had been a mind blowing event for both of them. After she broke the kiss to gain some air, she exclaimed, "Oh Lunn, I'm so pleased I'm safe here with you."

She went for his lips once more, and he truly started to enjoy her soft lips and her wonderful fresh smell. Her excitement and feeling the warmth of her body made him want more as well. He moved his hand up from her bottom to caress her back and was shocked when he felt something wet and cold attached to her back.

He roughly broke the kiss and commanded, "Andena, stand as still as possible. There's something attached to your back."

She frowned and said with a pouting expression on her face, "But I don't feel anything."

Lunn carefully moved sideways and saw a glistening miniature lollipop plant stuck to her back. It looked like it was about to fall off her back and Lunn rushed into the adjacent room looking for a plastic container which was big enough to hold it. He found one, but it was fully stocked with ammunition. With no other option, he removed the lid and dropped the packages with the bullets on the table before rushing back to Andena, who was still standing there with a funny smile on her face as if nothing serious had happened. He placed the container on her back and tried to prise the lollipop from her back with the lid. The plant slowly peeled away from her sweater and finally fell into the container.

Lunn placed the lid firmly on the container and made sure it was sealed properly. Meanwhile, Andena had turned around to see what was on her back, and she said cheerfully, "Oh what a pretty thing. I thought I felt one of the anchors hitting my back."

Lunn felt strange; it was as if the lollipop which looked like a beautiful, crafted rose on a stick had mesmerised him. Andena purred as she pulled her sweater off, "Maybe you should check my back to see if I'm hurt or not."

Andena's tight fitting top revealed her beautiful body. However, Lunn was still surprised by how his desire to take Andena here and now was so intense. With a smouldering smile, he agreed with a dark voice, "It would be my pleasure to fulfil my duty."

She snorted and kicked her boots off. Her eyes twinkled as she teased, "Well soldier, perform as requested. On all fronts."

Lunn couldn't wait to pull her top over her arms and raised his eyebrows playfully as he asked, "You want to test all my skills?"

Andena nearly moaned when she said, "Yes."

Her moan made his desire rocket to an unbearable level, and even though he knew, in the back of his mind that he shouldn't comply with her demand. He wanted her gorgeous body next to him in his bed.

Completely naked.

Andena woke up slowly, and she felt that her nose was ticklish. She lazily moved her hand to her nose, and she realised that she was lying with her head on a warm hairy chest. It slowly dawned on her that this wonderfully sculptured chest belonged to Lunn and the memories of an incredibly long and hot night flooded back into her mind.

Her face broke into a satisfied smile as she remembered the unbelievable skills Lunn possessed: how he was able to satisfy a woman fully. Andena was so pleased that she had bought a new birth-control scheme when she decided to join the rebels. She didn't want anything holding her back or tying her down. She was surprised at how fast Lunn had fallen for her flirtatious behaviour and his desperate need to devour her.

She winced a little when she moved away from his gorgeous body. The sex with him was mind-blowing and had an animalistic feel about it. The first two times they hadn't exchanged any words. She had never felt so satisfied and exhausted when they had finally fallen asleep.

The only thing she found scary was the feeling of being out of control which had happened when she entered the office last night. She would normally never kiss a man full on his lips to express her joy unless it was her lover. She had kissed Lunn and practically forced her tongue into his mouth. It was as if she had no inhibitions which made her feel uneasy. She had thought that he was a little reserved at first, but he somehow allowed her to be so frivolous. It was only after they had stored this amazing flower away that he made the incredible sexual advances to her. She had swooned when he had kissed her so passionately and gave her body fully over to his magical hands. She turned her head to glance at the ancient clock which was ticking the time softly away.

With a start, she remembered what day it was and sighed glumly. She didn't want to leave his wonderful body, but she had to get up because she couldn't afford to be late for her Martial Art class.

She looked for her flimsy thong, but she couldn't find the little piece of fabric and decided that Lunn could have it as a souvenir of their incredible night. She had to hurry home to take a quick shower and change into her training gear. Her master was a man in his eighties, but he wanted his students to be immaculate: everything had to be as he had told them. Even though she was his favourite student she had to comply with the same strict rules.

As she silently stepped out Lunn's bedroom, she saw her carbon suit lying in the doorway of the office. As she carefully folded it, she could barely remember taking the suit off. As she passed the container with the small lollipop flower she had the urge to open it and smell the wonderful smell again but she knew there was no time to waste anymore. In fact, she was probably going to work up another sweat because she was going to need to run, in order to be on time for her class.

CHAPTER FOUR

Danette was in an extremely bad mood. Her plans had gone completely wrong. She had hoped to have all ten androids up and running by now but of the three from the last batch, only two were good enough to endure the heavy stress test. On top of this, she had to deal with an impatient CEO of Bionex, which had annoyed her considerably and then Lunn had crushed her last bit of dignity to pieces by insisting that his little bitch, Andena, should stay on the team. It wouldn't have happened if she had been running the show, but Lunn had refused to let the girl go. His obvious physical attraction to the other woman made Danette feel extremely uneasy, and she readily admitted to being jealous of the girls' beautiful vibrant red hair and flawless pale skin.

She was furious when he not only overruled her say on this matter but as a result also deprived her of a bit of fun with him. The way in which he had lifted her out of his lap had been embarrassing, and she had been stunned by the fact that he made no attempt to hide his arousal from the redhead. It had caught her totally off guard. Danette wanted his attention but not this way! She wasn't in the mood for sex any more after he had pulled that ridiculous trick. She hoped that his balls had been heavy and aching for the last two nights and that hopefully he would give in to her demands.

The problem was that by withholding sex, Danette now felt sexually frustrated. She reluctantly had to admit that Lunn was the only man she wanted. No other man could live up to the incredibly high standards that he set. They didn't even come close to satisfying her, and it was this that was weighing heavily on her mind as she walked to his quarters. Danette hated the fact that she was so dependent on Lunn. It scared her to think about how badly she wanted him; craved him. There was no denying the fact that having sex with Lunn was always mind-blowing, but was it healthy that he made her feel like this?

She sighed and inhaled deeply for a few times before entering Lunn's quarters. When she arrived in his office, she was surprised that he wasn't behind his desk. He was always such an early bird and lying in was just not his thing. Her eyes fell on the container with the lollipop and was instantly mesmerised by its colours. She examined the flower from all sides and was intrigued by the smooth and shiny texture. Danette wanted to know whether the flower was wet or whether the surfaces had been polished into an incredible shiny sheen. Lifting the lid carefully from the container, she was startled by the little puff of air that escaped. The smell of the perfumed air reached Danette's nose, and she greedily inhaled the lovely scent. The scented air made her head a little dizzy, and it was as if the flower's scent had narcotic qualities.

She lifted the container to have a better look, and she was fascinated how the little petals shimmered in the rays of the upcoming sun. She wanted to study it more closely but in the back of her mind, she was aware that it might be dangerous. However, the need to take a peek was so compelling that Danette ignored all of the warning signs and removed the lid completely. Carefully taking the flower in her hand, she realised that it was covered with a slippery substance. She knew that she should have worn gloves. However, the slippery substance was irresistible. Her reverie was broken by the sound of Lunn coughing, and she knew he was still in his bed. Her heart started beating a little faster as she decided to sneak up on him.

She placed the container back on the desk and, like a tiger hunting for its prey, Danette slipped silently into his bedroom hoping he was still asleep.

As she peeked around the door, she saw that Lunn was naked, and lying on his back. Her eyes became fixated on his divine body and she felt a burning desire to kiss his muscled chest. As she approached the bed, she noticed that Lunn's breathing was steady, and she assumed he was fast asleep. Lowering herself slowly down onto the mattress, she moved her hand up and down over the hairy skin of his chest. She realised it was the flower's secretions that were making his skin appear so shiny. She felt a thrill of excitement when Lunn started to moan softly. Spurred on, Danette pressed her lips onto his skin as she marvelled the rippling of his strong muscles under her hand. Lunn's breathing became more erratic as he groaned, "Oh Andena, this is so good."

Danette was so annoyed that she had a strong urge to

sink her teeth into his flesh. As she looked up, she grabbed his crotch firmly and growled, "What the fuck did you just say, Lunn?"

He gasped, and his eyes flew wide open. Less than a second later a sly smile appeared on his face, and he said, "Got ya!"

Danette knew she had received her just desserts but didn't have time to think about it any further because Lunn grabbed her blouse and pulled her to him for a scorching hot kiss on the lips. After they had both had a chance to catch their breath, he nibbled her softly in her neck, whispering greedily, "Why do you still have your clothes on?"

She gasped, "Didn't have time to get undressed yet."

As he caressed the inside of her thigh, he grumbled, "Do it quickly or I'll take care of it."

She shivered with desire and knew she would have the exquisite fun that she had been aching for these past few days.

Lunn felt a warm body cocooning his back and a slender hand resting on his arm. He took a few deep breaths to clear his head and then realised that Danette was sharing his bed. He chuckled inwardly, as he recalled the moment that she had caught him unawares. He had genuinely thought that Andena was caressing him so nicely. He was relieved that he had managed to cover his tracks but nevertheless, still felt guilty about the scorching hot night that he had shared with Andena. He had given Danette his word, and he had somehow ended up breaking his promise the next day.

He was still very groggy when Danette asked him what he had said. The fact that Danette was holding his crown jewels firmly in her hand instantly woke him up, but it also reminded him how he had felt the last two days. It was his saving grace that he had remembered to use her trick against her. He loved the fact that Danette adored his body, and he had been taken aback at just how aroused he was given that he had spent the previous night with Andena. It had taken him every ounce of effort not to rip Danette's clothes off her back.

Andena had brought the animal out in him, and the sex was amazingly rough. He had enjoyed her devoted attention and was completely astonished when Andena managed to get him ready again after three extremely intense and tiring times. It had blown him away, and he fell asleep while she still was on top of him. Lunn sighed blissfully as Danette stirred and she snuggled even closer to him. It was always amazing to feel Danette's firm yet soft body rubbing against his back. His mind wandered back to the intense sex they just had. Even though it was the best he had had in a long time, something wasn't quite right. It was as if his levels of arousal had been artificially affected by an aphrodisiac.

It had to be the lollipop! He had touched the flower when it was on Andena's back, Andena's carbon suit had a wet patch where the flower had been and he was convinced that Danette had touched the lollipop as well.

Desperate for a shower, Lunn moved carefully away from Danette. Who would have thought that sex could be so demanding on his muscles? His body ached as he limped to the bathroom and as the warm water cascaded over his back he considered the significance of the lollipop. It was very tempting to harvest the potent liquid and use it at his convenience but he knew that it might be dangerous to keep. After all, the lollipop was part of a plant and, therefore the liquid might be organic and it could change over time. Lunn considered the slippery liquid to be quite dangerous because it had compromised his common sense twice in a row which he, as the leader of the group, couldn't afford.

He knew he had to store the flower in a safe place or destroy it before irreparable damage occurred. He decided to put the container in his vault for now until he had time to take a sample to his scientist.

When he looked up, he saw Danette walk into the bathroom. She had a sleepy smile on her face, and as she was stretching her body she asked, "Can I join you?"

Lunn admired her beautiful body and loved to wash her soft skin, and he replied eagerly, "I'm always happy to share a shower with you."

She laughed while she was fixing her hair into a bun on top of her head. Aware that he was watching her, Danette winked suggestively and asked, "You like what you see?"

He pulled her into the cabin and kissed her passionately. While the water was running down his hair, he murmured, "You have such a divine body."

She moaned softly, as he slid down the front of her body leaving a trail of gentle kisses. Even though he would have loved to linger, he needed to get that lollipop flower out of his office as soon as possible.

Danette was a little flustered when he stepped out the shower and asked, "Leaving me alone already?"

He took a towel, and as he was drying himself he asked Danette, "Did you touch that lollipop in the container?"

She looked surprised when she retorted, "Yes, I did. How did you know?"

He chuckled softly and gave her a mischievous smile. This confirmed his theory that the fluid from the lollipop contained an aphrodisiac, and he smiled indulgently at her, "Hmm. I'll tell you later. But I think I should store it in a safe place, for now."

Her expression turned to one of worry as she asked, "Is it harmful?"

He saw her concern, and he responded quickly, "Only if you are exposed to it too often."

Her smile reappeared, and she said, "You'd better clear it up then."

He knew he had to watch his words around Danette. It was vital that she never found out about the night of passion that he had enjoyed with Andena. So, as he walked out of the bathroom he replied casually, "Will do!"

As soon as he had finished dressing, he stepped into his office and noticed the amazingly sweet smell of the flower. Danette must have forgotten to close the lid of the container. Lunn needed to be certain that the effects of the aphrodisiac wouldn't consume him again, and so he decided to fetch some latex gloves.

The amazingly sweet smell was making him dizzy, and he had great trouble to keep his mind focused on storing the container in the vault.

He was grateful for the fact that he was able to control the airflow in his office and changed the settings to a high level which would refresh the air very quickly. It would cool the room a bit, but the fresh air would clear his mind as well. He sat for a while and contemplated what he should do with the flower. However, even though it pained him to do so, he knew that the only viable solution was to destroy it.

With a sigh of discontent, he logged onto his computer to see if there were any messages but there was nothing that needed his attention straight away. He was sure it was going to be another mundane day. He had reclined his chair because he was still affected by the smell and the escapades with the two women had taken its toll on him as well. Hearing footsteps from behind, he knew it was Danette. He asked, "Enjoyed the shower?"

Her hand slipped over his shoulder, and she rubbed his chest. "Yes, but it was a bit lonely."

He felt a pang of guilt, but he was pleased he had freed the room of its aphrodisiac potential. He looked up into her eyes and said, "I had to clear up here a bit. Someone left the lid off the container. It smelled wonderful, though."

She squeezed his arm and said softly, "Oops."

But then she gasped as if she had remembered something important and asked, "Tell me what happened with Andena. Did she survive?"

He turned around and said with a huge smile on his face, "Yes, she did, and that flower in the container is from the field."

She raised her eyebrows and demanded, "I want to hear the whole story."

Danette was horrified when she saw the video footage of the field. What she had seen was way beyond anything that she had previously thought possible. She had to agree that the people who had been captured by those plants looked happy, and they seemed not to have suffered any visible harm. However, watching the scene hurt her to an almost unbearable level. Lunn kept so much from her these days, and she felt increasingly left out. In the beginning, she had been actively involved but because of her other activities she had been forced to relinquish a lot of the work to others. But she was intrigued by the special mini lollipop, and she asked Lunn, "How did you know I had touched the flower?"

His eyes twinkled when he countered, "What happened when you opened the container?"

Danette had known that he would ask that question, but she didn't care because she would win this time and she said meekly, "The scent of the flower was amazing, and it made me feel dizzy."

Danette became visibly uptight when she saw the smirk flash across his face as he queried, "And then what happened?"

He was so patronising!

She forced herself to remain calm and took her time in answering his question, "I took the flower in my hand but then I realised it was wet."

His grin was mean looking as he asked, "You just touched the flower without taking any precautions?"

She blushed because she knew that she had made a rookie mistake and that it was something no trained security officer would ever do. Her anger made her see what Lunn had discovered: the flower had a powerful aphrodisiac in the liquid. It was as if all the little pieces of a puzzle fell into place in one rush of anger. Danette knew exactly what had happened to her when she had entered Lunn's office. As soon as she had opened the container she had been bewitched by the smell and the second her hand had touched the flower, she had become affected by the aphrodisiac. It had only taken a matter of seconds for it to kick in and soon the effects of the aphrodisiac were running through her veins. It had made her need for sex even greater which had, in turn, led to the steamiest sex session that she had ever enjoyed. She was beginning to wonder whether she would ever again experience such a morning. She knew she only needed to ask one question and then she would have him by the balls. Taking a deep breath and dreading the answer, she tried to sound as innocent as possible, "How did Andena bring the flower here?"

She could tell by the expression on his face that Lunn knew that she made the connection, and he said, "The lollipop was attached to her back. Apparently one of the plants had shot her with the flower in a last desperate act to disable her, but her carbon suit prevented that."

Danette didn't need to ask the next question, but she knew it was necessary to make it crystal clear to Lunn that she understood what had transpired. As she stared at him, she asked him softly, "Lunn, did you touch the flower?"

Lunn gulped, but he kept his eyes on her and said as neutrally as possible, "Yes Danette, I have touched the flower as well."

All this time, she had kept the little piece of fabric with the strings hidden in her hand. She could feel her nails digging into her skin because she had been clenching her fist so hard. She was shocked at how severely crestfallen she was, and she couldn't understand why he had broken his promise. It truly hurt that she had to find out he had sex with Andena in this way, and it was even worse that she'd found the thong when she had made up his bed. Something she had never done before because she hated those stupid routine chores but she'd somehow felt the urge to do it. It choked her throat for a few seconds, and she had to take a deep breath before she was able to confront him. Her hand was trembling when she opened it to show the little heap of fabric and whispered, "You really thought it was Andena this morning, didn't you?"

Danette didn't bother to prevent the tears from escaping her eyes. Lunn cleared his throat before saying hoarsely, "I'm sorry Danette."

Those few words turned her sadness into a maddening fury. The outrageously weak attempt to cover up his infidelity created an explosion of hatred in her mind. She stamped her foot on the floor, and she screamed, "Say it you asshole! I want to hear you say that you have fucked her and that you fucking thought it was her who was fondling you!"

His eyes darkened as he exclaimed, "After we were both affected by this stupid flower, I fucked Andena senseless and yes, I thought it was her."

His words stung her deeply and she had trouble not to cry. Danette spread the strings of the thong and laid the little piece of fabric on Lunn's nose. With her voice dripping venom, she said, "From now on you can relish the thought that she was wearing this pathetic item of clothing. We have a deal and I'll make it very simple for you Lunn: either she goes or I go."

She saw Lunn's face getting redder as he angrily grabbed the thong from his face, "Tell me, Danette, could you control your craving for me, after I had said her name? Or were you just so horny already that you didn't give a fuck as long as you could have me."

Danette was taken aback by his insulting question but the pain she was feeling overwhelmed her completely. She hesitated just for a second before stomping away without looking at him as she hissed, "Fuck you, Lunn!"

CHAPTER FIVE

Andena was pacing around in her small apartment not knowing what to do with her excess energy. She desperately wanted to feel useful. After her two incredibly successful adventures she craved more excitement.

She wanted more!

More excitement and more of Lunn's gorgeous body. She needed to find an excuse to visit his quarters again and her mind went back to the moment when the two vines had tried to puncture her with their thorns. Andena wondered if those vines were still there because she wondered whether it was possible that the thorns could have administered a sedative drug. She knew that if she took them to Lunn that there was a strong chance that he would offer to help her. It was a perfect plan because one thing would inevitably lead to another and it shouldn't be difficult to wind up back in his bed again.

The problem that she faced right now was how to find a safe way of transporting the vines to Lunn's quarters. She needed a tube of some sort, one that was sturdy enough and would enable her to store the vines safely. With a smile, she rushed to her cupboard and found her old battered aluminium roll in which her drawings were stored. She emptied the pipe by tumbling the drawings on to her bed. It was the perfect way to get the vines to Lunn without being detected.

There was still plenty of time before the curfew kicked in and it didn't take her long to get to the corner of the road. Unfortunately, there didn't appear to be any way of walking towards the field without being detected. She wondered why it was so busy, but then she realised it was the end of the afternoon shift. There were four small factories in the street and there was a steady flow of women walking back to the residential areas. Luckily Andena's clothes were as scruffy as theirs which made it possible for her to blend easily into the noisy crowd.

As she walked aimlessly up and down with the constant stream of women, it exhausted her patience to wait until she could pick up her pace and stroll towards the field. Constantly checking to ensure that she hadn't been followed, she sprinted towards the field and to her delight both vines were still lying on the road. When she was approximately fifty feet from the field, she took her binoculars from her pocket and studied the fence. As she had expected the cut she had made in the gorse was not there anymore. Now she was completely sure that there was something special about those fields.

Lunn had told her the previous night about the horrors that lay beyond the fence, and to be honest, it hadn't surprised her all that much. Apart from the fact that the people who had been captured, looked like they were enjoying their stay. She always had her suspicions that something was very wrong with those fields. Now that she had seen that it was all clear, she walked towards the vines. While keeping a safe distance, she carefully walked around them. They appeared to be sturdy rods and had clearly lost some fluid on the tarmac. There were some significantly darker spots on the tarmac directly under the ends of the vines but to her surprise, the cuts that she had made seemed to have been covered up. It was as if the vines had sealed the ends preventing the loss of more fluid.

Andena used her roll to separate the vines and she waited for a minute, to see whether or not, the vines would react to the separation, but they just lay there like two sturdy branches. Squatting down she slowly moved towards one of the vines and lifted it with her thumb and index finger close to the thorn. She reckoned that, in the same way, that you should grab a venomous snake just behind its head, it would be the safest way to get the vines into the roll. She was surprised how light the vine was and that she could slide it effortlessly into the tube. Even the second vine, which she had to turn a bit, slid into the roll without any problems.

Andena sighed with relief when she finally closed the roll. The lid had a special seal to make sure that your paper and drawings remained in a pristine condition. Now the seal would protect Andena from any unexpected tricks the vines might choose to deploy. So far her little project had gone perfectly, although she noticed that her fingers were a little bit sticky.

She chastised herself for not using any protection when she had picked up the vines. However, she quickly set her concerns to one side because she was feeling perfectly okay. In fact, she would go as far as to say that she felt wonderful and was looking forward to surprising Lunn with her little present. It was still light, and she wanted to see Lunn's face when she presented him with the vines.

Her heart was beating a little faster as she remembered his warm embrace and it made her walk a bit quicker to his quarters. She was wondering what he would do if she asked him to spend the night with her. It wasn't long before she was standing in front of the door to Lunn's quarters. She was always surprised at how easy it was to enter his place. It looked like he never bothered to lock his door.

Trembling with anticipation, she was surprised when the door didn't budge. She tried again but the door failed to open, and the only thing she could do was knock at the door. When he still didn't respond, in spite of her knocking three times on the metal door, she angrily started kicking it. She was truly pissed off and was going to have to rush home to ensure that she was home before the curfew.

She was still feeling annoyed as she hastily prepared something to eat. Her plan was to retreat to her secret place where she would examine the vines without the risk of getting caught. She was confident in her ability to complete this task by herself and told herself that she didn't need Lunn! While she was eating her simple dinner, she remembered to get her set of scalpels ready for use.

Her secret place was just opposite her apartment, and she had to pass through the airlock to get there. She knew how to overrule the security and bypass the alarm at the airlock. The last time she had been there she had stayed for about an hour before her headache became impossible to ignore. It was a small room with a small desk next to the window frame which was only covered with foil. There was nothing to be gained from bringing a canister of oxygen because the seals of the window frame had basically rotted away.

After placing her flashlight into the holder, she neatly laid the set of knives on top of the desk. She knew she was about to conduct a dangerous investigation and she probably shouldn't do it, but she couldn't care less at that moment. She had to prove to herself she was smart enough to do this research. With trembling hands she opened the seal of the roll and carefully removed the lid.

So far so good: nothing had happened, and the vines were still as rigid as before. She let them slide down onto her desk and turned them in such a way that the sharp thorns were facing away from her. Andena was both fascinated and excited that she was finally going to get a close look. She was amazed to see how smooth the surface of the vine was and that the grey colour was a mix of different thin stripes. There were all kinds of different colours intertwined with thicker black lines.

Andena was mesmerised by the way in which the patterns gave the vine its lively grey colour. The soft lustre made the vine seem as though it were made of silk while in reality, it was a thin layer of a somewhat sticky wax. She was tracing one of the thicker black lines with her finger and was wondering what the inside of the vine would look like. As she was tracing the stick with her finger, she saw something moving in the corner of her left eye. Slowly turning her head sideways she saw the lines slowly turning towards her and was horrified to discover that the thorn had turned itself upwards.

This could not be happening! How was it possible for a dead and sturdy vine to suddenly become so flexible?

Before she could fathom what was happening she felt the vine latch onto her arm while coiling around her wrist and the next instant, she felt a wonderfully warm tingling sensation spreading over her body.

She gasped knowing that she was doomed.

It was over!

Andena was starting to feel dizzy, as she slowly collapsed against the window she heard the cracking of the seal which had become brittle.

She became even more euphoric when the second wave of bliss shot up from her leg. Andena sighed knowing that she had lost the fight but she didn't care anymore because she loved how she felt.

Then another tingling sensation soared through her relaxed body and when it reached her head, the darkness was upon her. She was too far gone to realise that the bottom of the window frame had given away and that she had started to slip through the gap. Her boot prevented her from falling for a few seconds until her ankle twisted a little and her lifeless body fell like a ragdoll from the nine hundredth level.

Lunn was travelling up in the lift to Andena's apartment. He had managed to overrule the control panel, and as such, it now wouldn't stop until it reached the designated destination. He hated the fact that he was the one that had to deliver the bad news to Andena by telling her that she was no longer on his team. He had considered ignoring Danette's demand, but her input and the massive amount of work she had done for the group was too valuable to ignore. He was going to have to hold his hands up and admit to Andena that he had messed up. Deep in thought, it was a moment or two before he realised that the lift had stopped. Gathering his wits, he walked in silence along the narrow hall to Andena's small apartment.

He felt rotten having to be the one to shatter her dreams: especially when she had given up her ordinary life to be part of their elite group. He sighed, aware that she was unlikely to ever forgive him for this. He knew he was on the verge of losing one of the best recruits he ever had, and that made him angry. If it hadn't been for the damned aphrodisiac and the fact that Andena had carelessly left her thong in his bedroom, then Danette would never have found out about their fling. Sometimes life could be extremely unfair. He breathed out forcefully. He knew it was time to face facts and start showing some leadership. Straightening his back he knocked softly but firmly on the door. He waited for a while and then knocked louder when Andena didn't respond. Perhaps she was simply reluctant to answer her door to strangers. After he had knocked for the third time, he called out in a clear voice. "Andena. It's me! Lunn."

When he still failed to get a reply he knew for certain that she wasn't in her apartment. Lunn took his phone from his pocket in the hope he could reach her in that way but to his dismay, there was no signal by which to connect with the normal communication network. He had forgotten how lucky he was and that most people in the city had no means of contacting anyone because network connections were just too expensive and as such, they couldn't afford it.

He sighed at the prospect of having to travel back down. He was annoyed by the fact that he had been unable to reach her and found himself wondering where she might be. He decided to visit the bar where she used to work in the hope that he would bump into her.

Danette was staring at the android lying on her worktop. She was having a difficult time focusing on what she was doing and found herself constantly thinking about what had happened earlier that morning. She had been shocked when she saw herself in the mirror when she'd first arrived at her apartment: her red face and puffy eyes were a gruesome reminder of the fact that she had been crying.

The long shower had helped, and she had managed to eat something despite not feeling hungry at all. She had been replaying the events in her head from the moment she had demanded that the little bitch had to go. Danette couldn't help but wonder what she had done wrong. Had she really behaved that badly while Andena was there? She remembered the shocked expression on Andena's face which had then changed into a strange combination of jealousy and determination.

It all made her feel very insecure.

She had seen the hunger in Lunn's eyes when he looked at the redhead. It was all the more unsettling because she had sensed that Lunn was almost oblivious to her presence. It drove her mad, and she knew that she had overstepped the mark when she had tried to fire him up by dry humping him. She had played with fire and lost. There was nothing left to do right now but lick the self-inflicted burns.

She knew that theirs was an open relationship, and while she had been happy with the arrangement in the beginning, it was no longer working for her. Now it felt as if someone had well and truly come along and burst their relationship bubble. It was broken, and Danette found herself struggling to believe that it would ever heal let alone be the same again.

While she didn't have all of the solutions she was clear about one thing: Lunn owed her an apology. It was down to him to admit that he had broken the terms of their agreement. He needed to understand that she had totally lost faith in their relationship. Even though the flower had clearly affected him, he had been wrong to have sex with Andena. Danette could feel her anger slowly building as she realised that the bitch had not just taken away her stud, but her best friend and slumping down into the chair she began to cry.

Lunn tried connecting with Andena's phone as he walked towards the bar. However, in just a few seconds he knew that her device was not responding. He sighed, and presumed that she was simply one of those women that lacked the organisational skills to keep their devices charged. This was not his lucky day. As he turned into the dirty street where she used to work, Lunn was shocked. He'd had no idea that the area was so run down. The buildings were all boarded up with posters attached, stating that they were to be re-developed. He leaned against one of the boards and pondered what to do.

He was out of options and hadn't the faintest clue where she could be. He tried reaching her again, but her device was still not connected to the network grid. He was surprised when he saw Danette's device pop online and wondered briefly whether he had the courage to contact her. Lunn knew that there was no point asking her whether she had seen Andena as it would only make the situation between them worse. He was going to have to hurry back to his quarters if he wanted to avoid getting into trouble with the authorities.

Arriving back at his quarters he noticed several black lines at the bottom of his door. It looked like someone had attempted to kick the door down. Feeling incredibly pissed off he quickly entered his office and checked the recording from the surveillance camera to see who was responsible for causing the damage. He was completely taken by surprise to find footage of Andena becoming increasingly frustrated as she banged on the door. He felt incredibly guilty by the fact, that nothing that he could have done or said would have changed the situation. He had removed her from the list of people who were allowed to enter his quarters. He had stopped the recording as soon as he realised that it was Andena kicking the door. He could see by her clenched fists she was furious, and he was relieved that he hadn't been home at the time.

He had seen enough angry women for today.

It was only then that he realised that Andena was carrying a metal tube on her back, and it took a second or two for it to dawn on him. She must have gone back to the field to retrieve the veins she had cut off with her machete!

He checked the time that she had visited and realised that they must have only just missed each other. He reckoned that she must have returned to her apartment, just as he was leaving. He also knew that he had no alternative but to go back and check that she was okay. With just minutes remaining before curfew, he ran out of his apartment, hoping and praying that he would be in time to prevent Andena from doing something stupid.

Lunn rushed towards her apartment and knocked urgently on her door. He waited for a short while and knocked louder when Andena didn't respond. Again there was no response and Lunn tried to open the door but it was locked. He knew he was breaking one of his own rules when he removed his special access card from his pocket to override the lock on Andena's door. This time, he had to know that Andena wasn't hurt or needed any help.

He carefully opened the door an inch and when nothing happened he pushed it open further with his foot. He slowly moved into the small place, and he quickly realised she wasn't there. As he looked around more carefully, he noticed the scattered drawings on her bed. He examined the beautiful drawings, and he knew that they had been stored in the drawing roll that Andena had been carrying on her back. He found it weird that Andena still hadn't returned, and he anxiously wondered just where the hell the woman could be.

He decided to wait for her in the hall because it was better that she didn't know that he had been nosing around in her apartment. As he sat down and leaned his back against the door, he figured that he might be in for a long wait. As he wondered what he would do if Andena returned with the vines, his eyes drifted to the airlock opposite her apartment. A little red light was supposed to flash every ten seconds or so, but it seemed that the lock was out of power. Lunn got up to have a closer look at the lock. He could see minute scratches which proved that the lock had been tampered with, and when he looked at the disabled security panel he became convinced that someone had used the airlock to gain access to the area behind it.

He consulted the plan of this building on his device and found out there was a storage room which was not used anymore because of a broken seal. Lunn knew he could stay there for a few minutes which would be enough to see if there was anything of interest to be found. He tested the lock, and he wasn't surprised to find that he could open it effortlessly. He took a few deep breaths before closing the door behind him and then slowly opened the other door hoping that it didn't trigger any alarms.

He noticed the cold air flowing into the small airlock, and he quickly moved out to find himself looking at a desk which was standing close to the only window in the room. The flashlight which lit the room was still bright and Lunn saw two sticks lying on the floor. He realised that the sticks were the vines that he had seen on the video, but had now lost their fullness. It looked like that the vines had lost all their fluids. Taking one of the vines he saw traces of blood on the thorn. When he looked at the other, he saw a little drop of blood on the floor at the place where the thorn touched it.

Now he was absolutely sure that the vines were responsible for administering the fluids into a human, but found the absence of a body puzzling. It looked like someone had been here before him and had taken the body away.

He knew that he needed to get out of here quickly as his breathing was becoming increasingly heavy. He glanced around one final time but didn't see anything that would tell him whether or not Andena had been here. Just as, he decided to go back, his eye fell on the little pouch next to the knives. He opened it and saw the text written at the rim, "For my lovely Andena. Dad. XX"

His vision was starting to get blurry which was another sign that his body had been severely deprived of oxygen for too long: he knew that he needed to get out of there as quickly as possible. As he slowly stomped back to the airlock, he looked around once more to be sure that there were no traces of him to be found. Although his special gloves wouldn't leave any traces, he had to be sure that nothing else would point to his presence here.

Lunn practically fell out of the airlock, and he knew that he had to go down to the ground floor as fast as possible to prevent an enormous migraine attack. He was amazed to find that one of the lifts was available, and as soon as he was inside the lift, he slumped down onto the floor and commanded the machine to descend without making any further stops.

After a few minutes breathing in more oxygen, his brain started to work again, and he began to wonder who could have taken Andena. It had to have been someone as observant as him to notice that the airlock had been compromised. The more he thought about it, the more he realised that there was only one person who had known that Andena had visited the field: Danette!

Lunn couldn't believe that Danette would have done anything to hurt Andena. She might be stubborn and difficult at times, but she would never do that to another person. However, he suddenly remembered that she had popped up online when he was in the bar. She must have been with Andena when he'd tried finding her. It all made sense and was proof enough for him that she had taken Andena.

CHAPTER SIX

Arnost was pacing up and down his office while he waited for his head of security to arrive. He had summoned him because there had been a breach of one of the fields. His emissary, Tancred had confirmed that someone had managed to take video footage and had escaped. As Tancred looked out of the window, he said. "Your plan to leave those vines in the hope that someone would take them has worked."

Arnost stopped his pacing instantly. He still had difficulty understanding Tancred's heavy accent and asked, "When did this happen?"

"Today."

"At what time?"

"That is hard to tell. Most probably this afternoon."

Arnost sighed because it was so frustrating to deal with Tancred who didn't have any sense of time.

He sighed and asked, "Okay. Can you tell me what happened?"

Tancred's smile looked strange as if he had copied it from a comic book and he said, "They have been moved, and both vines managed to administer the initial compounds for integration."

Arnost shuddered a little and asked, "Do we know where they have been taken?"

"Not yet we have sent two sniffers to trace the scent."

"Does Haruz know about this?"

"No, but I assume we are waiting for him?"

Arnost growled softly with frustration. Since Tancred had arrived the quality and speed of communications, in general, had diminished considerably. The well-oiled system had practically ground to a halt, but since assuming the highest possible position of the Archon he had managed to repair most of the damage.

A sharp knock sounded at the door of the room almost causing Arnost to jump, and he yelled, "Enter!"

Arnost looked at the man who had entered the room. He always had envied Haruz's spectacular muscles. The suit Haruz was wearing didn't hide the well-built proportions of his body.

Haruz nodded to Arnost and said, "Sorry for the delay, but I was called away."

Arnost grumbled, "Yes, yes, yes, the reason I asked you to come is to discuss what happened last night."

"If you're referring to the breach of field beta eleven I can tell you who did it."

Arnost was stunned and asked, "You knew about it? Why didn't you inform me?"

"I assumed that Mr. Tancred had informed you. After all, it's his department."

Arnost had to admit that Haruz was right, and he grumbled, "He did. But tell me who breached the field."

Haruz cleared his throat and said, "It was a woman who is known by the name Miss Andena. She also had the audacity to return to the fields to retrieve the vines."

"That is interesting. Did you arrest her?"

"Not yet. She has disappeared. I arrived at her place when the sniffers were waiting for clearance and oxygen masks to access an airlock opposite Miss Andena's apartment. It seems that the vines were in an old storage room which is out of use. The sniffers have already confirmed that both vines were completely drained in the process. When we were finally able to access the storage room, we only found the vines."

Arnost looked unfazed at Haruz's beaten expression, and said, "I assume you have your men on it."

Haruz sighed and said, "Yes but there's strong evidence that the rebels took her."

"You mean kidnapped?"

"No, everything points to her joining Lunn's rebel group."

Arnost started to pace around again and said, "Right. Lunn is rapidly becoming a serious pain in the backside. We need to eliminate him."

Haruz said placidly, "We can't."

Arnost yelled, "I don't care what you need to wipe this man from the face of the Earth, but just do it!"

Haruz sighed and said, "His quarters are based on top of the main energy source for the whole county. If we make an attempt to attack him, he will simply blow up the power exchange which will result in eighty percent of the city's population perishing."

Tancred chuckled and said, "He is harmless as long as

he thinks he is in control of his little group."

Arnost moaned, "How on Earth did he manage to get access to that property? I don't like this!"

Tancred replied slowly, so as to calm Arnost down, "That might be the case, but you know that the situation will change soon. Best not to give him any unnecessary attention."

Arnost commanded, "Haruz, I want you to keep an eye on this him and attempt to free the woman."

He nodded and confirmed, "I'm monitoring the group already, but I'll make it my priority."

Arnost nodded, and Haruz left the room.

Tancred said, "That woman is far more dangerous than the leader of the rebels."

"Haruz will find her."

"I hope so."

Haruz still didn't like Tancred. He might look like a human, but the fact remained that he wasn't, and his casual dismissal of Lunn's power made him feel uneasy. Haruz knew it was a dangerous game they were about to play. He was convinced that Lunn would start to investigate those fields more thoroughly.

It had been mind-blowing when the small alien ship had landed on the secluded terrace of the high- security complex. He was the first one who made contact with Tancred. He had looked a lot different then but had still been able to make himself understood. The aliens had chosen to come to the Earth to help restore the atmosphere's lack of oxygen. Arnost was interested and had happily agreed to the aliens' offer.

Haruz wasn't convinced that they had been told the complete story, and his gut feeling told him that the exchange wasn't completely fair: replenish the air with oxygen for the chemical endorphin.

To him, it looked as though a group of addicted aliens who were short of supplies for their ever-growing population was using them. He sensed that there must be a catch, and it troubled him that up until now at least, he hadn't been able to find one.

The alien ship had made the fields, but to Haruz's relief had eventually run out of supplies. It was hard finding volunteers who were willing to give up a part of their life in exchange for a cure for their disease or disabilities. He had heard on the grapevine that recruiting willing people was a tough job. The rumours about people disappearing were getting more persistent which made the process of recruitment an almost impossible task.

Haruz hadn't been surprised when someone had managed to escape the alien plants. He had seen the footage of the amazingly talented Andena cutting through the vines to free herself and had witnessed the moment that one of the plants had shot a flower at her. Normally the small needles would have been enough to disable a human in seconds, but she had apparently been wearing a protective suit.

He had searched for her in the archives and had been impressed by her skills. Everything she did looked so natural: as if she always had done it. He had seen how she managed to get the access code to section Gamma fifty-four, and he really envied the security guard. The Martial Art classes Andena attended were a pleasure to watch and the last time he had seen her sitting cross-legged completely on her own he'd had to fight the urge to walk into the hall.

Now she had disappeared, he had no idea where they had taken her. He had heard rumours that Lunn's assistant had fallen out with him and that she had started her own little group. He knew that she had close connections with the owner of Bionex, and that troubled him deeply.

The CEO of Bionex was a powerful and ruthless man who didn't take kindly to setbacks of any kind. Once he had set his mind on something it had to be done no matter what. It was nearly impossible to hack into Bionex's secure systems, but Haruz believed that he had enough hidden resources available inside Danette's quarters.

He had programmed his software to scan every face, and it would notify him as soon as Andena showed up. He had been awake for over twenty hours and was feeling incredibly tired. The boost pills only worked for a short time and could easily backfire on you at the most inconvenient times. He was pleased to be able to crash out for a few hours.

Danette grumbled when she was disturbed by the loud banging at the back door of her lab. She had no time to lose because she had to deliver the last android and she couldn't figure out what the hell was wrong with it. Nothing had gone according to plan today!

She opened the door and was utterly surprised to see Lunn standing there with his arms crossed. When she realised that he had no intention of apologising, her anger quickly hit a critical level. She knew, considering his angry look and her sub-zero mood, it wasn't going to be a friendly conversation, and she sneered defensively, "Why the hell are you disturbing me?"

Lunn pushed her aside and let himself into the hall of her laboratory as he shouted, "Where is she?"

"Hey! What the fuck is the matter with you, barging in like this?"

He totally ignored her accusing remark and bellowed, "Where. Is. She!"

Danette hadn't a clue what he was referring to and screamed, "Where is who? Who the fuck are you talking about?"

"Don't try to play dumb, Danette! You fucking well know who I'm talking about," he spat.

Danette had never seen him so angry and she knew she had to calm him down before he exploded. She was racking her brains when it finally dawned on her that he was referring to the little slut Andena! Something must have happened to her, and now he was blaming her for it. Her anger suddenly evaporated and she sighed deeply. She said very calmly, "Lunn, why would I know where your little slut is? Are you sure she isn't just out there somewhere?"

He snorted but had calmed down somewhat when he said, "Well, I would have believed that if it weren't for the huge amount of drugs in her system. I found the vines that had been completely drained. So, where did you hide her?"

She snorted, "Why on Earth would I hide your fuck bunny? And besides how did you come to the ridiculous conclusion that I was involved?"

"She isn't my fuck bunny! I know for sure you've been up there because you've been offline."

Danette was starting to get impatient and retorted, "Yeah, right! Maybe I had switched the bloody thing off so I could work without being disturbed by a guy who only follows his dick! You know what? I want you to leave right now. I don't have time for this. Go and do some more research before starting to accuse the wrong people."

"I'm not wrong because it must have been you!"

"Oh Lunn, stop this stupid shit! I want you to go. NOW!"

"Where is she, Danette? You are the only one who knew she was involved! So stop lying to me and stop this stupid revenge thing right now!"

That was the final straw for Danette.

Her roar came from deep inside her, as she charged at him. Powered by the build-up of utter disgust and pure hatred she managed to push him out into the hall. As she slammed the door shut she screamed, "Fuck you, Lunn!"

She had the feeling he had just shattered the last bit of their brittle relationship and shouted at the top of her lungs, "How dare you to think I would ever do such a thing! Get lost! I'm out! Go fuck yourself with your pathetic little group!"

He banged once more at the door and shouted, "Let me in! I'm not done with you!"

Danette had really had enough of him and said in a normal tone, which sounded quite hoarse, "Fuck off Lunn and don't you dare to come back. EVER!"

She heard his footsteps dying away as she rested her forehead against the door realising that this might be the end of her relationship with him. She was still trembling severely from the built-up tension. She sighed while she was shaking her head and for once she truly hated that slut of a woman who had driven them apart. Tears welled up, but her anger kept her from crying.

Danette felt tired and wanted to rest, but she needed to get the last android ready for Bionex. Still flustered by what had happened Danette walked back to her office and came to an abrupt halt when she saw the CEO of Bionex leaning against her desk.

She was shocked: how the hell had he got in? The realisation that he had bypassed three different security systems made her feel very unsafe. She instantly understood that she would never have any chance of outrunning this man. She tried to straighten up while she wondered how long he had been in her office. She truly hoped that he hadn't heard the whole fight between her and Lunn. Focusing on the ugly man in front of her, she said with a slight tremble, "Mr. Yousima, what a lovely surprise! I've heard you're a busy man who doesn't often come to pay a visit."

His grin made Danette's hairs rise on the back of her neck. His high-pitched voice didn't match his enormous posture. "Ah, my lovely Miss Danette! You're always so discerning."

"Thank you, I assume you wanted to know when I will deliver the last android."

"No, not really."

"What do you mean Mr. Yousima? You don't want the last one?"

He started to pace around and said, "How shall I put this. Hmm. Let's just say that we have gotten a gift from above. I can't reveal much more information at this moment, but we might have an exciting addition to the nine we already have."

Danette didn't like what she was hearing because she had invested a lot of time and effort in the last batch and because she had given up her job with the rebels she needed all the credits she could get. His lips turned a bit when he saw Danette thinking about the situation and continued, "Of course, we will take all ten androids and you will get the final instalment as soon as the last one is delivered."

Danette smiled and said with a warm voice, "Thank you Mr. Yousima. I'll be honoured to bring the last one tomorrow afternoon."

"That is not necessary my dear Miss Danette. You can keep it here, and I would like to offer you a position in our company. Am I right to assume you are available?"

Danette knew that he had at least heard part of her heated argument with Lunn, and with a sinking feeling in the pit of her stomach, she realised that she now needed this job offer to maintain her lab. The question was whether she would like to work at Bionex. Her skill as an android expert was not in demand anymore since the Archon had decided that androids were too dangerous to deploy amongst humans after several fatal accidents. She had to admit reluctantly that there was very little chance of her finding a job that paid a high enough salary. "Yes Mr. Yousima, I guess I'm interested in the position providing the package is right. "

"I know your credit flow Miss Danette, and I'm willing to double it," he said with a smirk.

She was quite taken aback: Lunn had paid her generously which was more than enough to maintain the lab and have a good life. She stammered, "That, that is a very generous offer, Mr. Yousima."

He continued as if he wasn't interested in what she just had said, "Your job will involve taking care of the ten including training them for specialised acts. Are you still interested?"

She couldn't believe what he was saying because she constantly wondered about what Bionex planned to do with the androids. It was one of the few things in life that she enjoyed doing, and was more than happy to answer, "I think I can do that Mr. Yousima."

He chuckled for a short moment but then he cleared his throat. Danette couldn't believe her eyes at how quickly his expression darkened. He said with an icy voice, "Good. I want to make really clear that from now on you report directly to me. I would consider it an act of disloyalty if you have any further interaction with Mr. Lunn."

She got goose bumps when he stared at her with a blank expression waiting for an answer. She was shocked about the fact that he had the guts to interfere with her private life, but she knew she couldn't go back anymore. He had her trapped in his sticky and remorseless web. Danette forced a smile and hated that she couldn't see his eyes because of his dark sunglasses. She retorted with an insecure voice, "Of course, Mr. Yousima, I understand."

It took all the strength she could muster to force her lips into a smile when he stuck his hand out to shake hers. His grin was sickening as he said, "Well, good luck with training the androids. I'm sure they are going to be in safe hands."

"Thank you for having faith in me."

He chuckled, "It's not faith Miss Danette, I just know you're going to perform as expected."

Danette laughed nervously. She hated it when she was put under pressure. He let her hand go, and as he walked away, he said, "I will see you tomorrow at seven sharp, Miss Danette."

Pleased that he was leaving, she retorted quickly, "I will be there Mr. Yousima."

She heard the heavy door slam shut and she knew that he hadn't even bothered to listen to her last sentence.

Danette collapsed onto her knees, retching heavily. She realised with regret that her easy life was rapidly turning into a nightmare.

Lunn was walking aimlessly around, and no longer cared that he was entering the curfew zone. He had been searching for Andena by checking the hospitals even though he knew it was highly unlikely that she would have ended up there. The fact that he had removed her from his access list pissed him off. If she'd still been on the list, then she would have been waiting safely for him in his office. He sighed with frustration, knowing that searching for Andena was like looking for a needle in a haystack.

He needed a drink and decided to go to his favourite pub. It had been a while since he had been to a public place for a drink. As soon as he entered the bar, everyone stopped talking. The music sounded distorted through the old speakers, and all eyes were on him. He shouted wearily, "Just keep on talking, it's just me."

There was a short burst of laughter, but most of the people continued their conversations. Lunn sat down on a chair at the bar and demanded, "Double scotch."

The bartender looked at him and said gruffly, "No credits, no drink."

Lunn sighed and put his thumb on the scanner knowing that half the world knew now where he was. He didn't care and asked, "Can you double that?"

The bartender smiled when he saw that he could reserve the credits for the order and said, "Two double scotch coming up."

Lunn pressed on the scanner again when the two

glasses with the golden liquid were put in front of him. He took one of the glasses and smelled the strong liquor and downed it in one go. The burning of the strong alcohol in his throat numbed the pain he felt in his chest, and he reached for the other glass.

He felt a hand on his shoulder, and a friendly voice said, "I have the real stuff at my place."

Lunn slowly turned to the man and recognised the face. He downed the glass and hissed when the alcohol made its way down. As he put the glass down he grumbled, "I must admit, you're pretty good. I thought I would have time to have a few more before you arrived."

The voice chuckled and said, "You helped me by ignoring the curfew."

Lunn signalled the bartender for another round while the man said, "Come on Lunn, we need to talk."

Aware that the alcohol was starting to affect his brain he asked, "Why should I go with you Haruz?"

"Something is wrong if you are getting plastered and I think I know what it is."

"Oh, really?"

"Yes, and I don't think the rest of the pub needs to know what it is."

Lunn snorted and said, "I don't give a fuck about that."

"I do, and I know you do too. The longer we delay, the more difficult it will be to put it right."

"Ah, stop the nonsense: you don't even know what has happened."

"Do you know where Miss Andena is at the moment?"

Lunn took one of the new glasses of whiskey that the bartender had provided and moved it slowly to his mouth. He gulped the whiskey down in one go again. Coughing and spluttering, he raised his arms in the air, and he said with a placid face, "Nope. I have no idea where she is right now. She has disappeared."

Haruz grabbed Lunn's shirt and clenched his teeth when he asked, "What the hell did you do with Miss Andena?"

Lunn replied with a grin, "Apart from fucking her senseless last night. Nothing!"

Lunn didn't have time to react as Haruz punched him squarely in his face. He slammed backwards against the bar and slowly slid down to the floor.

Haruz was shocked by the intensity of his rage when Lunn had told him indifferently what he had done. He hated settling disputes with brute force but this time, he had at least, felt a degree of satisfaction. It was time to get things sorted, and he straightened his jacket ensuring that he looked decent.

Haruz flashed his card to the bartender and said with a smirk, "Take good care of him if you want to stay in business. I'll send someone to pick him up."

The bartender responded with a crooked smile, "Yeah, no problem."

Haruz walked towards the door, and before he left, he turned to the bartender again. He said with a smile, "Oh yes. Don't try to be smart. I'll know if he's paying for other drinks."

As soon as Haruz was on the street, he took his device from his pocket and wrote a message to his office, "Activate all channels in the country including the ones in Miss Danette's lab. Miss Andena is missing."

He was getting agitated by the fact, that this lovely girl had disappeared seemingly without trace. He had hoped that Lunn would cooperate, but it looked as though he couldn't care less. He would have more information tomorrow, but for now, he needed more sleep. His system had woken him because it had detected Lunn in the curfew zone.

He hated what was happening, and he knew that he would have had trouble sleeping if he hadn't taken another pill. He felt his body complaining and he regretted taking that last pill. He would pay for it for at least two days.

CHAPTER SEVEN

Joshua hated being exposed out in the open with all the delicate equipment. He knew that it was highly unlikely that anyone would turn into the secluded area, but he still had a bad feeling. He just wanted to wipe everything clean but needed to wait until the casualty was mounted on the table inside the cabin.

The fact that Mr. Yousima was personally paying a visit made him feel extremely nervous. This was clearly a high profile project, and it was vital that everything went according to plan. There was no room for mistakes. He shuddered involuntarily when he remembered the look in Mr. Yousima's eyes. His colleague had messed up badly and lost his job in the most horrendous way possible.

Joshua had been shaken, when Mr. Yousima had stepped in front of him and said, "Joshua, the pretty girl's neck is now secured and she is ready for the full upgrade."

He knew he had to behave as if Mr. Yousima knew what he was talking about and he replied submissively, "Perfect, Mr. Yousima. It will be done."

Mr. Yousima touched his glasses as he grumbled, "Now, don't mess up this time. I don't want to waste time on removing the equipment from a corpse again. Capisce?"

His heart was thumping loudly in his throat. He had made a fatal mistake the last time even though it wasn't completely his fault. He didn't dare meet Mr. Yousima's eyes and meekly replied, "Yes, Mr. Yousima I understand."

He patted Joshua on his shoulder and said, "That's my boy. Let's write history today and be nice to Olga unless you want to do the job on your own."

Joshua nodded, and was pleased when his boss walked away. He knew he had been very close to losing his job when he saw Mr. Yousima reaching for his glasses.

With a trembling hand, he swiped his card over the reader to open the door and pushed the cabin into the narrow hall.

He was glad that he had prepared everything already which would make the job quick and easy. The only thing he hadn't anticipated was that Olga would be there as well. He would have loved to kiss her pretty mouth with those juicy red lips, but he knew for sure it never would happen.

He jumped when he heard her icy voice saying, "Mr. Yousima asked me to assist you. I'll keep the door open so you can move your stuff."

He couldn't help but look at her fantastic body which was so beautifully contoured in her immaculate white slim-fitting suit. The white suit made her pale skin look much better, and her red painted lips stood out even more. He both adored and loathed her at the same time. She was horrible to deal with especially after spending time alone with Mr. Yousima.

He said meekly, "Oh, okay."

It took three trips to get everything he needed into the spacious room, and he was impressed at how elegantly it was decorated.

It took him just under a minute to get the cabin online and load all the modules into the pockets. He felt uneasy because Olga had watched his progress all the while sipping at a mug of coffee. The smell of the cheap surrogate coffee made Joshua a bit nauseous, and he asked her, "Do you really like that stuff?"

She stared at him and said, "No, but there's nothing else except this horrible tea which looks and smells like cat pee."

"Whose place is this anyway?"

Olga replied indifferently, "I have no idea, except that Mr. Yousima knows her well enough to offer her the penthouse suite at the hotel."

He hadn't seen the table yet on which the person was secured, but he was curious by what had happened. He asked, "So, how come we are here and not at the company?"

Olga sighed, and her face indicated that she was sick of telling this story. "The girl plunged straight through the conservatory."

"What? Here at level seven hundred fifty?"

"Yup."

"She must have fallen a long way it's practically impossible to break those windows."

"She didn't break a window. The whole structure of the conservatory collapsed. The girl was lucky that she didn't bounce off this one because the next conservatory is five hundred levels lower."

Joshua wondered how the girl had fallen out of the building in the first place. He asked, "How bad is she?"

As Olga walked towards the door, she said, "Apart from her broken neck, a few bruises. I reckon she must have fallen from the eight-hundredth level or so. I guess she must have bounced off the three other conservatories before she crushed this one. She was lucky not to hit any construction beams."

As he followed Olga into the room, he saw the table on which the girl was strapped. He couldn't believe his eyes when he saw her naked body.

She was the most beautiful woman he had seen for years, and it was also evident that she prided herself on taking good care of herself. He marvelled at the girls' beautiful well-toned body and was mesmerised by her vibrant red hair. Her full lips and her petite nose were in perfect proportion with her eyes. Her nails were immaculately painted, and her hair felt amazingly soft when he secured it into a net. It was impossible not to become aroused as he saw her pert breasts moving up as she breathed rhythmically. He needed to divert his gaze from the girl, and as he saw the discarded clothes lying on the floor, he said quickly, "These carbon boots are custom made, and they are much better than the ones with the outfit. She should keep those."

Olga answered indifferently, "Yeah, whatever. Let's get on with it. I don't want to be here the whole night."

Joshua chuckled and said, "I don't mind because I've brought my air bed with me. There's plenty of room for two."

She shot him a look which made him decide to stop trying to be funny. He saw Olga's eyes grow dark as she chided, "The longer you keep on chatting the later I'm back in my quarters."

He moved the girl into the cabin and closed the seals. He was not sure how well they had sedated her and decided to create a feedback link with the anaesthetic pump and her heartbeat rate. The faster her heart beat, the more anaesthetic fluid would be administered, which was the best solution in most cases.

He looked at the cabin display and chose the final option on the menu: 'Full Upgrade'.

He double-checked that all the connections and all indicators in the top row of the display were green. He knew that the girl had no chance of returning to a normal life with a broken neck, but he still questioned whether it was legal to administer a full upgrade to her without her consent. He knew she was very lucky to be alive. He had seen shocking pictures of splattered bodies from people who had jumped or fallen from those buildings. Olga had a senior position at Bionex, and he didn't want to mess up again by not asking whether they should do the upgrade on the girl at all. He sighed deeply and said, "Well, it's all set to go."

Joshua heard her snort. "Well, what are you waiting for?"

"You have to agree that I start the upgrade."

She moaned and said, "What do you think? Why the hell are you here? Why did I volunteer to be here on my free day? Is it because I like spending time with you?"

He hated her patronising tone and asked, "So, I assume you agree?"

She screamed, "YES! For fuck sake start the bloody upgrade!"

He winced and with a trembling finger he tapped on the screen. The screen showed a countdown from ten which had been built into the system as an extra precaution. He was staring at the screen while the numbers flashed by nine... eight... seven... six... five... four... three. His finger hovered above the button 'Abort' hoping that she would ask him to stop, but the numbers went steadily down to zero at an agonisingly slow pace.

Danette was drinking the last bit of the horrible tasting cold coffee while feeling dismayed as she closely studied the inner structure of the latest android. The bloody thing was still as dead as a squashed fly. She had been overjoyed when Bionex had first offered her a contract to create ten androids. Even though Lunn had warned her about Bionex's dubious practises, she had felt unable to turn down this once in her lifetime opportunity. There was no way that she would willingly let this slip through her fingers!

She finally had the opportunity to prove to herself that her specially developed Artificial Intelligence program was revolutionary and met the necessary requirements. She had spent the last fifteen years perfecting her program for the Artificial Intelligence core and by tweaking just a few parameters she was now able to convince an untrained person that they were talking to a real person.

She still hadn't worked out why Bionex had ordered so many androids, and she had been even more surprised when she'd received the 3D information folders. Bionex stipulated that not only did they all have to be female but they had to be unique! Danette was pleased that when she had calculated the price for the quote, as a precaution, she had based her price on them all being female. Female androids are composed of considerably more outer polymers than a male.

She was lucky she had managed to get hold of the most sophisticated skin renderer available and for an extremely good price. The outer skin produced by this renderer was as close as it was possible to get to human skin, and it was next to impossible to tell the difference between them.

She'd never been presented with an opportunity to prove that her androids were better and much safer than the others. She had been too late in submitting her evidence, and the board of the Archon had refused point blank to listen to her arguments. Her attempts to get another review were rejected and to her dismay, she had received an official warning for practicing illegally. It was an incredibly challenging time for her as she attempted to make ends meet. In desperation, she'd resorted to stealing and working as an escort.

Mercifully, Lunn had saved her from totally self-destructing. It saddened her that their relationship had deteriorated so rapidly, but she understood that she needed to focus and so shook her head to clear her mind of the disturbing thoughts. She was deeply troubled by the fact, that when it came to Bionex, she felt totally out of her depth. She shuddered as she recalled the foul expression on Mr. Yousima's face. Nothing about that man made sense, and that fact disturbed her on several levels.

She was beginning to think that she had made a serious error of judgement. The moment she realised that she'd been denied access to Lunn was incredibly disturbing. She mentally berated herself for the fact that she hadn't challenged him in any way. For this failure now meant that Mr. Yousima had even greater control over her life.

Her stomach was churning, and she knew she needed to eat something soon, but she probably wouldn't be able to keep anything down. Danette realised that it was no use staying at the lab because she hadn't the energy to focus on her work. The ridiculous brawl that she'd had with Lunn was rattling around agonisingly in the back of her mind. It was all just so fresh and painful. It was too much to comprehend, and Danette was aware that her anxiety was affecting her ability to think straight. She closed off her lab and rushed out of the door desperately wanting to be in the fresh air. Her stomach was still hurting from the retching which in turn conjured up disturbing images of the obese Mr. Yousima, staring viciously at her: penetrating her mind.

Danette needed to go home and eat before crashing out. She felt dirty, and the only thing she wanted right now was a long shower and to forget all about recent events. She was so preoccupied that she nearly forgot to show her ID-card to the curfew camera. She had a special dispensation to be late provided that she travelled only from her laboratory to her apartment.

When she turned into the hall before her apartment, she was perturbed to see a man leaning against the door. She stopped and instinctively reached for the pepper spray that was attached to her belt. This was exactly what she hated about her apartment complex: it was open to the public, and as such anyone could wander in. She gasped when she recognised Lunn's slurred voice, "So, have you done it?"

Danette could smell the alcohol lingering in the hall, and even though she presumed that he was too drunk to give a coherent answer, asked, "Have I done what?"

He chuckled, as he slid down the floor, "Never thought that hiding a dead human body would make you dumb."

Her anger was starting to get the better of her anxiety, and she decided that the best course of action was to ignore him completely. There was nothing to be gained from arguing with someone who was drunk. As she walked over to him, she could tell that he was in a terrible state. His shirt was covered with blood, and his left eye was badly swollen. It made her think about her actions and for a brief moment, she felt a pang of guilt. He'd clearly been involved in a fight, and his eye needed urgent attention. However, Danette had no desire to become involved in a lengthy discussion with him as she couldn't deal with this right now. The overpowering stench of alcohol was making her feel sick. "Lunn, go home. You're drunk."

"I don't want to go because I want you."

She instantly remembered Mr. Yousima warning her to stay away from Lunn. She looked at him, and said dryly, "Forget it, Lunn. Go home."

He laughed, and he stated, "I'm not going anywhere. I want you, Danette."

She knew how stubborn he could be and loathed the situation that he had created. She sighed and pushed firmly with her foot against his shoulder. He lost his balance and fell sideways. She had hoped she had time enough to enter her apartment but before she had the chance to open her door she found herself slammed up against it.

She felt his hard body pressed against her back. Normally this would turn her on, but his foul smelling breath made her even more nauseous.

She knew she was no match for his strength even in his present state. She groaned and pleaded, "Lunn, please don't."

"Don't you want it from behind anymore?" he hissed.

Danette was fighting against the urge to vomit, and she croaked, "Please stop, Lunn."

He started to grind his hips against her butt which increased the pressure on her stomach. She whimpered loudly when her stomach couldn't hold it anymore and with a loud retching noise the content of her stomach splattered forcefully against her door. Spatters of surrogate coffee mixed with stomach acid landed on Lunn's face and to her relief he staggered backwards.

She quickly opened her door and stumbled into her apartment. Just before the door slid shut she heard him say, "Oops, that went well."

With trembling hands Danette emptied her pockets on her side table and walked zombie-like with her clothes still on towards the shower.

She turned on the water and stepped straight into the cold spray. The cold water made her shiver as it ran down her body. She didn't care that the water was cold because she wanted to get rid of the awful rancid smell as soon as possible. After a short while, the water began to warm up, and completely exhausted, she slid onto her knees. She was so miserable that she began to cry.

Meleda heard her brother stumble into his bedroom. She felt for him: ever since he'd became the head of security, his nights were often disturbed. She knew that Arnost was very fond of him and treated Haruz as a son, although he would never show his emotions in public. She was regularly visited by Arnost asking her to make sure that

Haruz took care of himself. She thought it was sweet of him but after Haruz had pointed out that Arnost did it for self-preservation her regard in which she held him had plummeted considerably.

Nothing could have prepared them for the arrival of the alien ship. She had noticed that her brother was getting more and more restless which made her concerned that he was hiding something from her. Sighing, she got up from her bed. It was rare that she was unable to drift back to sleep, and feeling increasingly restless she opened her balcony doors and walked out to see if there were any stars.

Looking up at the stars felt different now that she knew there were other beings out there. She rarely went out onto the balcony these days: ever since Tancred had decided to place the last field so close to the main quarters.

The sudden hissing noises that occurred erratically always made her jump. However, tonight something felt different. The temperature was nice, and the air seemed to be crisp. She inhaled the air deeply and marvelled at the delicate and pleasant smell which she figured could only be coming from the field. She looked down at the massive square structure of the gorse which was glistening in the moonlight. It hadn't even occurred to her that it was a full moon tonight, and she couldn't believe her eyes when she saw someone walking directly towards the field.

Meldea ducked instinctively to ensure that she wasn't seen by whoever it was out there. As the man came closer to the field, she heard him humming a strange tune. His voice was low, and the melody was a simple one that he repeated constantly.

The song had a soothing quality, and Meleda wondered why he would risk standing so close to the gorse. Her question was quickly answered when the man was suddenly surrounded by four vines. He was still humming the tune and the vines seemed to be caressing his legs. One of the vines slowly moved up to his face, and the man stroked the vine as if it was a cat.

She was mesmerised by the gentle: almost loving movements of the vine and was shocked to the core when the man gently guided the vine to his neck. Meleda heard him gasp and shortly after that he slowly collapsed but the vines wrapped around him to keep his body straight. The vine at his neck shot away as if it had been bitten and the man quickly regained his posture. As soon as he stood up straight, the vines retracted back into the field, and with sturdy paces the man walked away from the field.

She realised that it could only be Tancred, and it suddenly made sense to her why he had asked to remove the cameras. Meleda knew that Haruz had complied with his request, but she wouldn't be surprised if he had other means of secretly recording everything. She knew that she was going to have to be discrete when speaking to her brother later.

Meleda suddenly felt cold, and longed to be back in the comfort of her warm bed. She stepped into her room and closed the balcony door as quietly as possible hoping that she wouldn't wake Haruz.

As she was lying comfortably in her bed, she couldn't help but mull over what she had witnessed. It looked like Tancred had been injected with something, and she was certain that he had been unconscious for a short while. Meleda was convinced that the vine, he had stroked, had administered some kind of potent drug.

The fact that the aliens had downgraded Earth to a planet where it was easy to get a quick fix, terrified her. All she wanted to do was sleep but was unable to quiet her mind. Why had Arnost allowed the aliens to build those fields? Did he know about the drug production? The one thing that surprised her most was the fact that the fields weren't guarded. Even though she had heard numerous rumours about people disappearing she struggled to believe that people weren't curious enough to take a look. She continued to toss and turn, and it was a long time before the reassuring veil of sleep descended upon her.

Lunn had the hangover from hell. He knew that he had messed up big time. He had never felt as depressed as he did at that moment, and he didn't blame Haruz for knocking him out like that.

He had ordered two more whiskeys to ease the pain of his bruised eye when he had regained consciousness. He desperately wanted to speak to Danette, and he had stumbled while still bleeding from his nose to her apartment. It felt as though he had waited for ages, and the effects of the whiskey quickly began to take hold. Staying awake was a struggle, and he had forced himself into an upright position. He knew that if he were to sit down, then he would quickly fall asleep and had been completely drunk by the time Danette had arrived. He was angry that she had dismissed him so abruptly and that she seemed to be unfazed about Andena's unknown fate. He was sure she knew what had happened to her.

It was only when she threw up so violently that he realised just how badly affected she was. Her stomach was her weak point. Whenever something wasn't right, her stomach played up. But this time, there was something else: something that he was unable to put his finger on.

She was hiding something from him, but he would probably never find out. He had gone too far, and he was sure their relationship had ended. He knew she would never forgive him. Now he had lost two women that he liked.

He could blame the alien flower but knew that his behaviour was to blame. He sighed as he distractedly massaged his neck in a desperate attempt to alleviate the throbbing pain in his head. A light knock on the door interrupted his reverie. Believing it to be his head of security, he shouted a little gruffly, "Go away. Let me be."

The soft melodic voice replied, "As head of security I need you to let me take a look at your eye, Lunn."

"It's nothing, just a little cut."

Lunn loved Alice's soft voice: conceding that her voice was the primary reason she had secured her job. However, her seven foot height body and her masculine build came in a close second. She had already entered the office, when she said, "You think it's nothing but the state of your shirt says the opposite and I think that I should have a look."

Lunn felt her large and strong hands on his shoulders pulling him softly away from his desk. She slowly reclined the chair, and Lunn was able to look straight into her eyes. She looked concerned, and there was more than a hint of compassion in her eyes as she asked, "Why did you decide to have a fight?"

"I didn't."

She briefly stopped her ministrations and slowly raised her eyebrows, "That was not what I've heard. When I got the message to pick you up from The Haggert, I knew you were in trouble. Now lie still, this will sting a little."

Lunn snorted, "The guy who sent you the message had knocked me out cold."

"Did he now? I bet you provoked him," she chided softly.

The cold cloth on his open wound stung, but was also refreshing, "Hmm, I don't know why he reacted so strongly to what I said."

"Who was it?"

Lunn opened his eye and asked surprised, "Haruz. He didn't tell you?"

Again Alice held still for a brief moment, and she clicked her tongue before she answered, "He sent me an anonymous text message. So I checked your quarters and after that, I tapped into the grid."

"What did you see on the grid?"

"You were leaving The Haggert so I assumed you were fine."

There was a silence while Alice was cleaning the last bit of blood from his face. She suddenly asked, "Do you know why he was so emotional?"

"Emotional?"

She chuckled softly, before she retorted, "Men don't just punch you in the face for nothing."

Lunn sighed again deeply and moaned, "I don't know Alice. All I know is that I have fucked up big time."

Alice slowly moved the chair up again, and as she handed him a glass of water, she ordered, "Here, drink this."

As he drunk the water, he looked at her blue-grey eyes and was pleased to see that he could trust her. He felt a pang of anger rising again. What had happened to Danette? Why was she so indifferent to the fact that Andena was missing? Why was she so extremely annoyed with him?

Why was she so jealous?

They had an open relationship where sex with other partners was tolerated. He still couldn't believe that Danette was so upset about it all. She was certainly short-tempered, but he loved to play with her fickleness.

Lunn was startled out of his thoughts when Alice asked, "Can you get up?"

He grumbled, "Of course I can. I'm not that drunk anymore."

He heard her stifle a giggle and her voice sounded joyful, "All right then! Get up, big boy, off to bed. You need to sleep off the alcohol."

It took him more effort to climb out of the chair than he had anticipated and he was grateful when Alice kept him steady as he stood. Still dizzy he walked, accompanied by Alice, to his bedroom.

When he saw his bed he knew that he was going to have difficulty sleeping, and he asked somewhat meekly, "Can I ask you for a favour?"

She stopped walking and hesitantly replied, "It depends on what you want."

He knew that she thought he wanted to have sex, but he was too whacked to even think about that and answered, "I would like you to listen to my story and perhaps even give me some advice."

Alice queried, "Why here in the bedroom?"

He had to chuckle inwardly: his reputation was seriously returning to bite him on the backside. However, his voice was calm as he replied, "Because I'm too tired to sit in a chair."

He flopped down on his bed, and as he lay down with a soft moan, he patted his hand to indicate that Alice should sit down too. "Please sit down. I won't bite."

She slowly sat down and stared at him for a few

seconds and then reminded him, "I'm listening."

CHAPTER EIGHT

When Andena woke up, she was alarmed by the fact that she was unable to move her body. Her breathing seemed to be controlled, and she couldn't feel anything. It was as if her body was detached from her. Only her main functions seemed to be present: she heard her heart beating, and knew that the very fact that she was conscious meant that she was being given enough oxygen.

She tried to open her eyes but she couldn't. To be honest, she didn't care that she was unable to do anything. Being in a void felt strangely relaxing. The only awareness Andena had of the outside world were the sounds of her heart beat and her steady breathing.

Even smells were lacking.

She had no recollection of the events that had led her to this and no great urge to find out either. She was happy to simply wait for the next event.

Assuming of course, that there would be a next event.

Haruz was unable to stop his face from contorting into a painful grimace as he sat down at the breakfast table. He could also see by his sister's huge grin that he had failed to hide his discomfort from her. They were too close for secrets. Ever since their parents had died, they had decided to stay together until one of them had found a partner. He had expected to be alone by this point, but it was still just the two of them. He thought that his sister was smart, beautiful, elegant and she exuded a confidence that made every man desire her. He was surprised that she never went out on dates, and whenever he raised that subject, she made it crystal clear that the subject was off limits.

As soon as the servant had left the room, Meleda said, "After you had returned home last night I went out onto the balcony, and there was an amazing full moon."

"Oh, I'm sorry that I woke you up Meleda. I'll try to be a bit more silent."

She smiled and said, "Don't. It's nice to know when you're home safely again."

She leaned closer to him and whispered, "I want to know if you have any recordings of what happened next to the field last night."

Haruz was flabbergasted by her question and looked at her for a moment wondering how she knew. Her smile was a joy to watch when he nodded slowly. Her voice was hardly audible when she asked, "When do you have time?"

It was strange speaking in hushed tones, but Haruz understood that she was wary about placing him in an awkward situation.

He took a sip of his coffee and said, "You know, it's been ages since we had lunch together. Why don't you come to the office at noon?"

Meleda said enthusiastically, "That sounds wonderful! It'll do you good to have something substantial for a change."

Haruz laughed and pulled himself to his feet after he had finished his coffee. Meanwhile, he reflected upon her words and knew that she was right; he needed to pay attention to his health after taking so many booster pills. He put his hand on her shoulder as he said, "See you at twelve. I'll make sure that the front desk is aware that you have permission to come to my office."

"Good," she said with a twinkle in her eye, "At least I can drag you away from your monitors."

As he walked away, he murmured, "It might be the other way, my lovely sister."

It was only a brisk short walk to his headquarters, and he liked that he had to take a road which was outside the complex. The smell of the outside air was always different, and since they had created the field, the air had a pleasant sweet tang. Haruz was convinced that the field was deliberately releasing the specific odour to make people relax so they would accept the structure more easily. It made him uncomfortable that alien technology was controlling the population on such a subtle level. Who knows what else they were capable of?

He couldn't wait to see what Meleda had witnessed. It would take some time to generate the pictures, but he was very pleased he hadn't removed the particle array.

He was happy to see that Gwendy was manning the front desk when he entered the headquarters. She was one of the few who only needed a few words to understand what he really wanted.

"Hi Gwendy, good morning. My sister will be visiting me around noon."

"Hello Mr. Haruz, Good morning. I'll arrange the necessary steps for Miss Meleda. May I assume she will have lunch with you?"

He loved how attentive she was, and he smiled warmly at her as he said, "You're right, Gwendy. Do you have any suggestions about where we should go?"

He could listen to her talk all day, "Oh yes I do! There's a new lunchroom which is said to be very special. I'll reserve a table right away."

Haruz chuckled pleased that she was always so straight forward, and he said approvingly, "Perfect Gwendy. I'm looking forward to that."

She purred, "You're welcome Mr. Haruz. Have a nice morning."

"You too, Gwendy." Haruz nodded and walked to his office in a much better mood.

At his office, he started his special program to extract the visual data from the particle array that was mounted on the wall close to the field. He knew the exact time that he had arrived home last night, and he reckoned that Meleda would have gotten out of bed a few minutes after he had closed his bedroom door. He entered the time and estimated that half an hour would be sufficient. After he had started the extraction, he checked his messages and was a little disappointed that Alice hadn't come back to him. It was a little strange because she was consistent in the fact that she sent a brief report early every morning. He sincerely hoped that she wasn't caught or compromised in any way because she was the only source he got to keep an eye on the major rebel core. He got up to get himself a cup of coffee and reckoned that by the time he returned the particle program should have finished.

Lunn woke up feeling warm and sweaty. He realised that he was holding a hand which was as large as his. It dawned on him that the large, warm body that was cocooning him from behind was Alice's. He felt the soft fabric of her cardigan, and he was pleased that they were both still dressed.

They had talked for a long time, and Lunn had come to respect Alice more than ever before. The situation with Danette was the most delicate subject they had talked about. He could sense that Alice was uncomfortable expressing an opinion about it.

Lunn wasn't surprised that she made him arrange to clean up the vomit at Danette's door and leave a bunch of roses. She agreed with him that he had messed up massively, and he could only hope that Danette might be a forgiving person. He knew Alice was wrong about that, but he couldn't blame her for not knowing Danette that well.

When she found out that Bionex was involved, she became nervous and lowered her voice as if she were afraid. It still brought goose bumps to his skin when he recalled what Alice had told him about Mr. Yousima the CEO of Bionex. He had always known that the CEO was ruthless, but he had underestimated his ability to manipulate people with his power. It also helped explain why Danette had insisted on continuing with the androids: Danette was no longer in control of her own mind.

Together with Alice, Lunn came to the conclusion that Bionex was now a serious threat, and he learned from Alice that Datanex, a provider of secure data connections, was owned by the same man. That news blew him away because it meant that Bionex was eavesdropping on roughly eighty percent of all secure connections. They certainly had the resources to harvest whatever information they desired; enough to take control of the entire country. Lunn now understood that it was going to be a race against the clock to see who would be the first to develop a deadly weapon.

He sincerely hoped that the schedule to complete the ring was still on target. He had kept it from Alice, and wanted to keep it that way because it was too dangerous to share such sensitive information with anybody else.

Alice was very intrigued by the story of the alien flower. In fact, she was visibly upset that Lunn hadn't shared that information earlier. He knew she was right, and it took him a lot of carefully chosen words to prevent a breakdown in trust. They both agreed it was unwise to investigate the flower at this moment, and he was very pleased that she understood the potentially lethal power of the flower. He realised that being an effective leader required a wide range of skills.

After Lunn had shown her the video of the field, Alice was in shock because she had seen her brother intertwined with one of the plants. It was agonising to see her with such conflicted emotions; her brother was still alive but held captive in one of the fields.

It felt strange when he was holding her to comfort her. It was very soothing and felt just right. They had been comfortably silent for a long while and apparently they had fallen asleep.

He had been stroking her hand absentmindedly and was a little startled when she squeezed his hand softly. She took a deep breath and said with a dark and sultry voice, "Good morning."

Lunn was surprised when she didn't move away from him. He had to admit that he liked the way they were lying and decided not to change his position either. He replied with a warm voice, "Good morning Alice."

"You don't mind me lying like this?"

Lunn thought about it for a moment and then decided that it didn't feel strange: it actually felt rather nice. This was totally new territory for him. He had never experienced this with any other woman. Squeezing her hand softly, he retorted, "No, It feels very comfortable."

Alice asked with a little voice, "Can we stay like this a little longer?"

Strangely enough, he was very happy that she wanted to stay like this as long as she felt right with it. He softly rubbed the palm of her hand as he said, "Sure, why not."

Danette was hurrying to her laboratory and dreading the fact she had to fix an unknown error with the last android before it was able to go to Bionex. She felt like she hadn't slept at all, and felt dreadful. She looked at her watch and realised with a sinking feeling in the pit of her stomach that she had even less time than she'd hoped for.

The only positive thing she had encountered this morning was that her door had been cleaned until it gleamed and there was a bunch of red roses on the brand new doormat. She had smiled knowing it was typical of Lunn to do such a thing. She had taken the roses with her and had given them away to one of the female beggars at the main square. She reckoned that the beggar could earn some credits if she were to sell the roses separately.

Feeling apprehensive, she entered her laboratory where she saw the android lying on the table. She slowly walked around the table looking at all the details and checking them minutely in the hope that she would find the flaw. She opened the little hatch where the main computer core was mounted and examined the connections of the core. Then it suddenly dawned on her: maybe the main software wasn't uploaded into the AI core.

Danette was relieved when the upload program confirmed that the core was empty. Something must have distracted her that made her forget to initiate such an important step. After she had started the upload program, she checked the time, and she was very pleased she had enough time to arrive at Bionex five minutes early. As she left her laboratory, she walked to the office of Bionex in a much better mood.

Olga had read the message from Joshua that the girl had been transported to the recovery room at Bionex. She was pleased because it had saved her a lot of time in the morning, which she had gratefully spent in her comfortable bed. As Olga walked into the corridor where the recovery room was, she found the empty cabin neatly parked against the wall. She looked into the operation tube of the cabin, and she was surprised at how immaculately clean it was. She heard footsteps, and as she turned around, she saw Joshua looking at her. He looked fresh: as if he had a decent amount of sleep. He said cheerfully, "Good morning, Olga. It's a wonderful day today."

She was always amazed by how cheerful he could be in

the morning because most of the time she suffered a bad case of morning mood. She murmured, "Good morning, I assume it went as planned?"

"Yes, even better than that. It went perfectly. During the whole upgrade her heartbeat kept steady as a rock. I don't know what you've given that girl, but it was a hell of a narcotic cocktail."

"What?"

"She is still out like a light, and so far I haven't needed to give her any anaesthetics."

She was surprised because she hadn't administered any drugs at all. On balance, she decided that it wasn't all that important and replied, "Oh okay."

Joshua was behaving a bit nervously, and he said, "But…. I really would like you to come and have a look at her."

His request didn't appeal to her at all. She knew from previous experiences how the girl would look after the upgrade. She had seen the ghastly cuts on the others and said, "I don't think I want to see her body at the moment."

"Don't worry: she is completely covered."

Olga didn't understand why she had to come and asked, "Why do you want me to have a look at her?"

"Just come. I promise you; it's not disturbing."

Feeling queasy, she took a deep breath and muttered, "Okay whatever you want to show me had better be good."

He smiled, and as he walked to the recovery room, he said, "She is on the respirator getting some extra oxygen to increase the healing speed."

When she saw the girl lying there, she felt her stomach contract a bit. She wanted to leave as soon as possible, and she asked, "What is so urgent that it can't wait?"

He lifted the sheet away from the girl's feet and said,

"We inserted muscle and joint enhancers for nearly every single joint. Have a look at her skin."

Olga looked closer, and she couldn't see any scar tissue at all. She moved her hand over the girl's foot and felt the small bumps of the enhancers. The skin was amazingly soft which made Olga feel quite awkward. She lifted the sheet higher and experienced a pang of jealousy when she saw the perfectly shaped legs. The girl looked as beautiful as before the upgrade and her skin still looked amazingly smooth. She whispered, "That is impossible!"

He said with a sigh, "I know. She looks so amazing. I don't know what has happened, but as far as I can see, she doesn't have a single scar."

She asked, "Did you check her? Has she had all of the upgrades?"

He nodded slowly and said, "Yup. She does have all the upgrades, and I checked them all."

She was taken aback by that remark and asked, "Right. So what now?"

They walked back into the hall, and he said with a meek smile, "Take a few cups of coffee and wait until she wakes up."

Olga said resolutely, "Not for me. I have other work to do. I need to get those androids up and running for Mr. Yousima's new trainer."

He sighed, "Okay, I think I can deal with the situation here."

Olga felt better now because she had seen that the girl didn't look mutilated at all. In fact, she was envious at how fantastic her skin looked. It was weird that she had no scars at all. She thought it was wise to keep it silent because she couldn't explain it all. Before she left, she warned Joshua, "Don't tell a single soul about the lack of scars. Make sure that she is covered at all times."

He nodded, "Don't worry, my lips are sealed."

She left in a hurry because she had already lost valuable time and she knew that she needed as much time as possible to get the nine android girls into shape. It was the first time that the girls would receive their initial training. Up until now, they had been offline and stored in Bionex's dungeons. Olga had received a message from Mr. Yousima this morning that she should bring the androids to the main hall. She knew that as long as she wasn't disturbed anymore she would have enough time to complete this task.

Danette arrived at the Bionex building five minutes early because she hated being late. The thought of upsetting Mr. Yousima made her shiver. As she entered the intimidating huge entrance hall, Mr. Yousima stood there waiting for her with a ghastly smirk on his sweaty face. The lighting in the hall was reflecting in his dark sunglasses making him look ridiculous. Danette had great trouble stopping herself from bursting into fits of laughter, and his voice had a sing-song quality to it when he said, "Ah my lovely Miss Danette. Ever so punctual."

The scent of his cheap aftershave overwhelmed her, and she had to force a smile. "Mr. Yousima what an honour to meet you again!"

His smile changed into to laughter that sounded like a castrated monkey, but it ended abruptly, when he said placidly, "It is my custom to welcome a new employee personally Miss Danette."

Danette was taken aback by his abruptness and

stammered, "I, I see Mr. Yousima."

He looked at her as if he was pondering whether he would say something about her appearance. Danette felt uneasy because she had spent quite some time deciding what to wear for the first day. She had decided to wear her suit because it was smart but stretchy enough if she had to work with the nine androids.

He walked to a desk and picked up a badge which he handed to her. He said, "With this badge you will have access to areas that have been designated for you. Now, if you would follow me I'll introduce you to Olga, who will guide you around and will be your assistant for today."

After they had walked what felt like a considerable distance, Danette began to get concerned about her ability to find her way back out of the building. Mr. Yousima stopped at the door and asked, "Oh yes, by the way, did you have any success with the last android?"

Danette was very pleased to be able to confirm that she had managed to fix the android on time, and she replied, "Yes Mr. Yousima, it was something very simple that I had overlooked. It will be ready when I have the time to seal off the inner core."

"Good, the last instalment will be transferred to your account by tonight."

She was surprised by his statement and the only thing she could think of saying was, "Thank you Mr. Yousima."

As he opened the door, he said, "Behold and see what you have built in the last few months. I think you've done an excellent job, Miss Danette."

As Danette walked into the large hall, she was very pleased with what she initially saw: it was indeed an impressive sight to see the nine androids sitting next to each other: they looked like a group of young women waiting to be informed. Danette's heart was beating faster, and she was excited by the fact that Mr. Yousima was pleased with the final results.

A woman dressed in an immaculate white suit entered the hall, and Mr. Yousima said almost joyfully, "Miss Danette I would like you to meet our lovely Olga. She will guide you around, and she is responsible for ensuring that your androids are in pristine condition. If you need anything, just ask her, and she will help you."

The smile on Olga's face didn't meet her eyes, and Danette could sense that something wasn't right when she shook Olga's firm hand.

Danette didn't want to spoil her good mood and smiled as she said, "Nice to meet you, Olga. I never thought that the androids could look this fantastic."

Danette instantly knew that something was bothering the girl when she answered with a tremble in her voice as she joked, "Thank you! Clothes make the girls."

They were all dressed in an extremely dull grey suit which covered all of the skin except their faces and hands. They all wore black boots and the ones with long hair had a neat plait. Each android had a number embroidered onto the suit.

Danette laughed but stopped instantly, when she saw the sour expression on Mr. Yousima's face. She had trouble stopping herself from shivering when Mr. Yousima addressed Olga with an icy tone, "What is the status of number ten?"

Her answer confused Danette, "She is still in the recovery room. I reckon it will take at least another two days before she is deployable, sir."

"Why is that?"

"It seems that she is still unconscious, sir."

His nose flared as he barked, "What the hell has happened to her?"

Danette admired the calmness that Olga exuded when she said, "It seems that the full upgrade was much more taxing than we had anticipated, sir. But she will be the first who has survived it, sir. I can guarantee you that the full upgrade had been successfully implemented, and it might take just a little longer than we had planned."

It was clear that Olga was one of his favourite employees because his voice was in an instant a lot more pleasant when he said, "I see. Keep me informed and help Miss Danette by giving her a tour of this department."

Visibly more relaxed Olga retorted, "Yes Mr. Yousima, I'll see to it that Miss Danette will have everything she needs."

Again he didn't wait for Olga's answer and the door slammed shut the moment she had spoken the last word. Danette blew out some air forcefully before she said, "That was really close! I really thought you were in huge trouble."

Olga laughed while shaking her head. The next moment Olga seemed scared as she said in a barely audible whisper, "As long he doesn't touch his glasses you're fine."

Danette understood instantly the importance of her remark and nodded slowly, as she asked, "What about that woman you were talking about? Who is she?"

Olga's face darkened as she said, "It is best not to ask too many questions."

Danette didn't like her answer at all and retorted, "If I'm going to be involved in the training of the woman, I rather would like to know who she is."

Olga sighed and said desperately, "You don't understand the policy and I advise you not to question Mr. Yousima's decisions. He gave the order to implement the full upgrade and besides the girl would have been paralysed from her shoulders down because of her broken neck. From what I've heard, she wouldn't have survived the injury at all if we hadn't intervened."

"We?"

"The medical team of Bionex."

Danette was shocked when she realised that they had implemented a 'full upgrade' - whatever that might be - on a woman without her consent. Even if that poor woman would have died because of the severity of her injuries, Bionex didn't have the right to 'fix her' in that way. She said placidly, "So this so called 'full upgrade' helped the woman to survive."

Olga's face changed into a hardened expression when she nearly growled, "In a way yes."

"And why is she going to be 'deployed' together with the androids?"

Danette had used her fingers to air quote the word deployed, and she wasn't surprised when Olga said in a dismissive tone, "You'll find out soon. Now, follow me so I can show you around."

She wasn't at all satisfied with the answer, but she could see by Olga's posture that she had nothing more to say on the subject. She knew that Olga wouldn't give her any additional information. Danette knew she was getting deeper and deeper into Mr. Yousima's murky web and to her horror she realised that she no longer had a way out.

CHAPTER NINE

Olga had trouble keeping her anger at bay. She thought that this Miss Danette was a stuck up bitch. She might be skilled to build those androids but who was she to judge her and her team? It was obvious that she didn't like it that she had to deal with a woman as well as her beloved androids.

As she and Miss Danette were walking back to the hall, she was thinking about what she had read in the information folders for the androids. She knew she was fortunate have had access those highly secure folders especially when it became clear why they were so secretive. It was typical of Mr. Yousima to masquerade his sinister goings on in a confused muddle. Olga thought that using the androids to cover up the errors was a smart move: provided, of course, no-one became too inquisitive.

Olga was shaken to the core when Danette broke the

silence by asking the question, "Do the androids still have their original program?"

"Yes, I haven't had the chance to make a start, and I'm pleased that you're taking over."

"I see. Too busy with other tasks?"

"Mr. Yousima always manages to fill my day to the brim."

Danette had smiled weakly and said softly, "I can understand that some days might be incredibly challenging."

Olga hated when people tried to sympathise with her. If they only knew what she had to endure on a daily basis, they wouldn't make stupid remarks.

She snorted, "I can assure you that from now on your days will never be boring. Let me show you the room where the androids are stored, and I'll brief you about the training program Mr. Yousima has set up for the androids."

Olga didn't like the woman's sour expression, and she couldn't wait to leave her with it.

Danette was pleased that she could finally start training the girls, and as she arrived in the hall, the girls were still sitting on the benches all looking dazed at the opposite wall. They hadn't moved at all, and Danette knew what would happen when she shouted, "Attention!"

All the girls stood up within a second and waited for instructions. Danette couldn't stop a little yelp coming from her mouth. She was super excited to see her hard labour bear fruit. It made her feel happy, but she knew that it was going to be hard work getting them ready on time.

Mr. Yousima had set quite a challenge, but she was convinced that she could pull it off, especially with her neatly designed androids and she instantly took command of the group, "Right! At ease! Sit down on the bench."

They all complied in an instant. Danette stood in front of the girls and studied the numbers embroidered on the suits. Hoping that the android was wearing the correct suit she asked, "Zero One, who am I?"

The girl replied with a ringing voice, "You are Miss Danette, our trainer."

"Good. Now listen carefully and store the next instruction: If you're in this hall, and I enter the hall, I want you to stand to attention immediately."

Danette expected a confirmation, but she realised that they had to learn everything from scratch. She didn't know whether to sigh or chuckle with frustration.

"I want to hear 'Yes Miss.' if you have successfully received and stored an instruction."

Again her remark was met with a deathly silence, and Danette said, "If I say at ease, and we are in the hall you sit down on the bench."

A chorus of nine female voices said, "Yes Miss."

She had to test whether or not her instruction had been received in good order and she shouted, "Attention!"

The women all jumped up again, and Danette grinned as she said, "At ease."

The women sat down on the bench in one smooth move. It was still intimidating to see nine androids moving as one. She left the hall and walked back after she had waited for a few moments.

As she entered the hall, the nine android women instantly got up which made her feel a little bit better. Now the time-consuming part of her job was about to start: making the androids ready for the task Mr. Yousima had assigned for them.

She pondered for a few seconds and said, "When I say 'go for it' you're going to run at a pace of two steps per second following the blue line around the hall, counter-clockwise. Since your body is different to the parameters stored in your memory, you will need to recalibrate. I will place cones and other obstacles in the route which you must avoid. You'll need to learn to overcome them as efficiently as possible. If you fall you will need to analyse what went wrong and adjust your patterns accordingly."

Danette looked at the androids and was quite excited by the fact that she finally had the opportunity to test the capabilities of her carefully designed androids.

With a big smile, she shouted, "Go for it!"

She hadn't anticipated the huge and laughable spectacle which unfolded right before her eyes. All of the androids got up at the same time and started to run. However, the first two instantly lost their balance and stumbled over their own feet. With a muffled thump they fell to the floor which resulted in the others falling over too. Danette realised that she hadn't anticipated that they would all start at the same time, but she was fascinated by how quickly the androids were adapting and before she knew it the androids were running at an equal distance from each other. It was impressive to hear the drilled sound of nine feet landing on the floor at the same time.

Now it was time to mix things up a bit! Danette placed a cone on the line. She was impressed when she saw that it took only four androids to wobble a bit before the others smoothly avoided the cone.

She was flabbergasted how quickly the androids were learning from each other! She was proud of the fact that the AI software was working so well. She couldn't wait to make it much more complex.

Olga walked into the hall where Miss Danette was training the androids and was taken aback by what she witnessed. The nine androids were running around the hall at a dazzling speed while they swerved and jumped over objects. The sight was mesmerising because of the women's light-footed tread. To all intents and purposes, it looked as if they were gracefully dancing over the obstacles. She couldn't help but laugh when she heard Miss Danette shouting, "Okay, now smile!"

Olga wouldn't have believed it if she hadn't seen it with her own eyes when the graceful dancing women started to tumble over each other. Within a few seconds, all of them were piled up into an impressive heap of mangled androids.

She heard Miss Danette commanding, "Okay! At ease and process what just happened."

It took the droids a considerable amount of effort to untangle themselves before they were able to walk silently to the bench to sit down.

Olga said to Miss Danette, "That was very impressive."

"Are you referring to how easily you can disrupt them with one command?"

She realised instantly that she had witnessed an unforeseen failure and that Mr. Yousima would have gone berserk if he had seen this. "I'm sorry if I have caught you at a bad moment, but the way in which they were moving was incredible."

Miss Danette's face turned into a brief smile as she said, "Well yes, you have an impeccable sense of timing, but I'm glad that I found it out before I made a complete fool of myself at the demo!"

Olga laughed as she imagined an unseemly pile up of androids in front of the whole company and she said, "I think you would have Mr. Yousima after you."

"Yes, I guess so. Anyway, what brings you here?"

Olga hated to dump unfinished work on somebody, but Mr. Yousima had insisted that she had to go back to the task of investigating the security breach. He had said that Miss Danette could take care of number ten.

She sighed, and she couldn't prevent the tremble in her voice as she started to speak, "Mr. Yousima wants my complete devotion to a pressing matter which means I have to dump something on you."

She heard Miss Danette huff, "Oh great. Don't tell me I have to take care of Jane Doe as well!"

Olga thought about how to respond because she wasn't pleased by Danette's bitchy answer. However, in a moment of blinding clarity she realised that she would have done the same thing. So, instead of losing her temper, she calmly retorted, "Well, yes, but Joshua will help you with it, and he is quite capable. If we hurry, we might catch him before he is done with her."

As they walked at a sturdy pace towards the recovery room, Danette asked, "What is Joshua doing with her?"

Olga had to laugh. She knew that she had used a strange turn of phrase and that clearly Danette hadn't understood its meaning.

"You know, the usual: checking her vitals and, if necessary, washing her."

Danette snorted and said, "I bet he finds it necessary

to wash her every day."

Olga felt her anger rising again because of her prejudiced opinion, but she knew Joshua wouldn't let an opportunity pass to examine that beautiful body.

Being in the same room with Joshua and the girl made her feel uncomfortable. She was relieved that Miss Danette was going to be there as well, and she murmured more to herself than to Miss Danette, "I can't blame him."

As they arrived at the door which led into the recovery room, Olga blew out some air before saying, "Right, here we are. Jane Doe is still connected to a respiratory device which might look a bit disturbing."

"Why is she on a respiration? Can't she breathe on her own?"

"She is on special medication to speed up the healing, and it is a lot more effective when she is breathing air with a higher percentage of oxygen."

Olga knocked on the door realising that it was more a warning for Joshua. She had the authority to barge into the room, but she wanted to spare Miss Danette an awkward introduction to Joshua.

He opened the door and said, "Olga! I didn't expect you to be here!"

He walked into the corridor and closed the door behind him. His face was beetroot red, and as Olga deliberately glanced at his pants, she knew that his embarrassment would get even greater.

She wasn't fazed by his arousal and said with a smirk, "I want you to meet our new colleague: Miss Danette. She will train the androids and your lovely girl."

Olga turned her head to Miss Danette to see that she was looking at Joshua with amusement.

Miss Danette licked her lips before purring, "Nice to

meet you, Joshua."

He cleared his throat, and as he took Miss Danette's hand with both his hands, he tried to deepen his voice when he replied, "The pleasure is all mine, Miss Danette."

Olga had to grin as she realised that he was failing spectacularly in his attempt to impress Miss Danette.

"Shall we have a look?" she asked abruptly.

Olga heard Miss Danette reply instantly, "Oh yes, I can't wait to meet our lovely Jane Doe."

Joshua tried to prevent Miss Danette from opening the door, but she marched straight into the room.

Olga rushed into the room after she heard Danette scream, "What? No! No! It can't be true! Where the fuck did you find her?"

She saw Miss Danette sink onto her knees and begin to rock. "Oh shit! This is so fucked up. This is so fucked up."

Olga realised that Miss Danette must have recognised the girl and that it had clearly had a huge impact on her. She hated finding herself in this situation because she was duty-bound to report anything unusual to Mr. Yousima. It was always unpleasant to bring him the unexpected news because of his erratic behaviour. She needed to know if Miss Danette knew the girl. Placing her hand carefully on Danette's shoulder she asked in a very gentle voice, "Miss Danette, do you know her?"

Danette stopped rocking and turned to face Olga; a look of bewilderment on her face. Olga felt a shiver running down her spine when she saw Danette's pale face change into an unnaturally placid expression. Her dark brown eyes seemed to pierce her soul; making her feel incredibly uncomfortable. It felt as if they were sitting there for hours until Danette forced a crooked smile.

She placidly responded with a croaky voice, "No, I have never seen her before in my life."

Haruz sat down at his desk with his coffee and saw that the video had been successfully generated from the particle array. He eagerly started the video and watched as the screen flickered briefly before showing the glistening gorse and the grounds between the field and the buildings. Just as he was about to take a sip of his coffee, he saw someone walking to the field and was mesmerised as the vines wrapped themselves, almost lovingly around the man. Tancred was clearly in control. "Damned Tancred! You are a conceited bastard!"

Haruz hadn't forgotten that Tancred was an alien, but he had up until this point, overlooked the fact that he was also a drug addict. He now regretted his decision to allow the field to be built so close to the quarters. However, he conceded since Arnost had been the one to grant Tancred's wish, then it would have been impossible to dispute.

With a big sigh, he fast-forwarded the recording and timed the complete event. He then deleted the file from his system to ensure that no-one else got their hands on the footage. As he was waiting for it to delete fully, it dawned on him that his sister must have witnessed Tancred with the vines. He had hoped to keep his sister out of this for as long as possible. However, he now had no alternative but to tell her everything. He smiled as he remembered the look of excitement on her face when he had suggested that they have lunch. He wouldn't be surprised if she had it all worked out already and that he only had to confirm her theory. The lunch was going to be interesting! Haruz was pleased to see that Alice had finally sent her report which he opened eagerly. His mouth fell open when he read the ultra-short message. Her demands were simple:

You are a major asshole! I am withdrawing my services until you have rescued my brother and killed Mr. Yousima.

A.

He had totally forgotten about her brother, and the truth was that he had no idea where he might find him. Alice's note clarified that. However, he wasn't surprised. Her brother had always been a thrill seeker and was constantly placing himself in dangerous situations. A knock on the door prevented him from giving it any further thought. Closing down his secure application, he called out, "Enter!"

A young man entered the office, and Haruz's smile was genuine when he exclaimed, "Baxter, what do you have for me? Did you have any success in finding anything? Did you find Miss Andena? Any feeds from Miss Danette's lab?"

Baxter looked tired, and his smile was a little forced. He cleared his throat several times before saying with a hoarse voice, "Um yes, Mr. Haruz we did. We didn't find Miss Andena but straight after you had sent us the message we activated the channels in Miss Danette's lab. We have recorded footage of a conversation between Miss Danette and Mr. Yousima."

Haruz had trouble hiding his disappointment at the fact that there had been no sightings of Miss Andena and said glumly, "Oh, I see."

"But um, it seems that a particle array was available,"

Baxter continued.

Haruz was surprised and asked, "A particle array? How's that possible?"

"I'm not sure and because we had some trouble to get the sync-line aligned I haven't had time to investigate it thoroughly. However, it seems that we sold that building to Miss Danette's grandfather."

Haruz laughed and said, "Those arrays are really old! No wonder you had trouble getting anything decent from them."

Baxter's grin was wide when he said, "Well we had some problems in the beginning but um, we finally solved that problem Mr. Haruz."

Haruz couldn't believe what this young man was saying, and he asked eagerly, "Did you? How far back can you go?"

"Up to eight hours, after that, it becomes too grainy."

Haruz slumped back into his chair and exclaimed, "That is amazing! Congratulations! I'll see to it that your team get a bonus! Send me the names of those involved, Baxter."

Baxter smiled and said meekly, "Thank you Mr. Haruz, I will. Um, I've made a video where I've combined the array and the other capture devices. It starts with Mr. Yousima coming into the lab."

"Thank you, Baxter."

Baxter walked to the door and before he left the office he said, "Have a good day Mr. Haruz. I'll send you the names of my team."

"You too, Baxter."

Haruz hesitated for a few seconds before he slid the memory stick into his terminal. He took a deep breath and started the movie. He was surprised by the confident manner in which Mr. Yousima walked into Miss Danette's office. The array followed him into the laboratory where he examined the android which was lying on the table. Haruz stared at the footage with disbelief. He shook his head in disgust when he saw Mr. Yousima groping the breasts of the naked android. Sickened, he was about to stop the recording, when he saw Yousima remove a small module from the android's head and then slip it into his coat pocket. A moment later he saw him replacing it with another one. As Mr. Yousima reached for the android's breasts once again, Haruz stopped watching the recording.

Haruz was so angry that he thought that he would explode. Instead of learning Miss Andena's whereabouts he had been forced to watch, while the perverted CEO of Bionex violated the android! Clearly Mr. Yousima had lost any sense of dignity. However, to his annoyance, Haruz realised that there was nothing that he could do to put this vile man behind bars.

In his frustration, he slammed his fist on the table. He was deeply concerned for Andena's safety. However, he also knew that he needed to reign his emotions in if he was to stand any realistic chance of finding her. Time was running out: the longer Miss Andena was missing, the greater the chance that she was dead. Haruz shook his head trying to keep his mind focused; he still had an hour before Meleda was due to arrive and he needed to find a way of venting his anger. He stored the memory stick in his safe and left his office for a serious workout.

Alice marvelled at Lunn's strong body. She had felt the muscles ripple when he had moved his body into a different position. It was the first time in her life that a man had made her feel so comfortable, and she couldn't help but wonder why this should be the case. She felt Lunn's fingers rubbing the back of her hand; it was incredibly soothing, and it gave her the feeling that he somehow cared for her.

Last night had been amazing; both shocking and revealing at the same time. As a result, Alice had now changed her opinion about Lunn completely. She had believed him to be a super macho man who slept with any available woman, but she was quite taken aback how sincerely concerned he was for both Andena and Danette. She hadn't expected him to confide in her. It had felt special but awkward when he had asked her for her advice. It was clear that he had strong opinions of his own about the best course of action, and it had been difficult trying to keep her emotions under control. Never had a night been so revealing and she had been pleased to find herself in complete alignment with Lunn for the first time ever.

Seeing the video footage of the field had shaken her to the core. Seeing her only sibling imprisoned by the vines had broken her heart, and it was hard not to burst into floods of tears. It was at that moment that she had made a decision. Under the circumstances, there was no way that she could continue to act as an informant for Haruz. He had betrayed her by lying to her! When she had asked him if he knew what had happened to her brother he had lied to her face! After two long, agonising months, Alice had assumed that her brother had most likely been murdered, and his body dumped at sea.

When Lunn had hugged her, she had been surprised at how comforting it felt. However, just at the point when she had started to become aroused, she realised that Lunn had fallen asleep. Disappointed, she had listened to the regular beating of his heart for a while and couldn't remember when she had also fallen asleep.

But now here she was; snuggled up against Lunn's muscular back and it felt wonderful! The innocent stroking of her hand had become more intense. Alice began to feel pleasant, tingling sensations in her whole body. Her belly was full of butterflies, and she loved the little jolts of desire that she felt in her core. She revelled in the way her body was responding to the mere thought of having sex with him. The heat of their bodies enhanced the wonderful musky smell of Lunn and she couldn't get enough of it. She pushed her chest against Lunn's back and couldn't resist the temptation to kiss him in his neck after she had inhaled his smell again.

Lunn turned his body slowly around, and she saw his eyes full of fiery desire. It was also clear by the manner in which his hands were beginning to explore other parts of her body, that Lunn knew exactly what was going through her mind. She knew that she couldn't deny her body's reaction to his wonderful assault any longer and if she didn't stop him now, then she was going to very quickly pass the point of no return.

She needed to make a decision.

The more he touched her, and the more he kissed her, the more she wanted him. If she didn't stop him now, then she knew she would be in deep trouble. Kissing him on the forehead, she whispered, "If we don't stop now, I might end up doing something that I regret."

His words threw her off guard, "Why would you regret something that your body craves, Alice?"

She thought about what he had said for a few moments and knew that he was right. It had been a long time since she had felt this way. She was speechless, and, this time, having anticipated her dilemma, Lunn asked, "Don't you trust yourself?"

That wasn't the problem. It was more about where this was leading. Looking him in the eye, Alice said, "I need to know what you expect to get out of this."

He chuckled and moved her hand to his lips. She felt herself go weak and moaned softly as he responded lazily, "I would like to see it as the icing on the cake. The perfect end to a perfect evening."

"Nothing more?"

"I will always remember it with a smile even if you want it to stop right now."

She pulled him closer, and she knew that she could have the best of both worlds; that she could enjoy a night of passion with Lunn and then move on with her life without any regrets. Flipping him onto his back, she straddled him, locking his lips with her own. When they finally came up for air, he asked with a smirk, "What flavour icing do you want, Alice?"

She purred, unbuttoning his shirt, "Vanilla will be fine."

CHAPTER TEN

Feeling drained, Danette plumped down on her sofa with a bowl of instant noodles. Her head felt as if it was going to explode. She knew that she would feel better after she had finished her bowl of food that had been enriched with some concentrated vitamins and enhanced proteins.

It had been a taxing day working with the nine androids who needed to re-learn the smallest things, but that was nothing in comparison to the heart-stopping shock that she had experienced when she saw Andena lying there in the recovery room.

It was as if her whole world had collapsed into a pile of shattered dreams. Seeing Andena's lifeless but stunningly beautiful body made Danette slump down to her knees: she couldn't bear to look at the woman who was responsible for compromising her in this way. What's more, she'd had to bury her pain. There was no way that she could tell Olga, or anyone from Bionex that she knew the girl. She shivered, as she thought about the potential consequences of anyone finding out. It was for her the hardest decision she had ever had to make, but she knew she had no choice. Luckily, she had managed to convince Olga that it was seeing Andena lying there with all those tubes that had freaked her out.

She had been racking her brains all day thinking about just how Andena could have ended up at Bionex.

Now she was going to be forced to deal with this woman every day, and couldn't confide in a single soul. Knowing how desperate Lunn was to find Andena, how could she ever look him straight in the eye again? Thinking about it made her stomach churn.

Feeling a sudden urge to be sick, Danette put her bowl down and pulled herself to her feet hoping that her nausea would settle down.

She knew that she needed to eat and have a proper rest.

She knew that she had ruined her life by getting involved with Bionex.

She knew that she had to continue to train the androids.

She had no idea how to handle the situation with Andena.

However, what scared her more than anything was the realisation that she would more than likely wind up like Andena if she annoyed Mr. Yousima. It was this that brought her back to her senses, and she forced herself to finish her noodles before reaching for her sleeping pills. She hated taking the drugs, and had been proud of herself for gradually weaning herself off of them but knew that unless she got a good night's sleep, then she was doomed to fail. Telling herself that she would dispose of the remaining pills first thing in the morning, Danette hastily swallowed two and flushed them down with a glass of water before calmly undressing. She had this down to an art form and knew that she had around five to seven minutes before she would pass out.

She was startled by the knock on her door, and she automatically shouted, "Who is there?"

She was unsurprised to hear Lunn's voice, "It's me, Lunn."

A pang of guilt shot through her body and was coupled with an over-arching sense of anger. She didn't know what to do. However, her feelings for him were still strong, and against her better judgement, she opened the door. As she walked unsteadily back to her bedroom, she tried to sound indifferent as she said, "Thanks for the roses."

She realised that it sounded more like an apology and decided not to say anything more.

His voice sounded strange as he said, "You're welcome. It was the least I could do."

When she turned to her bedroom door, she saw Lunn leaning against the door frame looking bewildered. The sleeping pill was making her behave girlishly, and she began to giggle.

"What's so funny, Danette?"

"The look on your face," she responded aware that she was slurring already.

Those damned pills!

She dropped down her sweatpants and pulled her sweater over her head without being the slightest bothered that Lunn was watching. Dressed only in her underwear, she sighed blissfully, as she crawled into her bed and said,

"I've taken two Dormancans. You'd better tell me quickly what you want."

"I owe you an apology. What I've done was….. Look: I want to talk to you."

"You're wasting your time," she answered sleepily.

"Then I'll come back tomorrow."

She suddenly remembered Mr. Yousima's intimidating threat and tried to keep her voice as calm and steady as possible. "Don't bother Lunn. We don't have anything to say to each other."

Danette was surprised when Lunn crawled onto the bed. With his face pressed against hers, he kissed her softly on her left cheek he whispered hardly audible, "Datanex belongs to."

Then he kissed her right cheek, and again he whispered, "Yousima."

The name blasted into her brain like lightning, but in her drugged state she couldn't fully comprehend what Lunn was trying to tell her. The name 'Datanex' was familiar. Her brain was starting to get sluggish because of the pills. She really needed to understand his message! It was frustrating that she couldn't place the name Datanex. What does it mean? She repeated the name over and over in her head.

Datanex, Datanex, where had she heard that name before?

Then it dawned on her, and she could barely keep herself from gasping. She was using Datanex for her secure connections! Now she understood the enormous impact of what Lunn just had revealed to her. It also explained how Mr. Yousima had managed to bypass her security systems with such ease!

She had always laughed at Lunn's suspicions about

using anything other than his software for secure connections. He had given her the software to set up her secured connections, and she remembered the funny name that he had given it. She had no idea what had possessed him to call it 'Captain Hook.' Danette inhaled deeply trying to fight off the effects of the sleeping pills and did her best to look him straight in the eyes. She couldn't keep her eyes open anymore and whispered, hoping that he understood the hidden message, "Farewell skipper."

She smiled when she thought she could feel the barely noticeable squeeze on her shoulder. The darkness descended rapidly, and she didn't even notice that Lunn tucked her in.

It was difficult for Lunn to leave Danette's apartment knowing that he wouldn't be able to come back. She had made it clear that she didn't want him to be a part of her life anymore.

It was over.

He felt a pang of sadness, and it hurt to watch her falling back into her old habits. He had helped her with a lot of personal issues, and he had been proud when she had managed to kick her drug habit. He was also hurt by the fact, that she was clearly moving on with her life: with a life that didn't involve him. Lunn thought it was incredibly telling the last words she had said were influenced by the drugs because it was clear she saw him as a captain running a ship instead of a leader of the rebel group.

He sighed, and he needed to hurry to be on time for the monthly meeting with his financier. It would be the fifth time that they had met each other in person in the cave near the shore. Lunn knew the man was using a device to distort his voice and that he deliberately stayed in the dark. It didn't bother him much that the financier wanted to keep his identity secret as long as the credit flow remained steady. It had made life a lot easier and had helped transform the group into the well-oiled machine that it had become.

Lunn was careful when he reached the steps down to the cave. They were slippery due to the continuous spray of the crashing waves. He loved the place: far away from luxury and the hassle but easily accessible in fifteen minutes on foot. The moment he entered, he heard the metallic sounding synthesised voice echo around the cave "You are late."

Lunn answered, "I know, I'm sorry. I forgot that a part of my route is in the curfew zone now."

The man clearly wasn't interested in his excuse and came straight to the point by saying, "I want you to speed up the launches."

Lunn was surprised because this was the most expensive project and he always had to wait for the financier to release payment. "That will be a major undertaking," he remarked.

"What is your schedule now?"

"The ring should be ready in six weeks. I doubt if we can reschedule the launches."

"Hmm. Does the ring need to be complete to target a very small area?"

Lunn was taken aback by his question and said, "I don't know. I think it might depend on how small you're talking about and where this area would be."

"Not larger than a soccer field and the location would

be a few miles from the central county."

Lunn was intrigued, but he knew there would be some complications if the target was so close to town and he said, "I have to consult my team to be sure if we can do that. We are moving the systems to the new protective headquarters tomorrow. So the earliest that we could start would be three days."

There was a long silence which made Lunn feel uncomfortable, and he was dying to know what the target would be.

The man said, "The timing will be sufficient."

Lunn asked, "May I ask what the real target will be?"

The man's chuckle sounded sinister. His demeaning answer blew Lunn away, "Bionex is going to be a real danger to our society. Your former assistant is training a small group of androids and a hybrid."

"A hybrid?"

"Yes, a female who has been enhanced with implants. I have just received confirmation that it is a woman."

Lunn was not surprised that Bionex would do this. However, it was still disturbing to know that they had managed to create a hybrid. Alice was right: the CEO of Bionex was balancing on the rim of ethical illegality.

Then it hit him: it was a woman! Andena's lovely face popped straight into his mind, and he hoped that the financier could provide him with the information that he so desperately needed. "Do you know who she is?"

"No, and it is not important," he said dismissively and continued, "My intelligence says that they will start to train outside at the Bangly plateau soon. It's a perfect opportunity to disable them all in one go."

He knew even if it were Andena, that there was nothing that he could do to prevent this from happening.

He had to bite his tongue, and it took him considerable effort to remain calm as he grumbled, "I see."

He still had trouble accepting that this man had no qualms about murdering a human. Even if she was completely mutilated by Bionex, she was still made of flesh and blood and had probably led a normal life.

As a rebel leader, Lunn knew that he needed to set his emotions to one side. Slowly exhaling, he forced himself to focus on the financier and was impressed by how well informed the man was. "All right. I assume that my technicians can pull this off. I'll ensure that we are ready on time."

The man spoke slowly as if he was double checking his plan and said, "I'll contact you. But be prepared to act fast. They won't stay on the plateau the whole day."

Lunn wanted to talk about the adventure with Andena and the alien fields and said, "I have video footage of the inside of one of those fields."

"I know. I've seen it."

Lunn was totally gobsmacked. How the hell could the financier have seen the recording? Lunn realised that the financier had somehow managed to access his network.

He tried looking into the man's eyes, but could only see his legs. Still dazed by the indifference of his financier he had trouble finding the right words. The man continued, "I'm on to it."

He couldn't believe what he just heard the man saying and started to wonder what on Earth was wrong with him. Lunn blurted, "What? You're on to it? Those plants are fucking alien, and they fucking use people to flourish!"

The man asked calmly, "Who said they are alien?"

Lunn huffed, "Have you ever seen plants which can attack you with such an incredible speed?"

He replied stoically, "No, but they seemed to have been specially cultivated."

Lunn snorted while starting to get a foul taste in his mouth, "Yeah by aliens! I refuse to believe that anyone on this planet has the knowledge to pull this off. Tell me: how do you explain then the sudden appearance in one night?"

The man's chuckle sent chills running down Lunn's spine. "With the right amount in credits, anything is possible. I've seen things which would blow your mind. So as I said before: I'm on to it."

Lunn had to admit that he, himself, was just an experienced guard with ambition and brains enough to maintain the group he was leading. He also knew that he had only been in this business for a very short time. He had to force himself to calm down! Lunn shook his head and chuckled with frustration. He said sarcastically, "So what we are doing is just peanuts."

There was a brief silence, and Lunn knew he had upset the financier considerably. The man was clearly annoyed as he snarled, "The ring will be the most sophisticated weapon on Earth when it is completed! I would hardly call disabling the entire Earth with just the push of a button, peanuts."

Lunn knew that the ring was the financier's pet project and that he would be wise not to get too carried away by his emotions. He knew that the man was right, and he retorted, "Yes, just by the sheer numbers."

When the man spoke again, he sounded calmer. "Lunn, as soon as the ring is ready I will be able to answer your questions more fully. At the moment, I must remain the plain financier."

Lunn understood the delicate situation his financier was navigating and said, "All right, I'd better scoot on because Haruz is still on my back."

The man retorted, "He was. He has other, more pressing things, to take care of."

"Oh well, good to know I'm a free man again. I think I'm going to have a drink."

"All right. I'll contact you in a few days."

Lunn didn't need to reply and stepped out the cave. He walked up the steps pondering what the financier had said about Haruz. He was constantly surprised by how much the financier knew. Where did he get the information from? Who was his informant?

He was also very surprised by his lack of interest in the fields. Lunn was certain that the financier knew a lot more than he was telling and this frustrated him enormously. He was in desperate need of a strong drink.

Haruz was happy that he could finally relax. He had walked back home from the meeting with Arnost, which was tiring because of the long and intense discussion about the awkward situation that Bionex had created. The potential threat of the newly created android army was making Arnost almost irrational. It was Tancred who pointed out to him that as long as the small group of androids refrained from manifesting in public, nothing had to be done about them.

Haruz was pleasantly surprised by Tancred's simple but clear remark, and that Arnost had been left in no doubt that in terms of the law, Bionex had not committed a crime. In fact, the more that he thought about it, the more Haruz wondered why Tancred had interfered at all. There had to be a reason why Tancred had suddenly decided to involve himself in the heated discussion. He had noticed that the alien was becoming less tolerant of Arnost's outbursts. Something about the manner in which Tancred was behaving at the meetings had changed, and it bothered Haruz that he was unable to figure it out.

He smiled as he remembered how Arnost had stared at Tancred with a dumbfounded expression on his face. Feeling happy, Haruz entered the apartment and was surprised by the fact that Meleda was still up. He silently slipped into the kitchen, where he found her enjoying a small plate of snacks.

He could see the contours of her body when the light of the fridge shone through the thin fabric of her nightgown as she opened the fridge door. He was shocked by how thin she was and asked himself whether she had always been that thin. The last time he had seen his sister naked was when they were teenagers. He had accidentally walked into the bathroom when she had forgotten to lock the door.

He was sure she was not as thin as she was now and wondered why she was starving herself that much. When she had seen him standing in the doorframe of the kitchen her face had turned a little red, and she said, "Oops! You've caught me red-handed."

"Hmm, I thought I was the only one who raided the fridge at night."

Her laugh made him remember his mother's laugh: the same sweet sounding but oh-so-controlled laugh. As if it was an art to satisfy someone's ears with a pleasant sounding laugh.

"I felt too full after our wonderful lunch, so I decided to skip dinner. However, I started to get a little peckish."

Haruz grabbed a sandwich from the plate: they were

the same as those served in the restaurant that they had visited earlier in the day. "How was your afternoon? Have you recovered from the shocking information I gave you?"

She smiled and popped a morsel of food into her mouth, presumably to give herself more time to formulate her answer. "I already had my suspicions, Haruz. I think that we need to be very careful. I don't like the fact, that Tancred is an addict."

He gave her answer some thought but instinctively knew that she was right. He knew from experience how devastating the effects of an addiction could be. Both their parents had died as the result of an overdose. He sighed. "Yes, Meleda but I'm not in a position to question Tancred's integrity. In fact, he managed to put an end to one of my useless conversations with Arnost."

A small sigh escaped from Meleda's lips and gently tapping his arm she said, "Don't forget Haruz, addicts will do everything to protect their habit. Don't you see that he is manipulating you?"

He re-ran the events of the last meeting in his head and recognised the techniques that Tancred had skillfully deployed.

"Damn! You're right. I still don't know when the others will come."

Meleda squeezed his arm and whispered, "We have to find a way of preventing Earth from being turned into a druggie's paradise. We will all be doomed if we don't fight back against those aliens."

Haruz hadn't yet mustered up the courage to tell Meleda what was really happening in the fields and was shocked when she asked, "Do you know why those plants need to feed off humans?"

He was speechless for a moment and couldn't believe

that his sister knew. He whispered while hardly daring to look into her eyes, "How do you know?"

He saw the look of disappointment in her eyes when she responded, "Why didn't you tell me?"

Haruz looked down at his feet, at a loss for words and was genuinely remorseful. He heard her sigh and her voice sounded darker when she uttered, "There is always an element of truth in rumours. The fact that there is no-one guarding those fields makes sense. They would be taken by the plants too! How many people are in the fields, Haruz?"

He was shocked by her determination to get to the truth. When he looked up, he saw that she was genuinely upset. He had totally underestimated her. It didn't take long to fill in the blanks. "I don't know the exact number, but I think maybe three hundred sixty. The majority of them were volunteers."

"Volunteers?"

"Yes, you see, in exchange for being a part of a plant, the plant would cure their illness."

Haruz could see the disbelief in his sister's eyes and wasn't surprised when she asked with a quiver, "That sounds too good to be true. What is the catch Haruz?"

The fact that he was unable to give her a satisfactory answer made him feel stupid. "I don't know." He said softly, "The plants generate oxygen and create a drug. In exchange, the plants need human bodies."

Her voice was hoarse when she said, "If we can't stop this, we will all end up attached to a plant."

Haruz hated that Meleda immediately opted for the most negative possible outcome. "That's not going to happen."

Meleda had taken her hand off his arm, and he felt the sudden loss of her warmth. She inquired with a stern voice,

"Do you know how many aliens will come? A couple? A hundred? A thousand? Ten thousand? A billion?"

There was a silence which he was desperate to fill, but he couldn't give her a satisfactory answer. She pressed him by asking him insistently, "How many Haruz?"

He had to admit that he had totally misjudged the severity of the problem, and he wondered why they had agreed on this plan with Tancred.

Meleda looked at him: her eyes full of fire, as she asked, "How on Earth did you come to agree to this? Were you out of your mind? What were you thinking?"

Why didn't he manage to see this himself? Why was it that this talk with his sister had opened his eyes, and revealed the full extent of the problem?

Meleda was pacing around the room, and she suddenly stopped. Turning to face him, she asked, "Have you ever had a meeting with Arnost or the board without Tancred?"

Haruz had to think hard and started to realise that the memories of those meetings were blurred. It dawned on him that he and Arnost had been manipulated by Tancred from day one.

"Good grief! No, he was always there!" he gasped.

"Right. That means Tancred is using something to manipulate your brains."

Haruz exclaimed, "I, I can't believe this! This is really insane! How the hell didn't I notice?"

"He is dangerous if he can manipulate us so easily without us noticing that anything is amiss."

"This has to stop. I need to get rid of him, but how?"

He was taken aback when Meleda put her hands on his face as she said, "Haruz, I want to investigate Tancred, and I want to have Carte Blanche."

He knew it was probably the best way to get a grip on

the situation without raising Tancred's suspicions and he conceded, "I see where you're going with this. I'll take care of it tomorrow."

"No, I want you to organise it now Haruz, because I don't know if you will still agree to it tomorrow or whether you will have completely forgotten our conversation."

He thought about it for a moment, and because he had no way of understanding the full extent of the power that Tancred had over him, he had no choice but to agree with her.

At this moment, his mind was clear and he understood what was happening. As he took his memory stick out of his pocket, he said, "Okay my dear sister, let's go over it, right now."

There was a small smile on her face again which made him feel a lot better.

He now understood that Tancred was far more dangerous than he had realized and that preventing himself from being manipulated again, was going to be a challenge. There was only one solution: he needed to capture Tancred. Alive.

CHAPTER ELEVEN

Lunn walked into The Haggert and as he had expected no-one paid any attention. The bartender had a crooked smile on his face when he asked, "Same as last time?"

This time, he wanted to go easy on the alcohol, and he replied, "Yes, but just one."

While he was waiting for his drink, Lunn thought back to what his financier had said to him about the woman who was mutilated by Bionex. He sincerely hoped that it wasn't Andena and wondered how he could find out who this woman was. He realised that Danette might have information, but the thought of another confrontation with her filled him with dread. However, he began to wonder just how Danette could have any useful information. There was no doubt that his financier had paid an exorbitant sum of money for the highly classified information.

But who from?

Danette, as a new employee at Bionex, was unlikely to have the relevant security clearance. The best course of action was to wait. However, Lunn ruefully conceded that waiting was not something that he was good at.

He knew that the ring was complete except for the North Pole region. He was more concerned about the location: even a highly concentrated narrow EMP might damage sensitive equipment and trip some fuses in an area so vast. Lunn wasn't surprised that Bionex had chosen the Bangly plateau as their practice area: it was high, out of sight and had no security cameras.

But as the financier had pointed out it was a perfect opportunity, and he knew that with a strong enough EMP, the androids, and the woman wouldn't even know what had hit them. Bionex indeed would suffer an enormous loss which might bankrupt the company completely.

He was a bit startled when the bartender planted two glasses with the amber coloured liquid in front of him and grumbled, "I thought I said just one!"

The bartender held his hands up in a gesture of defeat, as he pointed with his thumb to the left, "Hey! Calm down, calm down. The lady bought you one."

Lunn sighed and hung his head. More than anything else, he wanted a quiet night to himself, and he realised that coming to The Haggert had been a huge mistake. He knew that he was in deep trouble as soon as he heard her sultry voice, "I thought you would be pleased to have some female company, especially if that also means free drinks."

He chuckled because he recognised her voice. She was one of the county's most desirable prostitutes and a night with her would cost about a month's salary. He turned towards her and remembered how he had always thought she looked so beautiful. She was as stunning as ever, and the aging process apparently hadn't begun to take its toll on her. Her radiant blue eyes were still as mesmerising as before, and her skin complexion was flawless as far he could detect. She had clearly invested in her appearance because Lunn was sure her breasts were considerably larger than the last time he had seen her. He considered for a moment whether he should give her what she wanted but, strangely enough, he was not in the mood to bury his face into her fake tits tonight. He smiled and clunked his glass against hers. He was a little embarrassed that he had forgotten her name when he asserted, "I appreciate that uhmmm."

"Lily," she purred with a naughty smile.

"Lily, a nice name."

Her smile changed to a mesmerising gleam as she said softly, "Thank you, Lunn."

He finished the glass in one go and took the other glass in his hand. He marvelled at the fact that she had done her homework and knew his name. He was flattered by her attention.

"You're welcome," he said after he had taken some deep breaths to recover from the burning sensation from swallowing the alcohol.

He saw she had done the same, and as he pointed at her empty glass he asked, "You want another one?"

She smiled showing her perfect, brilliant white teeth and happily agreed, "Hmm yes. It always makes me feel nice and warm, in my tummy."

Lunn hadn't looked at her lower body, and he admired her flat stomach. Her crop top barely hid her gravity-defying breasts, and her ultra-short skirt showed most of her smooth, toned legs. Lily looked incredibly sexy, and she seemed to be ready for some mind-blowing sex, but Lunn was not attracted to her at all. He slowly looked up and saw she was biting on her lower lip as if she was turned on by his gaze.

It was a strange situation to find himself in.

However, he didn't crave her fantastic body and the only reason for this, that he could think of, was the emotional roller coaster he was currently on: Andena was missing, Danette had practically dumped him and then he had enjoyed an incredible time with Alice. The steaming hot morning with Alice was still sizzling in the back of his mind which made him feel quite insecure. He needed to stop making his life so complicated. Having sex with Lily right now would do more harm than good.

He decided, to be frank with her and smiled as he said, "Lily, my lovely girl. I'm here to get a little drunk, and then I am going home. I don't mind if you want to stay and drink with me, but I am going home alone."

He wasn't surprised that her smile never faded as she countered, "You pay double if you find me in your bed tomorrow, my dear."

He laughed and downed the other glass. "Okay, challenge accepted on one condition."

Her beautiful face changed into a wild cat which was assessing her pray. Slowly sliding her hand up his legs, she growled softly in his ear, "And what would that be my gorgeous man?"

Lunn lifted her hands gently off his legs and said, "No touching, no body contact."

She pouted and asked with a girly voice, "I can't kiss you?"

He had to laugh at how she had changed from a predator into a little girl. He turned his cheek to her, and as he pointed with his finger, he smirked, "If you insist."

She playfully pushed his face away and chided, "Oh stop that Lunn. I'd rather have another drink than peck you on the cheek."

He chuckled when he signalled the bartender for another round and said, "Well, you've had your chance. So, are we game?"

He saw the horny smile disappear from Lily's face as she looked up. Her eyes became bigger, and she said with a little tremble in her voice, "Maybe another time."

Right at that moment, Lunn felt two big hands gently grabbing his shoulders and he was relieved to see the black nail polish out of the corner of his eye. It was Alice, and it felt uncomfortably strange: as if he had been caught red-handed for doing something wrong. Lunn stubbornly ignored her by picking up the two glasses from the bar.

As he handed Lily her drink, he said, "Don't worry. She is nice."

Lily's smile was weak and mumbled, "I know who she is Lunn, and I think I'm going to let you be for now."

He took a huge swig from his whiskey, and he was annoyed that Alice had managed to scare Lily away. At that moment, the burning sensation left by the cheap alcohol was starting to annoy him, and he murmured glumly, "I see."

Lunn turned around to study Alice's face because he suddenly realised that she might be pissed off by the fact that he was spending his time with a prostitute. He was taken aback by her warm smile, and he could only stare at her. She bent down, and she whispered in his ear, "I hope you're sober enough because we have a major issue at the new headquarters."

He had expected to hear something completely

different but her words impacted his jolly mood. He cursed inwardly that he was being deprived the chance of playing with Lily for a bit longer, and he was remarkably relaxed: aware that Alice had a tendency to exaggerate the severity of a situation. Lunn patted Alice's hand to confirm and said after a big sigh, "Hmm yes, Lily. I'm afraid I'm needed somewhere else, but I really enjoyed your company."

Lily got up from her barstool, and she smirked as she said, "Too bad. I was looking forward to having some fun."

Lunn kissed her hand, and as she turned away, he said to the bartender, "Two more drinks for Lily."

Lunn marvelled at how graciously Lily walked to the other end of the bar. The bartender's smile was crooked when he teased, "It's a shame you're going. I would have loved to see you fail miserably."

Lunn was surprised. "Is she that good?"

"She drinks alcohol like water without getting drunk."

Alice quipped, "I'm so pleased that I had arrived just in time. Come, Lunn, let's go, the guys weren't happy when I left, and I hate to think what state they will be in when we arrive."

Tancred was humming the special tune when he arrived at the hidden entrance to the field. He rarely visited, but today he needed more information. He was starting to get nervous about what could be taking the others of his species so long to come.

Arnost, was becoming a nuisance, and today he nearly lost control. It was hard keeping both men under control and at the same time, leaving strong enough imprints in their brains to reassure them that that everything is all right.

The vines opened the gorse just wide enough for Tancred to slip in. As soon as his senses told him that nobody was watching, he stepped into the field. The view of the human bodies intertwined with the plants made Tancred's stomach turn. The Earthlings physical appearance repulsed him, and he quickly walked towards the centre of the field while using his hands to shield his vision of the horrible naked bodies.

He was pleased to be able to step into his vessel. As soon as he entered, he knew something was seriously wrong: the whole internal structure was gone, and the ship was no more than an empty shell.

"What?" he bellowed hoarsely.

His booming voice echoed strangely into the spacious hull, and he was startled when a female voice said placidly, "You are always so blunt and forget to greet us."

Tancred had trouble recognising the female voice, and he screamed at the top of his lungs, "Who are you, and by Hondas what happened with my vessel?"

It took a moment before the reverberation in the empty hall had died down.

The female voice cleared her throat.

He couldn't believe what was happening and groaned with frustration. A male voice sighed and said, "Greetings Tancred, what can we do for you? You need your Joy already?"

Tancred finally realised who was speaking to him: The ship's servants. They were normally integrated with the ship, but since everything had disappeared they were most likely somewhere out in the field, but the strange acoustics of the empty hull were making it seem like those voices were talking directly into Tancred's head.

"No, I don't," he rumbled, "By Hondas, what have you done with the ship?"

"You told us we are staying here so we are building permanent housing," the female voice explained.

He sighed as he was shaking his head. He still couldn't fully fathom that his ship, where he had spent a good deal of his life, was gone. Completely gone!

He longed for something recognisable from his own planet: hearing a voice or seeing an image of his own kind would give him the strength to cope a little longer in this backward place. He asked while he was trying to keep calm, "Am I still able to contact the main fleet?"

The ensuing silence made Tancred feel very uneasy. He repeated the question and bawled, "Hello! I asked a question! Am I still able to contact the fleet?"

A darker male voice sounded reluctant, "No, not at this moment."

Tancred felt his anxiety growing bigger by the second as he yelled, "What do you mean, not at this moment? By Hondas! When do you think I can?"

"I don't know."

"What do you mean? You don't know?"

The darker voice started to speak faster, "It depends on when I find the transmitter again. I have no idea where I have left it, and even when it does turn up, I will need to find the antenna and the other parts to make it work again."

Tancred couldn't believe what had happened, and he screamed, "What by Hondas did you do with all the equipment?"

The female voice said calmly, "All unnecessary

equipment has been used to build our living quarters and a medical facility."

He had to lean against the wall because his rapid breathing was making him feel dizzy. He didn't understand why they needed living quarters because as far as he knew servants of a ship didn't have a physical body. He was dumbstruck when he saw three bodies walk into the empty hull.

They were humanoid, but their features were vaguely defined as if unfinished. One was female while the other two bodies had the male form and one had darker skin than the others.

Tancred was completely flabbergasted and stammered, "By Hondas, what have you done?"

The female stepped forward, and he looked with disgust at her body. She had female curves like an Earthling, and her face was harsh and scary just like the females that he encountered on a daily basis. Her smile made him feel very uneasy and he groaned, "Why by Hondas did you choose to manifest yourself in those human bodies? They are so disgusting!"

She snorted again and asserted, "We *are* on this planet where these humans are living, and since you have changed into their humanoid form we thought it would only be appropriate to do the same."

"How did you get into the bodies?"

Tancred couldn't believe his eyes when a dozen vines appeared from behind the three servants and started to weave themselves around their bodies. The female started to caress one of the vines which was coiled around her middle, and she said, "The Cerasus found us and helped us to create new bodies."

Tancred suddenly realised how his body was

responding upon seeing the vines caressing the three bodies. His need to relax and enjoy a soothing moment with a shot of Joy was there in an instant. However, he became anxious when he saw several Cerasus vines moving closer to him and he queried, "Why are the vines coming to me?"

The darker male said with his baritone voice, "You seem to make them curious. I guess the Cerasus sense your elevated state. Maybe it is better to follow us to the medical facility. We can investigate what we need to do to calm you down."

Tancred's eyes grew bigger when two vines gently wrapped around his wrists. He knew that resistance was futile, and he had to use all his willpower to stay as calm as possible. He said meekly, "I guess that would be the right thing to do. I'm curious to see what you have done."

His mind was working at top speed. He wanted to get out of the field as soon as possible. He wondered how this could have happened. His decision to hide his vessel had resulted in unintended consequences.

He shivered at the prospect of being stuck on this horrible planet until the rest of his nation arrived. He followed the assistants towards a large heap of shredded material which he recognised as the remains of the padded surfaces. However, his eyes almost fell out their sockets when he passed the heap which was a mixture of vines, wires and other parts of the ship woven into a solid structure that was nearly as high as the gorse.

He murmured, "How remarkable."

The darker assistant said, "Not really. The Cerasus are using the parts to extract the necessary chemical compounds to finish off our bodies."

Tancred counted that at least four Cerasus had been

used to create the structure, and he wondered whether the production of the chemical Joy was being impacted in any way. The baritone voice shook him away from his thoughts. "The other Cerasus have the humans who were on these four, so you don't have to worry about the production."

"So we are still on target?"

"No, we are not."

Tancred was getting nervous again and hissed, "Why is that?"

The female snorted, "You decided that the fleet's ration scheme wasn't good enough for you, so you increased the doses yourself."

He knew she was right and that he had occasionally adjusted the ration for his personal benefit. He sighed, "How many units are we short?"

"If you consider all the delays and all the legitimate losses, we are about three thousand units short."

He gasped aware that he was in big trouble: The fleet's ration was one-hundred units per day which meant that he would need to stop taking Joy for at least twenty-five days.

He could get away with a shortage of five hundred units, but anything higher than that would cause him severe difficulties. He was aware that the fleet could turn up at any time, and they would definitely arrive within twenty-five days. He sighed and asked, "Is there any way we can increase the production?"

"No, the enhancer is at maximum capacity," said the woman placidly.

That answer made him shiver.

Tancred reckoned he could survive on twenty units every two days, but he knew he would get very sloppy with his tasks. The main reason he had been chosen to recruit a new planet was because of his skill to manipulate beings with his mind-bending capabilities. He had found out that humans were much harder to keep under control. He felt worn out, which was one of the reasons why he had been taking Joy more frequently than normal.

Without this wonder drug, he would have failed long ago. However, he was smart enough to realise that by taking the drug he was severely abusing his body. He needed to re-assess the situation, and decide the best way to tackle the problem. He was so lost in his thoughts that initially he didn't realise that he had entered a spacious room with a table placed in the middle.

The woman said, "Tancred, I think you should lie down."

Totally flabbergasted he stammered, "What? Why? There's nothing wrong with me! I need to go because I have a meeting soon."

Both men guided him to the table, and he knew it was best to cooperate. The table felt cold on his back as he lay down. He shivered with fear and disgust when the woman smiled at him as she said, "Relax Tancred. It will be over soon."

Tancred saw one of the vines hover over his body and before he could say anything he felt the soothing rush scorching through his body. His last thought was forgotten as the blackness took hold.

For the first time since meeting her, Lunn felt awkward as he walked with Alice back to the new quarters. He still felt like he had been caught red-handed with another woman, which was ridiculous. He glanced at Alice, who had a huge grin on her face. He didn't understand why she was smiling so broadly, and he asked her with a slightly annoyed tone, "What?"

She started to giggle and shook her head.

Lunn could feel himself becoming increasingly annoyed. The alcohol was starting to influence his thinking, and he sneered, "Alice I am really starting to get pissed."

She burst out laughing as she pushed him into an obscure-looking bar. He was surprised when the wonderful aroma of fresh ground coffee caressed his nose. Lunn allowed himself to be guided to a small table in the corner of the dimly lit place, and as soon as they were settled, two mugs of hot coffee were put down in front of them.

He looked at Alice who was still looking at him with a smile, and he was surprised when she said softly, "As head of security I should have been there earlier. I'm sorry Lunn."

He took a sip of the coffee and enjoyed the rich flavour of the hot, bitter liquid. He pondered her remark and asked, "What do you mean, Alice?"

"When I discovered you were Lily's next victim I should have left immediately, which I didn't."

"Victim?"

"Yes, you see, there's quite some betting going on as to how long the next one would last if Lily decides to play her game."

Lunn snorted as he realised that he had fallen into Lily's trap and said sarcastically, "How funny."

"At least, I have saved you from a huge hangover."

He didn't know whether that was true because he hadn't wanted to get completely drunk especially as he hadn't fully recovered from the excesses of the previous night. His mind was clearing, simply by drinking the strong coffee and he remembered what Alice had said about the problems at the new quarters. He wondered whether she had used it as an excuse to get him away from Lily and he asked, "So there are no problems at the new headquarters?"

Alice was tracing her finger around her empty coffee cup as she said softly, "There are, but it can wait until you have finished your coffee."

Lunn sensed a small change in Alice's mood as if she was less relaxed. He asked himself whether he fully appreciated the extra attention that she was giving him. Her attitude towards him had clearly changed since their sexual encounter. Then it struck him: Alice had always been attentive but because of Danette she had kept her distance. He was wondering if that had changed and queried, "How did you know so quickly about Lily and me?"

"She is my sister."

He thought she'd answered too quickly, and he shot back, "Your sister? I don't believe that."

He looked into her eyes which were just a little wider when she confided, "She is, same mother but a different father."

He recalled how Lily had looked up to Alice, and he realised she was her protector. Lunn stared into her eyes and said, "I bet you have helped her out several times."

Alice nodded slowly and retorted, "In the beginning, yes, but it wasn't long before everyone knew that I was her sister because I kept those assholes alive so they could spread the word."

He realised that Lily knew him because of her which made him wonder why she had come on to him.

He was amazed when Alice said, "I guess you're wondering why Lily did it?"

"Yes."

He noticed a slight hesitation before she said one word, "Danette."

He slumped back stunned that it was widespread knowledge that Danette had dumped him. He whispered, "I can't believe it."

He saw that Alice was looking him straight in the eye when she asked tentatively, "Uhm, were you planning to....?"

Lunn cut in straight away hoping she would get his intention and said firmly, "No!"

"Oh."

There was an awkward silence, and Lunn felt the urge rising to explain the situation in The Haggert. He cleared his throat and continued, "I had challenged her that I would go home alone."

Alice's laugh was one of genuine relief, and she said with a broad smile, "Just as well I came to rescue you."

Lunn didn't know what to think about it all. He liked Alice but knowing what the financier had said he needed to get the headquarters up and running as soon as possible. After that, there would be plenty of time to figure out what he wanted. As he finished the last sip of his coffee, he got up and said eagerly, "Let's go to the headquarters. You can tell me what the problem is while we're on our way."

He looked into her eyes as she got up as well and he was pleased that her face had relaxed into a lazy smile. He reckoned she was okay with the situation they were in and was pleasantly surprised when she replied with a warm almost sultry voice, "Sounds like a perfect plan."

CHAPTER TWELVE

Danette's headache was returning with a vengeance as she entered the narrow hall that housed the recovery rooms. She had been free of it the whole day, but she couldn't delay doing something about Andena because the girl was still unconscious and this was having an effect on Danette's mood.

She had difficulty focusing on the fact that she was pleased with the work she had done with the android girls. They were in much better shape, and the overall condition of their additional subroutines was reaching a level which would soon be good enough to start field exercises.

As she stood in front of the door, she felt irritated that Joshua hadn't left a message informing her that Andena had woken up. She slowly opened the door hoping and praying for a miracle. However, Andena was still lying there, in a deep sleep, recovering from the massive surgical intervention. She still couldn't understand why Andena didn't have any scar tissue at all. From what she had read about the upgrade procedure in the paper, Andena should have numerous scars all over her body. Danette wanted to be absolutely sure that Andena had had the upgrade, and she decided to check the girl herself.

Danette shivered a little as her fingers traced the respiration tube which disappeared into Andena's mouth. With a trembling hand, she stroked her hair and was amazed at how soft and shiny it was. Danette was really jealous of the amazingly vibrant red colour which perfectly matched her mystical green eyes and her pale, flawless complexion. Indeed, it was a wrench prising her gaze away. Slowly moving the sheet down she admired Andena's naked upper torso. She couldn't believe how immaculate Andena's skin was: not a single mole or pimple was to be seen, and her skin had a silky lustre quality. She couldn't resist touching the soft skin and marvelled at the toned and flat stomach as she realised that Andena must have been working out for some time. Only the enhancers in her hands looked out of proportion because they were clearly visible. The little pointy bumps on each joint of her fingers looked like little studs.

It was because of the warmth radiating from Andena's body that Danette felt the uneasiness creeping up, making her stomach churn again: this was a real living human, made of flesh and bone. She slowly peeled the sheet away from Andena, feeling a conflicting sense of guilt and jealousy. Andena's body was beautiful: spoiled only by Bionex's bionic enhancements.

Danette sighed and quickly covered Andena with the sheet again because she couldn't bear to look at her body anymore. Instead, she studied the screen which showed the physical status of the girl: everything was within normal parameters. Nothing pointed to a reason why she wasn't awake, and she spent a long time pondering exactly what she should do.

Mr. Yousima had given her an ultimatum: the girl had to be awake by the day after tomorrow, or the enhancers would be taken out and reused on someone else. She hated to be in this predicament.

The noise of the respirator was getting on her nerves, and so she hastily left the room. It had felt eerie when she had closed the door because the intermittent hissing sound of the respirator was just about audible and sounded as if somebody was whispering. Her stomach was in knots, and she knew she had to eat something soon. With resolute steps, she hurried to her apartment hoping she could keep her food down.

"What is going on over there?" Lunn asked as he walked with Alice to the headquarters.

"There's a problem with the secure connections."

"Oh okay, how bad?"

"It seems that we are unable to create stable, secure connections," Alice replied.

"What do you mean by stable connections?"

"As soon as the connection is established it drops within twenty seconds. The boys have tried everything, but nothing stays online longer than twenty seconds."

"Hmm, sounds strange. I have no idea what that could be."

"John is pretty pissed off."

"No kidding."

Alice chuckled and kept her pace steady as if nothing would change her speed. Lunn knew that he couldn't draw any further conclusions until he arrived and decided not to ask any more questions about it. They kept on walking in a comfortable silence. He had no urge to talk which was, to his surprise, a pleasant feeling. He looked at Alice who still had a happy smile on her face making her seem even more desirable. She had noticed him looking at her, and quipped, "What is it with you and women?"

The question took him back to his late teens when he had practically a different girl every night until one of the girls had committed suicide. People had thought she couldn't cope with the fact Lunn had left her. Lunn had stopped seeing her because he didn't want to find himself trapped in a relationship. It was an unfortunate coincidence that it was at that time that he realised that he couldn't sleep with every girl he met.

It had taken a long time before they had found the girl's letter which stated that she had ended her life 'at the will of the gods.' Lunn was pleased that he wasn't the reason she had decided to commit suicide, but it had contributed to drastic change in his attitude towards life. He had made the decision then to be celibate and ignored the many temptations around him.

It had left him cold until Danette re-energised his love life with a steaming hot experience. He had been alone for a long time until Danette had managed to break his vow of celibacy. She was the first one he had allowed to be intimate with him, and it had amazed him how completely different it felt with Danette. Their open relationship had enabled him to enjoy a colourful sex life again although, apart from a few meaningless flings, Danette was still number one.

Then there was Andena. The sex with her was amazing, but he knew it had only occurred as a result of the heightened state of arousal brought on by the alien aphrodisiac. He enjoyed her company: she was different, not as self-indulgent as many other women. Now as he looked at Alice, he wondered what he admired most in her. He sighed and confided insecurely, "I think I like women who have high self-esteem."

Alice snorted.

"What?" he asked surprised wondering whether he had upset her.

"As if I have that."

He stopped walking and said, "Hmm. You surely act like you know what you want."

Lunn studied her aware that his comments had shocked her deeply. He kissed her softly on the lips and as he pulled away he whispered, "You *are* a strong woman."

She grinned as she rested her forehead against his and said, "Maybe."

"How so, maybe? You kick ass if it's necessary and you're not afraid to bare your teeth."

Lunn saw her fidgeting and realised that she wasn't comfortable with the way the conversation was going, he slapped her playfully on the bottom as he mused, "Right, let's move on before I'm accused of negligence."

Alice laughed, genuinely relieved as she retorted, "Yup, John is pretty pissed that you left him alone to set up the initial part of the new headquarters."

Lunn laughed and said, "He could have contacted me."

"Not when you leave your phone in your office."

Her answer made him jump, he just about managed to suppress a gasp as he remembered that he had deliberately left his device at the office. The financier had explicitly told him not to bring it for safety reasons. He confessed, "Hmm, you're right I don't know why I did that."

Alice looked straight at him, and he could see that she didn't quite believe his story and said playfully although with a stern undertone, "You just can't run away and hide. You're too important now."

As they entered the headquarters, Lunn murmured, "I guess I am."

Meleda had enjoyed a good brunch after a long lie in bed. She'd needed her rest after the long, taxing conversation she'd had with her brother the previous night. She was very pleased that Haruz had finally given her the necessary access to the main system. At least now she could easily browse around without the fear of being caught. She had been using other means to get the same information, but now she could dig a little deeper, which was what she planned to do today. She knew she wouldn't be able to access all the information that she needed but with her neat set of little program bots: she could gather most of the data without being noticed. Once the little bots were started, she could relax and wait for the results.

There was one thing in particular that she wanted to find: the contract which Arnost had signed with Tancred as the emissary of the aliens. But she reckoned, considering the conversations she had had with Haruz, that it was doubtful whether there would be a contract at all.

The other major challenge that she had already spent quite a lot of time attempting to overcome was finding a way to breach Bionex's security gates. It was only after several frustrating nights of rigorously reprogramming her bots, that she had finally gained access. She discovered that their systems were far more complex than she'd thought they would be but had loved the challenge, and she was incredibly pleased with her success. With a sigh of contentment, she realised she'd got nearly all the information she was looking for, and that she needed just a little more patience before she could start reading the next batch of documents. She had been shocked to discover how far Bionex's technology had evolved.

She had checked the credit balance of her reserves, and there was still enough to fulfil the next installment. She knew there were two more instalments to pay and after that, she would have less need for the harvesting bots.

Now she had done the easy part of her to-do list, and there was one thing left to do, which probably would take the rest of her afternoon to get organised. She knew that nearly all the meeting rooms had their own particle array, but had never been used since the last civil war which had ended long before she was even born. Her knowledge of the quantum physics was limited, but she knew enough about how to connect to a particle array. The real challenge was to gain access to the heavily secured gate which had been purposely built to keep out nosy people like her.

Meleda had created a new program which could fool the security protocol by extending the network paths into the gate. Once she was in, she would be able to access the right time particles to create a grainy video. It took her a few attempts before the secured gate granted her the coveted green light and with trembling fingers she gave one of her bots the command to gather the ancient information. As soon as the bot gave her an acknowledgment of the fact that there truly was data to recover, Meleda slumped back into her chair with a joyful sigh. She could barely wait to find out what data the bot would come back with, but knew that for now she had to be patient. She estimated it would take at least six hours before the bot had enough completed data ready to use.

She was surprised when she saw how long she had been busy and suddenly realised how hungry she was. With a soft groan, she got up from her chair and limped to the kitchen to raid the fridge for food. She chided herself for going without food for so long and knew that she would suffer as a result, later this evening. She knew that she needed to be more careful because she couldn't allow herself to get too weak.

The sound of footsteps in the corridor woke Andena, and when the door opened, she heard a familiar voice say, "Why is she still not responding?"

A nervous sounding male voice said, "Because she has the full upgrade which meant she had to be sedated for a longer period for to heal fully."

The female voice sounded annoyed when she replied, "I see. When do you think we can deploy her?"

The man started to stutter, "I, I don't know because we have never successfully implemented a full upgrade before."

The female growled, "I've been waiting for her to be ready. Every delay is costing a fortune in credits, and she will be too far behind soon."

"But she doesn't need that much training because of the full upgrade. I'm sure she will come to within a day and then it will be a matter of another day or two before you can fully deploy her."

Andena listened to the conversation with a strange sense of apprehension, and she wondered what they had done to her. She still couldn't move any muscles: it was as if something had switched her off. Her mind was very sluggish, and she had great difficulty in comprehending what the two were talking about. The woman's high heels reverberated in the room as she walked away from Andena, and when she stopped, she sneered, "I'll give you one more day. After that, I will personally pull the plug."

The young man was clearly upset when he exclaimed, "You can't do that! That is first-degree murder!"

The woman laughed as she walked away, before shouting, "Come on now! You can hardly claim that she is still human!"

The man sighed. He moved closer to Andena and whispered in her ear, "Why oh why are you still not awake?"

It was strange for Andena knowing she was awake, but she couldn't do anything. She vaguely remembered the woman's voice, but couldn't remember her name. She was not afraid of what might happen but had no desire to die. She could hear the man pacing around the room, and he shrieked when something loudly played a short melody. She heard him nearly shouting, "Patrick! Did you find anything? What? What do you mean by resetting her core?"

The man walked closer to Andena, and he asked, "How can it be so simple? Are you sure? Do I need to do anything before I reset it?"

Andena heard the other voice now clearly because the man was hovering above her head, "No. Just connect to the core and type the word reboot. That should do the trick."

The man asked anxiously, "What if nothing happens?"

"Then we have messed up and killed this girl. A pity, though, she was a beauty."

The man growled, "Patrick, how on Earth can you say that?"

The voice from the telephone snorted and said, "You were the one who suggested giving her the full upgrade."

The man yelled, "Yes, I did because she had the most suitable body for it and she was incredibly fit."

"Hey! Calm down, Joshua! Just reboot the damn core will you?"

The man sighed deeply before he conceded, "All right Patrick, I'm sorry. I just had a bad conversation with that bitch. I'll hang up and call you back as soon as I'm done."

"It's okay, Joshua. Good luck, I'll keep my fingers crossed."

A short beep which reverberated in the room told Andena that he had finished the conversation, and she wondered what he was planning to do. As far as she knew she didn't have a core and why would you need to reboot a person? She heard him rubbing his hands while he said, "Right. Here goes, pretty one."

The next moment Andena felt a surge right in the middle of her head, and everything went blank for a brief moment. However, it wasn't long before she was able to hear her heart beating again, and she was stunned that she was able to see a row of text scrolling in front of her right eye. It went too fast for her to read it and she didn't have time to focus on that because she felt that she was lying on something soft. Something was wrong with her mouth and her breathing. Andena was getting more and more strange sensations and knew that something was very wrong. She grabbed her face and discovered a tube going into her mouth. Her instinct told her that it had to go out, and she started to pull at it.

She heard the man shout, "Stop! Don't pull it! Let me do it! It will only hurt much more if you do it."

Andena felt the man tugging at the mouthpiece and after that, the breathing immediately became more normal, however, when he hauled the tube from her mouth in one swift move she arched her back when the pain became almost impossible to bear. She turned on her side into a foetal position and coughed for at least a minute. Thick mucus dribbled from the side of her mouth, and she came to the conclusion that she must have had this tube in her windpipe for a long time. She was wondering what had happened to her and felt strange. Her rational mind told her that she should be afraid but she felt….normal.

Her mouth was dry, and she longed for some water. She sat up, and she opened her eyes for the first time and saw the man looking at her with a huge grin on his face. Andena saw lines of text appearing in front of her right eye. It said, "Joshua Killman, Tech. Opp. Bionex. Age 29. Weight 165 lb. Heart rate 150. Body Temp. 99.7."

He said, "Thank God. It worked! What is your status?"

Before Andena could think about his question, her display showed, "Status: 100% fully functional, all systems: green."

It was as if Andena had been taken over by something. She was forced to take a breath, and she croaked involuntarily, "I'm hundred percent fully functional and all systems are green."

Joshua jumped a little and yelled, "Yes!"

After she had told the information, the compulsive urge was gone. Andena looked at him, and the taste of the mucus was quite strong in her mouth, and she said, "I would like some water."

Instantly the display in her eye gave a red cross and under a text was blinking, "Water level: 102%. No water intake allowed."

Joshua looked at his device and said, "I see that your levels are sufficient, so you don't need water."

It was a strange feeling for her that her desire for water had somehow vanished into thin air. But again her mind acknowledged that this was an unusual situation that would normally have made her feel upset.

Joshua said in a commanding voice before leaving the room, "Stay here."

Andena was sitting on the bed still a bit dazed about what just had happened, and she couldn't put her finger on what was disturbing her. She didn't have much chance to think about because it wasn't long before Joshua came back carrying a grey suit and a pair of familiar looking boots.

"Put these on," he ordered and handed her the clothes.

It felt strange and quite weird that she had the *urge* to follow his orders. Without any hesitation and with a certain determination she started to step into the suit which fitted her like a glove. She noticed that her movements were a bit jerky, and she had trouble grabbing the zip's lever. She tried again, but her fingers were not responding as she wanted and she couldn't get hold of it.

Joshua noticed her struggle and helped her to zip up her suit. He followed the zip with his eyes and he slowed down considerably when the suit was pressing her breasts together. Andena was at the point of asking why he had slowed down, but he suddenly moved the zip up until her suit was completely done up.

She felt dizzy as a result of moving too quickly to put her boots on. Her hand shot to Joshua's leg in an attempt to prevent herself from falling over.

He gasped and exclaimed, "Ah! You're hurting me! Let go!"

As he was holding her wrist, she instantly loosened her grip and found that she was able to regain her balance. She used his hand to hold herself and with the other hand she took one of the boots. As she stepped into it, she noticed that it felt strange: as if it was too small and Andena struggled to slide her foot into it. Much as she tried, she was unable to get her foot into the boot and eventually heard Joshua ask, "What is the matter?"

Her voice was still a bit hoarse from the respiration tube when she replied, "It seems that the boot is too small."

"What? But they are yours, and they are auto fitters, it shouldn't be a problem!" he said getting irritated, "Let me have a look at it."

Andena handed him the boot. He fiddled with it until she heard a soft beep and he handed it over to her.

"Try again." he snapped.

This time, the boot adjusted to her foot as she was slipping into it. She vaguely remembered she'd had a pair of carbon boots which had been fitted for her feet, and it was strange they didn't fit. She didn't have any more time to reflect upon it because she heard Joshua say, "Come, follow me, I need to introduce you to your new commander."

Andena had some trouble initially walking, but within a minute, she felt as if her body was functioning a lot better. But still something was not right!

She knew something was different, but she couldn't put her finger on it. She thought it was strange that it didn't bother her at all and that every emotion she felt seemed to be flattened.

CHAPTER THIRTEEN

Lunn was walking back to the new headquarters after a few hours' sleep. It had taken nearly the whole night to set up the new secure connections. The previous owner had used Datanex as their provider. That wouldn't have been a problem if the physical connections weren't hosted by Datanex as well. It was a shocking realisation that they were obliged to use Datanex encryption to get a stable connection: all other forms of secure connections were dropped by Datanex within a minute. Lunn knew he had failed, and if they remained here, Datanex would finally gain access to everything. The new headquarters were utterly useless unless they found a way of keeping their information safe and hidden from Datanex. They had to come up with a solution because this was the only available space which could withstand an EMP.

He had slumped down on the floor holding his head

between his knees trying to fight the horrific visions. He dreaded the fact that he had to report the huge setback to the financier. He also knew that remaining in the old headquarters was no longer an option.

Lunn was flabbergasted when Alice came up with an incredibly simple solution, and he had real trouble stopping himself from hugging the wonderful and smart woman. He was still a little jealous of her brilliant but simple solution: encrypt the "secure" Datanex connection again with your own.

While Lunn and his team were building the new hardware, Alice had found another panel hidden in a cupboard. It was the original data connection to the national grid.

Lunn was pleased that they could change their provider eventually, and he planned on doing that after the planned EMP attack at the plateau. He still hadn't had the opportunity to have a talk with his main technician, John, about the financier's request.

He entered the quarters and hoped to find the technician there alone. As he passed through the secure main entrance, he heard a voice shouting, "Who's there?"

Lunn chuckled, aware that John was yet to be convinced of the accuracy of the entrance security Lunn had developed. He retorted, "It's me, Lunn."

John murmured, "I still can't believe you're solely using your access system."

"All other systems are hackable John."

"Yeah, yeah I know, but it still freaks me out that I just can walk in without using any kind of key."

"If we have more time, I'll let you into my secret, but now we need to discuss something really important."

John sat down and as he rubbed his face he grumbled,

"Here we go, again."

Lunn could see that John had had as little sleep as he had and he knew that John might be a little short-tempered.

"Well? Shoot." John said.

"How many satellites do we still need to launch?"

John squinted at Lunn as if he knew there was trouble coming. He blurted, "Two hundred and forty in the last two batches. The biggest, counting one-hundred and eighty satellites will be launched later today."

Lunn was shocked because he'd been unaware that the timing was so tight, and muttered, "Wow you're cutting it fine John! Is everything ready for that?"

John bragged with a sly smile on his face, "Yeah, we can do it from here, and I have my apartment as a backup. I've been sleeping with a satellite dish hanging just a few inches above my head."

Lunn had to laugh as he imagined John's little place stuffed to the gunnels with equipment, but he also admired John's commitment to the project. Lunn cleared his throat and asked, "What if we need to use the ring within a few days?"

John looked up and his burning eyes made clear that he was not happy.

"I assume it bloody can't wait," he scoffed.

Lunn heard John was about to explode into a tirade. He said calmly, "No, it can't wait another six weeks."

John sighed and shook his head. He revealed, "You're lucky I haven't ordered anything for the last batch yet."

Lunn was pleased that John hadn't exploded yet and mumbled softly, "Oh okay."

"If you want to use the ring we need to spread this batch to fill the gaps and after that, we need to initiate the ring. It is do-able, but there's a risk that it might fail if the gaps between the satellites are too big."

"I see," mumbled Lunn.

"Yes, and the other thing is, once the ring has been initiated you can't add more satellites."

Lunn started to understand what John was saying and wondered whether moving the activation forward was too great a risk. He also knew that the Bionex group wouldn't continue to practise for weeks on end on the plateau.

He sighed and said, "I think we should take the risk."

"I knew you would say that," John grunted.

"It's good that you understand."

"Yeah, but don't blame me if we have for five billion credit of worthless shit hanging up there."

Lunn had to laugh and smirked, "Don't worry John, I will inform him about the risks."

He was pleased that John had taken it so well. They still had a huge amount of work to do before the headquarters would be fully operational.

Alice woke up with a start. Bewildered she looked around the strangely decorated room, but it quickly dawned on her that she was in Lunn's bedroom. She fell back onto the soft pillow, and she realised she was still dressed. She remembered that they had entered the bedroom and that they both were too tired to get undressed. It was strange but also very comforting to fall asleep being cocooned by a person, especially when it was by Lunn. She turned her face into the pillow to inhale Lunn's strong masculine smell. She loved the spicy tones of his scent because it made her light-headed. She would love to be able to breathe in that scent every day.

With a start, she realised that her belief system was weakening. Her mantra was to keep herself at arm's length. It was simple but effective: better to be alone than suffer heartbreak.

She had always been able to keep her feelings for him under control, but ever since Danette had dumped him, it had become harder to ignore what was truly simmering in her heart. Deep down she knew that she was fooling herself because right from the first moment she had laid her eyes on his gorgeous body she'd felt an irresistible attraction to him. She couldn't keep her eyes off his beautifully developed muscles, and his strong facial features made him so incredibly handsome. He was so hot!

At the time, she had needed the additional job to pay for her place. It was practically impossible to live with her sister Lily under one roof. She could count the number of nights that she'd had a proper and undisturbed night of sleep on one hand. The fact that she was regularly bumping into strange men made her decide to live alone. She had enjoyed the life of solitude, but now her body and her mind were longing for something more. Her time with Lunn had made her even more aware of it. Alice knew she was trying to rationalise what had happened over the course of the last few days. It was her way of dealing with things that were bothering her but this time, it seemed that she was having great difficulty comprehending her feelings. That was something which never had happened before!

She desperately craved his warm touch, the comforting feeling that his strong muscles were protecting her. His smile and the twinkle in his eye were all so disarming. Thinking about it made her tingle all over. Could it be that she had fallen for him?

No! No!

With a gasp, she jumped from the bed, and rushed towards the door. She had to go! If she stayed here any longer, she would suffocate. It should never have happened! How could she have been so blind?

Andena sat on a bench in a large hall waiting for 'the others' to arrive. Joshua had instructed her to sit on the bench which clearly felt like an order. Her mind was still sluggish as if it was repressed in some way. While she was waiting she tried to make sense of it all: she knew that something wasn't right. The fact that she saw text appearing in front of her right eye was somewhat disturbing. It was as if she was being controlled by something and it felt unnatural. She had stumbled several times over her own feet and as far as she knew she'd never had such problems before. She was wondering if she could walk around the hall without stumbling if she were to concentrate hard on her movements.

As she got up, she found herself flying, at least six feet up into the air, and she barely had enough time to adjust the position of her body to break her fall. A little dazed she got up very slowly afraid that she might launch herself again. Andena was frantically trying to fathom what was going on with her body because it was abundantly clear something was really wrong. She knew that she should be scared, but was aware that her emotions had been considerably repressed somehow. It made her realise that she needed to be bolder and after a brief moment of deliberation, decided to explore the strangeness of it all. She had already discovered that her muscles were much stronger than before, and her initial jerkiness was starting to make sense. She needed to investigate her capabilities and decided to do some simple tests.

As she stood, she bent her legs and concentrated on making a small jump. She was surprised to see a little dial appearing in front of her eye. By tensing her muscles, she could manipulate the number, and she came to the conclusion she could vary her power. She practised with several jumps and quickly learned that the dial only appeared when she concentrated for a little longer.

Andena prepared herself to jump to the other side of the hall and to her astonishment the display indicated the exact amount of power she had to use to successfully complete the task. Her tensed muscles released the immense power, which felt like a small explosion and she launched towards the other side. But as soon as she was descending she realised she had forgotten that she needed space to come to a stop!

She knew she would collide with the door, and she brought her arms forward to soften the blow somewhat. At the moment she braced herself for the impact, the door opened, and Andena saw that she was flying straight at a woman she vaguely recognised.

As soon as she touched the floor, she grabbed the woman's shoulders which changed her forward momentum into a turn. The woman began screaming when she saw Andena flying towards her, and she didn't stop until she was lying, unharmed, on top of Andena's body.

As she scrambled up from Andena, she shouted, "What the fuck were you doing? You could have killed me!"

Andena was still a bit dazed from the blow she had

endured when she had landed roughly on her back. The collision with the angry woman's body had slammed all her air out of her lungs, and she could only whisper, "I'm sorry."

She ranted, "You were told to sit on the bench and wait for me. Who gave you the order to charge at the door at such a dangerous speed?"

Andena stood up and said meekly, "Nobody, Miss."

She looked straight into the woman's eyes and the display in her right eye gave the next information, "Danette Williams, Trainer Bionex. Age 31. Weight 140 lb. Heart rate 170. Body temp. 98.4."

When she saw the name, she vaguely remembered her being the associate of a very nice man she thought she knew. It bothered her only a little that her past was blurred and that she couldn't remember his name.

Danette sighed and said, "Right. Go back into the hall and sit on the bench."

Andena knew she had to be polite because Danette was her trainer and whispered, "Yes, Miss Williams."

As she started to walk towards the hall, Danette stopped her by sticking her arm out in front of her chest and requested grumpily, "How do you know my surname?"

Andena felt a little odd as if she wasn't supposed to know Danette's surname and she stammered softly, "I, I. If I look at a person I get information about them."

"Tell me what kind of information you get," Danette commanded.

Again Andena had no choice than to reply instantly and blurted placidly, "Name, occupation, age, weight, heart rate and body temperature."

Danette shouted, "Tell me my age! I'm curious as to

how the hell you know my age."

This time, the urge to tell Danette the information was as strong as before, but she also saw Danette's heart rate increasing even more. Andena knew she had to give an answer and decided to see if she could avoid giving her the information.

"I don't know how I know your age. It is just stated on the list," she replied. Andena was surprised that it wasn't that difficult to ignore the urge to comply with the demanded instruction. She wondered if it was possible to ignore it completely.

"Tell me my fucking age!" barked Danette.

The command was too direct for Andena to dismiss and said placidly, "Your age is thirty-one."

Danette sighed and said, "Right. Go back to the hall and stop using my surname."

Andena wondered if she might be able to dismiss any direct command in time. The urge to tell Danette her correct age was strong but she had the time to contemplate whether she should give a different number of years than her actual age. It made her wonder what was controlling her and if she could control it rather than being controlled. She wondered why she felt that there was still something she had to do and realised that Danette had given her an order.

"Yes, Miss," she said quickly and walked towards the bench in the hall with firm steps. She sat down on the bench and was utterly surprised when a line of nine women marched into the hall.

With resolute steps, they headed for the same bench where Andena was sitting, and she had to move quickly aside to avoid a collision with the first woman. Andena felt the bench shudder when the women, as if they were one, sat down when Danette shouted, "At ease!"

With great interest, she looked at the girl who sat next to her and came to the conclusion that she was part of the same team. She realised she was wearing the same outfit as the other girls except for her boots which were her own. Andena saw the number zero-one on the suit of her neighbour and noticed for the first time that her suit had the numbers zero-zero.

Arnost was pacing around the room impatiently waiting for Haruz to arrive. He was getting extremely anxious about the whole situation with Tancred and his alien race. The fact that Tancred was missing made it all worse because Arnost started to realise that he had been deceived. The longer he thought about the awkward situation the madder he became. Why had he never asked Tancred the question? How many of your kind are coming to Earth?

Arnost shivered at the thought that Earth would soon be overrun by aliens and that the whole population of Earth might be used for the production of drugs. He knew that the number of nuclear missiles available might be enough to disable a few ships but what if their superior technology could destroy the weapons in the blink of an eye?

Arnost slumped down on his chair feeling defeated: he had personally invited the aliens to come to raid his beloved planet. Even though a most of the population realised that Earth was facing ruin: the outcome in the near future would have been the inevitable extinction of the human race. There simply was not enough oxygen left to sustain the huge number of people living on the planet. He started to doubt whether those weird plants would ever be able to replenish the Earth's atmosphere with the necessary oxygen. How many plants would be needed to restore the level of oxygen?

Thousands?

Millions?

Arnost came to the conclusion that Tancred had manipulated the board right from the start, and the most devastating part of it all was that he had only just realised it this morning. It had been a full day now since Tancred had failed to attend their regular meetings. Arnost was almost certain that he had been manipulated by a mind-bending 'spell' Tancred had cast on him. His mind was cleared from a strange fog, and he could think much more clear by now. The sturdy knock on the door sounded like music in his ear, and he exclaimed, "Come!"

Even though he was pleased that Haruz had walked into the room, he couldn't muster up a smile. He felt the huge burden of guilt resting on his shoulders when he said, "Haruz, we are doomed. Tancred has deceived us completely. Soon we'll be swamped with others of his kind. It will be the end of our existence."

Haruz sighed and said, "We are not doomed yet, Arnost. If we can join forces with each group, we will have a chance of fighting them off."

Arnost snorted and shook his head several times. He murmured, "They will lynch me when they find out that I made this unbelievably hideous and fatal deal with an alien race."

"When is the next board meeting?"

"In an hour."

Arnost shuddered a little when he recalled the first

meeting when Tancred had given a very interesting talk which was received very well. He couldn't understand how the alien had fooled the whole board with his smooth talk. He was convinced that the alien had a special gift to create illusions which lasted for a long time. He knew he had to make certain that Tancred couldn't manipulate the situation anymore. He looked at Haruz who looked as agitated as he felt and he grumbled, "Make sure that this building is off limits. When we catch him, I want to ensure that he goes to prison, far away from any human."

Haruz retorted, "Hmm, that will be a challenge."

"How so? Just arrest him."

"If he can manipulate us, he can definitely manipulate guards."

Arnost sighed and asked, "How about the android guards? Can we re-deploy them?"

Haruz nodded slowly. He responded, "You mean the old ones? Maybe, if we use the remote controlled androids, we might have a chance. I sincerely hope that Tancred can't control the men who are operating the androids."

Arnost felt a sense of panic rising in his body as he commanded, "Find him, Haruz. I hate that this dangerous alien is nowhere to be found."

Haruz nodded, and as he left the room he said, "Yes, as soon as I have him, I'll let you know."

When the door was shut Arnost closed his eyes, but it was only for a short moment because he was disturbed by a vision of Tancred's ghastly face. He hated Tancred's strange narrow eyes which right now seemed to be dancing in front of him.

He had never liked Tancred. He had always felt that there was something creepy about him.

Now he knew why he didn't like the alien.

It was probably too late to change the destiny of his beloved planet, and he couldn't think of a solution that might save Earth from a horrible fate. With a deep sigh, Arnost went to his office to prepare for the board meeting. He knew he had to be honest about the catastrophe that was looming. He knew it was going to be the toughest meeting he had ever had in his life.

Danette was staring at the two pills which were lying in the palm of her hand. She didn't dare to think about how many pills she had already taken during the last few days. She knew the longer she took the Dormancans the harder it would be to wean herself off them again. The pills glistening in the light had a soothing quality, and she wondered whether the manufacturer had deliberately made them so shiny. She closed her hand to hide them for a while: they were distracting her too much.

Today was one of her better days, considering the progress she had made with the android girls. Joshua was right about the fast rate at which Andena was adjusting to the rest of the group, but there was something about her which concerned Danette. If she compared her with the rest of the androids, she wondered whether Andena's conscience, which had been overruled, was seeping through somehow. It seemed that she was starting to become more aware of what had happened to her. It was something she needed to pay more attention to because if Andena started to rebel against what had happened to her, she would become a real danger. Danette had already noticed Andena's small and hesitant delays when she had given the group a command. Sometimes Andena had asked her for more information which would justify why she had ignored the direct order, but there were a few times where it looked like she might have deliberately ignored the direct command.

Danette was wondering whether the remarkable recovery since Andena's full upgrade might have had an effect on the inserted computer core in her brain. From what she had read, it was the most sophisticated part of the upgrade. It had taken Bionex a long time to master the integration of a computer into a human brain. She shuddered when she thought about how many people Bionex had experimented on before they had fully mastered their technique.

She gasped when she realised that all of them had the same AI software and that Andena's full upgrade was the muscle and joint enhancers. Andena should behave like the others, but she was definitely interacting at a much higher social level! Something was not right with Andena. Was it possible that the AI software *had become* different from being implemented in a human instead of an android? She suddenly remembered the conversation with Joshua when he had mentioned that Andena would be deployable much faster, but he had never mentioned that the AI software would be affected as well.

Danette knew that she had two more days to investigate the situation before the girl had to perform at the big event: Mr. Yousima would pay her and the group a visit. She had informed him that the women would be ready for the next step of the training. She hoped that Andena would be prepared enough and that Mr. Yousima would be pleased with the progress she had made with the ten ladies. She was a little relieved that she was ahead of schedule because she reckoned that the training outside in the open would be much harder than they had anticipated. From her own experience, she knew that the rocky surface of the plateau would be a serious challenge. The loose rocks were not always obvious, and she had fallen several times when her father had trained with her there. Danette's stomach churned as she nervously realised that she would soon have to demonstrate the skills that the girls had acquired. She knew that she couldn't sleep because she would start to ponder if she had trained them well enough.

When she opened her hand containing the pills, she saw that the shininess of the surfaces was gone. They were stuck on her sweaty palm, and when she pulled them off, there were two little red patches visible where they had been all this time. She quickly popped them in her mouth and swallowed them down without any water. A skill she had to learn when she was too far gone to be able to get a glass of water.

She double checked her alarm and let herself fall on her bed. She didn't bother to get undressed. She would need a long shower in the morning anyway to awaken her.

CHAPTER FOURTEEN

Andena was lying in her bed still fully awake. The fact that she was confined to such a small room troubled her. She had tried to get out, but she couldn't open the door. Today's training was not that strenuous for her, but it had been difficult. Keeping her balance on a small beam took most of the afternoon to master. It was only after she had concentrated on the beam that she was able to walk across it without falling off. She saw the two lines appear which had followed the contour of the beam and when she stepped on the beam, at any small unbalance her arms waved just the right way to keep her from falling. Andena knew something was helping her, but it only happened when she concentrated on something.

While in the shower, she had found out that if she focused on the water, her display showed the temperature and that the water was potable. Once she had glanced at one of her classmates and the information on her display confused her. It was telling her which kind of model the girl was, and the power supply was green. She remembered how strange it was when she saw the text of her first status report appear at her eye after Joshua had asked for it. She was wondering if she could let it happen again by querying it herself and asked softly, "What is my status?"

Nothing happened. Strange.

Maybe she had to concentrate on the question internally, and she asked the question by projecting the words in her mind, "What is my status?"

Again nothing happened, and she thought back to the training when the lines had appeared. She recalled that she had focused inwards to block any outer influences, and then looked intensely at the beam. She had to try again and brought her attention inwards and asked the question, "*What is my status?*"

This time her display showed, "*Status: 100% fully functional, All systems: green.*"

Andena was pleased it had worked, and she was even more pleased that she hadn't been compelled to say it out loud. She wondered what else she could ask and without actually thinking about the implication of her question she asked, "*Who am I?*"

Andena felt a search of anxiety coursing through her body when her display showed:

"*Hybrid: 00, Name: Unknown Model: Female Full upgrade core: H_UNICS/AI version: 2.124 written by Danette Williams.*"

She had to ask the question again because she was too dazzled by the answer to fathom its meaning fully. It was completely unsettling that she still didn't know her name and the answer raised, even more, questions. Her mind told her that she must have a name, but she couldn't remember it. The other part of the message was telling her she *had* a core which was dampening her mood even more. Fighting against her rational precautions, she asked, "*What is H_UNICS?*"

She had to find out what those letters stood for, and she was somewhat surprised when her display showed, "*Operating system: H_UNICS, Hybrid Uniplexed Information, and Computing System. Better known as UNIX or LUNIX.*"

It became clear to her that she had connected with a computer. Her rational mind said she should be upset, but she found it interesting, and she wondered why she was connected to a computer. As curious as she was she asked, "*What is AI version 2.124?*"

"*Main program running: Artificial Intelligence by D.W. version 2.124.*"

Andena was confused, and she read the text once again. She was asking herself if she was part of the AI program. She vaguely remembered that scientists had come quite far with developing a good working AI program, but it had stopped when the Archon had banned all AI-based devices. She noticed that she was getting tired, but she wanted to know which other programs were running and she commanded, "*Give me a list of programs which are currently running.*"

She realised it was her first command, and she sincerely hoped that she would get an answer. Within a second she got a small list of programs with various names she couldn't place, but there was one which could potentially be interesting: a program called 'suppressor.' Andena wondered if it might help her to think a little better and more coherently if she could stop that program.

She asked, "*What does suppressor do?*"

"*This program is used for suppressing the brain activity of the person. Installing the program is a lengthy procedure because of scanning for brain areas affected. For more information type: suppressor more.*"

Andena knew she had found something which might help her to understand what had happened to her. She wasn't able to recall anything from her past even though she reckoned she must have one. All this thinking and reasoning was tiring, and she yawned fighting her sleep as she commanded, "*Suppressor more.*"

The text appeared and she started to read, but it was very detailed with terms she didn't understand at all. At the bottom of the text was the word 'more' and she knew she had to give the command to continue. Andena had lost count how many pages of text she had read already, but it was all as clear as mud. In the end, she couldn't focus enough to give the command in the correct way to get a new page of text. She tried it once more, but her mind didn't work anymore and totally exhausted she fell into a deep sleep.

Lunn walked into his quarters feeling totally exhausted but satisfied, wanting only a hot shower before crashing into bed. It had been an enervating afternoon in the new headquarters. The launch of the satellites was on schedule and had gone smoothly. Lunn was fascinated by how confident John was in monitoring the progress of the launch and when the satellites were released into space it had been amazing to see them joining the rest of the ring. The only moment when John showed some discomfort was at the point that the ring was to be completed. With sixty satellites fewer, all the others had to be readjusted which was a delicate job and after spending at least an hour double checking the positions, it had been time to initiate the ring. John had given Lunn the honour of pushing the button. Lunn knew if it didn't work that the financier would lose several billion credits and his relief was palpable as the ring came online. It would be around forty-eight hours before the ring was fully charged and ready to be deployed, assuming that the systems at the headquarters were ready as well.

There was still a major issue with the secure connections that had been provided by Datanex because they were not stable enough. During the repositioning of the satellites they had lost their connection with them several times but fortunately, it had never happened at a critical moment.

That was reason enough to stop using Datanex immediately, and it had taken John a few hours to get the local network facility to start the procedure to reconnect the original data connections. The man at the facility had promised that it would be done within forty-eight hours. They had ended the laborious day with drinks John had brought with him, and it was way past midnight before the two had left the headquarters.

With a satisfied sigh, Lunn stepped into the hot shower and felt his tense muscles relax as the warm water streamed over his tired body. Memories of Danette caressing his body flashed across his mind, and he felt a stab of pain knowing he had lost her for good. He wondered whether Danette had dumped him because of his obsessional involvement with Andena. His reaction to her disappearance had even shocked him, and he couldn't make sense of his feelings for her. There was no denying that she was very sweet and incredibly beautiful in every respect: a perfect body and mind-blowing sex-appeal. He regretted the fact that he had only ever had sex with her while under the influence of a mind-bending aphrodisiac. His recollection of the night with her was reduced to a shadow in his mind, and even though he knew what they had done, the experience was devoid of emotion.

Then Lunn's mind was flooded by the amazing, intimate and pleasurable moments with Alice. Those moments had been more genuine, and he realised that Alice was always there when he needed her. It dawned on him that she had secretly been harbouring a crush on him for some time, and he knew she would never have admitted it to him openly. He sighed as the soothing warm water cascaded over his body: he hadn't a clue what to do. He stepped out the shower and decided to sleep on it all because he was just too tired to do anything else. As he entered the bedroom, he saw a piece of paper lying on his pillow, and he smiled knowing it would be from Alice.

He unfolded the paper and started to read the text:

Lunn, I'm afraid I can't stay with you anymore. That means, to my regret, I have to resign, and I hope you find a suitable replacement for my position.
All the best, Alice.

He gasped realising he was about to lose another woman that he cared for. He moaned softly as he tried to process the note. He studied the paper intensely, and he noticed she had written it in a hurry. Her handwriting was usually more curved. Something must have happened, and he decided against his own better judgement to pay Alice a visit. He jumped into some clothes and looked up her address. He was surprised by how close she lived. He thought it was funny that he had never bumped into her as he passed her door on a daily basis.

Within a minute, he was standing at her door pondering what to do. Just as he had gathered up enough courage to knock on the door, he heard a sultry voice behind him saying, "I knew you would come back for me Lunn."

Totally flabbergasted Lunn let Lily pass him to open the door. She hooked her index finger, indicating that he should follow her and pressed him close against her voluptuous body. She nibbled on his ear and said huskily, "What do you want to do gorgeous?"

Lunn was pleased that he had bumped into her instead of being confronted by a sleepy and perhaps angry Alice. There were worse things in life than having to deal with a very hot and apparently incredibly horny woman. His groin reacted to her sensual assault, but he managed to keep a cool head and said calmly as he caressed her arms, "Talk."

Lily instantly stopped bumping and grinding her hips against his butt and asked wearily, "About what Lunn?"

Lunn tried to turn around, and Lily let her arms go just a bit which was enough for him to turn. He felt her firm breasts in his chest and she moved her hips against his excited girth. Her eyes pierced his while she waited for him to answer her question. Lunn had to fight hard against his urge to kiss her beautiful lips. They were almost the same as Alice's which brought his mind back to the present and he chided himself for being so weak. He turned his head away because he couldn't look into her eyes anymore as he whispered, "Alice."

She moved her hands to his chest and pushed him slowly away from her. He looked up and saw that her face had changed into an angry frown. She moved her hands to her hips and growled, "What the fuck did you do, Lunn?"

Lunn was taken aback by how hostile she suddenly looked. He sighed and said as he gave her Alice's note, "I haven't a clue."

With her fingers trembling, Lily unfolded the paper and started to read the note. Lunn saw the emotions flashing across Lily's face with each word that she read, and as she folded the paper several times, she took a deep breath.

She shook her head and whispered, "Oh dear."

Lunn's heart was in his mouth and asked hoarsely, "What is the matter, Lily?"

She looked at him and gave him an affectionate smile as if she knew exactly what had happened. She took his hand, and as she was guiding him to a room, she said with a friendly voice, "Let's have a seat and enjoy a bottle because we definitely need to talk."

Lunn followed her into a bedroom and said, "I figured that much but why are we in a bedroom?"

Lily smirked and said, "The living room is occupied."

"Oh?"

"Yeah, and don't you dare to ask!" she chided with a playful smirk on her face.

Lunn couldn't stop his chuckle and declared, "I don't even want to know."

Her smile was half-hearted as she chose to ignore his remark, "Let me tell you something about Alice that you should know."

Lunn sat down on the bed and gratefully took the drink Lily had poured him. He had the feeling it was going to be a long night.

Tancred felt somebody patting his arm and he had trouble understanding what the female voice was saying to him. The light in the room was not too bright which made him feel relaxed. The female voice addressed him again, "Tancred, Tancred it is time."

The soft mattress he was lying on was far too comfortable, and he turned away from the voice trying to prolong his pleasant state of mind. The patting on his arm was as persistent as the female voice that kept bothering him, and he had no choice other than to open his eyes. He instantly regretted his decision to give in: he recognised the horrible face that went with her voice. He moaned softly and asked, "Why do I need to wake up?"

The female voice answered joyfully, "You have had your well-deserved rest, and now it's time to get up."

"Well-deserved rest?" asked Tancred surprised.

"Well, yes. Your body showed signs of prolonged sleep deprivation."

He couldn't believe his ears, and was too afraid to ask the pressing question. His face must have shown his discomfort and the woman gently patted his arm again and said with a warm voice, "Don't worry! Nothing special happened during the time you were out."

Deep down he knew he had lost control over the humans, but he wanted to be sure and asked, "Can you tell me how long I've been out?"

The woman helped him to sit up as she said, "Hmm, I'm not sure but definitely longer than twenty-nine hours."

Tancred dipped his head in sorrow because now he

knew that all his carefully planned work had been for nothing and he knew he had failed massively. There was no way he could repair the cracks in the carefully constructed conspiracy pyramid. It was very fragile, and it had already been showing signs of crumbling before he was taken by the Cerasus vines. This planet would be the end of his adventure because he was sure that his superiors would kill him slowly. The woman gave him his robe, and he said still thinking what he could have done differently, "Thank you, human."

She frowned and chided, "I would like to be called Saida."

Tancred was taken aback by her sternness and raised his eyebrows. He had never thought he would have to address the assistants by a name. As the two males arrived in the room as well, Saida continued, "My partners would like to be addressed as Latif and Uso."

Tancred looked at the three people standing in front of him. They were still surrounded by several Cerasus vines, but their bodies seemed to be complete as far as he could determine. He had to laugh when he heard their ridiculous names and wondered how long they would survive when his kind ravaged this planet. They didn't have a clue how savage and uncivilised his race could be. He had only survived because of his powerful mind manipulating capabilities, but his superiors were even better at it. They could kill him in a blink by just looking at him. Tancred decided to retreat to his quarters and stay there until it was time to face his fate. He nodded to the three and mumbled, "Saida, Latif, Uso," and turned around, heading to the exit of the field. He wondered whether he could reach his quarters without being seen but he knew that Haruz was not to be underestimated.

As soon as he stepped out of the gorse, two people walked towards him, and the first of them addressed him by saying, "Good Morning, Mr. Tancred. Would you be so kind to walk with us, sir?"

Tancred couldn't believe that Haruz was so ignorant that he had only sent two of his guards, and he smiled at the two men and spoke calmly while imprinting their brains at the same time, "I'm not so sure. Why don't you both enjoy the wonderful morning and have a stroll on the beach?"

Tancred was surprised when the men started to walk next to him and gently laid their hands on his shoulder. The guard said with a friendly voice, "I do agree it's a wonderful day, but I'm afraid you will have to come with us."

Tancred was stunned by the man's indifference and focused all his mental power at him, "I want you to kill the other guard."

He was horrified when the guards walked on as if nothing could stop them. The guard looked at him and said, "Well Mr. Tancred, I'm afraid that is not possible. He is my friend. Oh, by the way, there's something dripping from your nose."

Tancred knew he had strained his brain too much and used his sleeve to wipe the blood away. He looked closely at the guard's face and to his horror he noticed the little cracks in the skin. He understood that he was staring at a machine which looked like a human. At that moment, he knew he had failed again, and he hissed, "Damned you Haruz! I'll ensure that you suffer the most!"

He was surprised when they stopped at a large old lorry. The guards helped him climb into the back of the old vehicle where two scruffy looking benches were attached to the floor. Another guard sat on the bench opposite. Tancred was too stunned to sit down, and he stared at the guard realising it was a machine as well. He was shocked when he heard Haruz's voice saying to him, "Do sit down Tancred. You and I are going to have a nice little talk."

Tancred startled a bit when the heavy doors of the lorry slammed shut. He hated dark and confined spaces, and he asked with a trembling voice, "What are you going to do with me?"

Tancred felt the sudden jerk of the lorry accelerating.

"Tell me, Tancred, when are they coming?"

"Who are you referring to?"

Haruz chuckled and said, "Always trying to avoid the truth aren't we Tancred? I'm referring to your race."

Tancred shivered when he recalled the angry faces of his superiors and whispered, "Soon."

"How soon, Tancred?"

Tancred sighed because that was exactly why he had gone to the field but he never had gotten an answer to that specific question. He said remorsefully, "I wish I knew, Haruz."

He repeated the short sentence but hardly audibly, "I wish I knew."

Haruz's voice stayed calm as he asked his next question, "Tancred, how many of your kind are coming?"

Tancred knew it wouldn't matter what information he gave because he knew they wouldn't have a chance of thwarting the attack and he said, "Everybody is coming."

There was a silence which Tancred used to continue, "Our planet is much smaller than yours, and it wasn't overpopulated but the Cerasus couldn't produce enough Joy for all of us."

"How many, Tancred?"

He didn't know the exact number and said, "Oh, I don't know. Perhaps a few billion."

Haruz's voice was a little hoarse when he reacted, "A few billion. Are we talking about two billion?"

Tancred had to think hard because he wasn't good at numbers and he answered tentatively, "No, more like three."

He heard Haruz sigh, and he wasn't surprised that the man sounded somewhat stressed when he heard him ask, "Are they all coming at once?"

Tancred remembered the euphoria of his kind after they had conquered the planet and said dreamily, savouring the good old times, "No, each caste has its own vessel."

"Do you know how many vessels there are?"

Tancred sighed because he was getting sick and tired of these useless questions and said with annoyance, "Does it really matter, Haruz? I don't know, but I guess it will be about twenty thousand or so!"

He couldn't stand the darkness, and demanded, "Where are you taking me?"

Tancred hated that Haruz didn't respond: it made him feel disregarded. The silence had become nearly unbearable, and he felt a little relieved when he felt the lorry slowing down. As soon as the lorry had stopped with a jerk Haruz's voice said, "You are in a cave now with enough food and facilities to keep yourself alive for at least ten weeks."

Tancred gasped because he realised he would start to suffer from major withdrawal symptoms within a few hours and pleaded, "You can't do that! I need my medication!"

"You will be fine. Don't try to get out unless you want to be electrocuted. We'll regularly check to make sure that you are still alive."

The android got up and opened the door of the lorry and sat down again. Tancred knew he had lost everything and shouted, "How dare you to treat an emissary like this Haruz! I'll kill you if I get my hands on you!"

Haruz's laugh was half-hearted, and he said, "I hope you're willing to share your food with the rats, although if you keep it all neat and tidy, you'll be fine. Have a nice time Tancred."

Tancred roared, "You are dead! You hear me Haruz? You can't stop us! You will fail!"

Meleda woke up with cramps in her stomach, and she felt sick. It wasn't the first time that she had to deal with the consequences of being fragile and not paying attention to the needs of her body. A hot shower was usually the best remedy. While showering, she recalled what she had read in Bionex's reports. It was fascinating and horrible at the same time. The research and experiments Bionex had conducted were amazingly advanced but from an ethical point of view, it was truly sickening and highly illegal. What they had done to the woman they had 'rescued' wouldn't have happened in a regular hospital. She knew that the poor woman probably would have died or been paralysed for the rest of her life. She thought that it was remarkable that they hadn't put any effort into finding out who the woman was, but then she realised the search would have brought unwanted attention from other systems.

The only thing Meleda couldn't understand was why Bionex had ordered ten androids. Why was a company investing an enormous amount of credits in machinery which has been banned? It didn't make any sense to train the androids as a small army unless Bionex intended to plan a coup. For her that was reason enough to disable them as soon as possible.

She had been looking for an update to Miss Danette's report, but she hadn't found anything new. Her bots hadn't come back with anything coherent the last time she had looked. Meleda had the feeling that she had to step up her encryption, and she had quarantined those funny files the bots had gathered. The disappointing results made her think that Bionex was onto her, but she still had her trump card left to play. It was tricky, but if she would time it correctly, she could have unrestricted access without them even noticing it.

She felt a lot better when she got out the shower, and she dried herself as quickly as possible. She needed to eat a good breakfast and after that, she would check her system for new results.

CHAPTER FIFTEEN

Andena woke up with a start because someone was banging on her door. It was Joshua who shouted, "Wake up! You need to be ready in fifteen minutes."

Her head was pounding because of the loud noise and the direct command she had received from Joshua. She sat up in her bed and to her surprise she noticed that the text was still there in front of her eye. She recalled what had happened the previous night and decided to continue to flip through the text as fast as she could give the command. She wanted to get to the end as soon as possible. After she had given the command 'more' for several times, she reached the end of the program's lengthy information. With growing interest she read, "*To uninstall type: suppressor uninstall. Warning: all stored settings will be deleted when an uninstall has been executed. Re-installing will take as long as the initial install. Press enter to close this text."*

Andena was reading the text again wondering what she should do. It was simple enough to uninstall the program and in the short description, it said it was suppressing parts of the brain. The warning was clear; quickly undoing an uninstall was not an option. She wanted to have a clearer mind to be able to think faster. She made up her mind, and she decided to uninstall the program. She lay down on her bed again and gave the command to close the text.

Not knowing what would happen she took a deep breath and commanded, *"Suppressor uninstall."*

A new text appeared, *"Uninstalling the program will discard all saved parameters. Are you sure? (Y/N)."*

She knew there was no return if she continued and hesitated for a moment but then she heard footsteps reverberating in the hall. To her dismay, she recognised the typical clicking sound of the heels which were definitely Miss Danette's. She knew it was too late to complete the uninstall because she didn't want to take the risk. Who knew what would happen if she gave the command. She sighed accepting the fact that she was probably going to have to wait until tonight.

At that moment, she heard Danette trying to open the door but it stayed shut, and she heard her murmuring, "What the fuck is this? Why is this still not organised?"

She heard Miss Danette stomping away angrily and realised she had gotten some extra time. Knowing it was now or much later she knew it was the right moment to go ahead, and she gave the command, *"Yes."*

She pinched her eyes closed and was startled when her display showed, *"Closing down the arrays......"*

She waited for a few moments, but nothing else happened. She decided to get up from her bed to get ready and dressed. She quickly got into the bathroom, and as she looked at herself in the mirror, she got the fright of her life. With trembling hands she touched her hair and came to the conclusion it looked like it hadn't been washed for weeks! She stepped into the shower and saw to her disbelief there was no soap and no shampoo! But then she realised she hadn't time for that anyway and looked feverishly around for a solution. Her eyes fell on a grubby hair brush which was lying on the sink, and she was relieved to find some hair elastics at the base of the brush. It took a full five minutes to get her hair into a decent enough plait, and she was quite upset by how much hair there was gathered in the brush. Andena was not at all happy at how she had been treated for the last few days. It suddenly sank in: the suppressor program had stopped working, and she was back to normal!

Although she still felt really strange.

She studied herself in the mirror and saw the numbers embroidered on her suit. She recalled that Miss Danette had called her 'Double Zero' instead of her name. She gasped when she remembered that she didn't know her name, and she started to wonder what had happened to her. The last thing she could remember before she woke up with this horrible tube in her throat, was being attacked by those vines. How she had ended up here was a total mystery, but she was convinced that something wasn't right. The fact that she was locked in this room was one of the things Andena was worrying about and *where* was she?

She heard Miss Danette's heels approaching her door again and within a few seconds, after the door had slid open, they stared at each other for a long moment. Andena was shocked by Miss Danette's dishevelled state and exclaimed, "Oh my, you look horrible!"

Miss Danette closed the door, and the expression on her face as she looked at Andena was one of bewilderment. Andena realised that she had made a stupid mistake by commenting. She needed to be careful to behave in such a way that it wasn't obvious that she had disabled the suppressor. Miss Danette's voice was shaky and raw which made the little hairs on Andena's neck stand upright. She spoke softly, "Double Zero, I don't want to hear any personal remarks from you anymore, do you understand?"

It was then she felt the scary and strange urge to obey, and she knew that Miss Danette still had considerable control over her. She whispered meekly, "Yes Miss."

She saw Danette pinching the bridge of her nose before she said, "I don't know why your parameters are diverting from the others, but I hope it's just a glitch."

Andena looked at Miss Danette whose face was now marred by a troubled expression, as she looked discreetly upwards. She wondered whether Miss Danette was trying to tell her something. On a hunch, Andena decided to look up slowly towards the ceiling of her room and saw to her dismay a camera which was mounted in the corner of the room. She knew she had to keep her facial expression as neutral as possible and thought long and hard about the most appropriate way in which to respond to Miss Danette's remark. In the end, there was nothing that she could say, except an apologetic, "Yes Miss."

Miss Danette squinted for a moment and turned around abruptly without saying a word. As she walked out the door, she commanded with a gruff sounding voice, "Follow me."

Andena understood that something major was at stake, and she didn't dare to screw it up. It made her feel uneasy that Miss Danette's direct order compelled her to follow her.

It undermined her free will, but she felt that she still was in control. She knew that a response was required, and so said, "Yes Miss."

He felt a leg slowly rubbing against his body, and an arm was resting in the nape of his neck. There was something soft but firm keeping the side of his body warm, but all these pleasant experiences were nearly overwhelmed by a horrendous headache. Lunn had to take a deep breath to fight off the urge to vomit, and he moaned softly. A warm body climbed further on his chest and hugged him tightly. It took him a few long moments to figure out to whom this wonderful feeling body belonged: Lily!

He was in no state to respond to her. The only thing he could do was move his arms on her back, and try to relax a bit longer. He had no energy to do anything else anyway, and he shut his eyes hoping he could fall asleep in spite of his throbbing headache.

Danette was shocked when she saw how much Andena had changed since the day before. It was as if Andena was suddenly much more aware of the world around her. The fact that Andena had combed her hair and had braided it into a neat plait made Danette wonder what was going on. It made her feel even guiltier that Andena was stuck on the program, together with the other androids. Danette started to wonder whether Bionex had altered the settings on Andena's AI program or whether her personality which was meant to be suppressed, had somehow managed to overrule the core.

As she was walking behind Andena, she couldn't help but notice the pungent sweaty smell coming from her, and she realised that Andena had no means of washing herself. It was clear that Bionex had never hosted a human.

Andena remembered that they had walked along this corridor before but now she was able to see everything in far greater detail, and she did her best to process this additional information. She was amazed by how immaculate and pristine everything looked. It was as if everything was brand new. She recognised the hall where she had been in before, and she wasn't surprised at all when Miss Danette ordered, "Sit down on the bench and wait for my return."

Andena responded in an instant placidly, "Yes Miss."

Miss Danette growled, "And no stupid tricks, this time, do you understand?"

Andena looked up to Miss Danette as she remembered she nearly had crushed her when she had tried to jump across the hall and said with an apologetic voice, "Yes Miss."

They stared at each other for a few seconds longer before Miss Danette turned away in a huff.

Andena mulled over what Miss Danette had said, but she still was keen to find out what had changed in her body. It suddenly dawned on her that if she concentrated on a certain move or action, she could summon a little dial. She was also a lot stronger, and that intrigued her even more. It was something she definitely had to try out!

She placed her hand firmly on the edge of the bench about a foot away from her. Slowly she increased the strength of her pull until she heard little cracking noises. She hadn't realised that there was a dial in front of her eye until it started to blink in red. It was clear that she had reached the maximum extent of her capabilities. As she glanced sideways, she was taken aback by how much she was bending the bench. Andena heard noises outside the hall and let the bench drop down again. The bench snapped back with a loud bang, and Andena felt the whole surface shudder for a moment.

The nine androids marched into the hall, and she had to move towards the end of the bench. Watching the androids all sit down in unison was an impressive sight and the bench not only shuddered from the sudden increase in weight but it also made a loud creaking noise. She looked at Miss Danette, who pretended that nothing had happened. She smiled and suddenly her voice reverberated loudly around the hall, "Right! Today we are going to do something completely different. We are going to practice leapfrog."

Andena remembered she had played the game when she was a little girl, and she couldn't understand why Miss Danette would choose to do such a strange and silly game. Her voice echoed against the walls of the hall as she commanded, "Stand in a line and make sure you're ten feet away from each other."

All of the androids got up from the bench and before Andena had decided where she would stand, the nine women aligned themselves with an equal distance between them. Miss Danette chided her, "Double Zero since you're a little slow you can start to leap over the rest. As soon as you have jumped over the last one, you distance yourself ten feet and stand still."

Andena walked to the beginning of the line and understood why they were spread so far from each other: she needed the space to avoid a collision with the next android. She looked at Miss Danette who clearly was short-tempered this morning because she yelled, "What the hell are you waiting for Double Zero? Go, go, go!"

Andena was a little startled, and she quickly made her way to the first girl. She jumped just a little too high and didn't have enough space left to jump over the next one. She had trouble avoiding a collision but managed to steer her body sideways enough. Flustered, she continued and jumped over the third, and it surprised her that her jump was just perfect. It was as if her body *knew* what to do with the result that the rest of her jumps were flawless. As soon as she had jumped over the last one, she heard Miss Danette shout, "Zero Nine you're next!"

Andena turned around to see how the android was copying her and was stunned when she saw the android collide with the one in front of it. Both fell with a loud thud on the floor, and Andena had trouble stifling her giggle as she watched the androids clumsy response. Miss Danette stared at her with disbelief as she shouted, "Analyse what went wrong Zero Nine and next time use your arms to compensate. Do it again."

The second attempt worked a lot better, and Andena could see that the android used her arms a lot to jump over the others. She gathered she had to ready herself for the impact when Zero Nine jumped over her. She had no idea how heavy the android would be. The thumps of the android landing on the floor were coming closer and then she felt a pair of hands resting on her shoulder for a very short time. Andena was surprised at how gracefully the android landed in front of her, and she got that the android had learned how to jump effectively. She heard Miss Danette shout, "Zero Eight, you're next!"

Haruz ended the remote connection with the android robot in the lorry and had to take a few deep breaths. He was still in shock about what Tancred had said with such indifference. He still couldn't fathom the sheer quantity of spaceships that would be invading Earth shortly. The chills ran down his spine as he remembered Tancred's statement that more than three billion aliens, presumably armed to the teeth, would attack the planet.

An utter and complete disaster!

The only comfort Haruz could derive from this conversation was the moment Tancred had realised that he was stuck in the cave without any drugs. Haruz could see the horror in his eyes when he knew he had to deal with his withdrawal symptoms on his own. It wasn't surprising he went feral when he understood how he had lost complete control.

Haruz sighed as he stretched his sore back. He had been up all night waiting for Tancred to appear. He had guessed that Tancred was hiding in the field, but it was very strange that it took him so long to leave the field again. Normally Tancred would never miss any meetings, but he had missed several. It was as if the emissary had been kept in the field against his will. It had changed the situation, and all the board members were as shocked as Arnost when they had come to the conclusion that Tancred had fooled them from day one.

Haruz walked towards the main meeting room while

preparing himself to deliver the bad news. He was certain that the board wouldn't object if he were to re-commission all the nuclear weaponry there was on Earth.

Andena was sitting on the bench biting a large chunk of her bar of compressed food. She was ravenous because she hadn't had anything to eat since she had woken up in this strange facility. It was only after her empty stomach had made a lot of noise that Miss Danette had stopped the training. She was visibly shaken when Andena had told her she was hungry because she hadn't had anything since she had gained consciousness. Miss Danette sat down next to her and asked softly, "Why didn't you indicate you needed food?"

Andena thought about that question because it was indeed strange that she hadn't felt hungry at all. Now she was eating the food: it made her aware she was very hungry but before that she had no urge to eat at all. She retorted, "I don't know Miss. I think I wasn't hungry before."

Miss Danette sighed and pointed to the empty mug and asked, "Do you need more water?"

Andena was only a little startled when her display showed, "*Water level at 75 %.*"

She hated that the display popped up just like that, but she was pleased she hadn't had the urge to tell Miss Danette what was on the display. She reckoned it was wise to drink a little more water because the exercises made her sweat. She nodded and said meekly, "Yes please."

Miss Danette got up and commanded with a relaxed voice as if she knew Andena wouldn't walk away, "Stay here."

Andena had taken a bite from her bar and nodded. She was busy chewing the dense food as she watched Miss Danette walk away again. She was staggered when the android which was sitting next to her asked, "Why are you eating?"

Bewildered Andena stared at the android. It was talking to her! The voice sounded nice and friendly, and she had trouble believing that it came from the android. She answered with a hoarse voice, "Because my body needs it."

The expression on the android changed a little, looking as if she was surprised, "Don't you have a power pack?"

Andena thought about the question and smiled at the android as she retorted, "Ah yes, I do and the food I'm eating will be used to charge it."

The android nodded and returned the smile. Andena was bemused when she heard the android remark, "You must be a newer model. We don't have an internal power source like you. We are dependent on an external power source."

Andena was intrigued and asked, "How long can you function on one charge?"

"My power pack was drained down to thirty-eight percent yesterday after the training. It is now at sixty-one percent."

"I see."

"How much is yours?"

Andena knew she had to make up a number, and she felt pretty good after she had finished the food bars Miss Danette had given her. She said, "My power pack is about eighty percent and rising because of the food I've eaten."

"Zero Five wants to know why you're not

communicating with us."

Andena was taken aback by the question, and she responded, "But I am talking to you now."

Zero One's smile disappeared and said, "Yes you are, but not via the wireless link, it is much more efficient."

"Wireless link?"

Zero Five responded, "Yes, we see you're there. You are node Zero Zero, but you are not connected to our ring."

Andena was speechless for a few moments and had to think hard as to what she would do. Zero One asked, "Is there a reason why you're not connected to us?"

Andena answered instantly, "No, not really. I just didn't know it was possible."

"Do you want to connect with us?"

She had to make up her mind quickly because she reckoned that Miss Danette would be back soon. It was a wild guess because she didn't know what she would get herself into but it might be something which might help her to get more information. She inhaled deeply and let the breath go again and answered, "I would like to, but I don't know how to do that."

The android smiled and said, "Just accept the requests to connect from each of us."

A second later her display showed, "*Node Zero One requested to connect with you. Do you want to connect (Y/N)?*"

Andena smiled to the android and gave the command to connect. After she had given the command nine times her, display suddenly filled with little sentences which scrolled up so quickly that she couldn't read them at all. Andena shouted, "Okay, okay! Maybe it wasn't such a good idea! I can't read that fast!"

The text messages stopped straight away, and Zero One asked, "Are you different because you're a hybrid?"

Then it dawned on her, and she whispered, shocked by the revelation, "Yes, I'm a hybrid."

She saw a message popping up, "*Miss Danette is approaching.*"

It came from Zero Nine which was the closest to the door and Andena just had enough time to compose herself as if nothing had happened. She decided to send them all a message, "*Thank you for inviting me to join your group.*"

Her display showed only one message from Zero One, "*You are welcome Double Zero!*"

She wondered whether she should ask them to address her with her real name but as long as she didn't know where she was and why she was here it probably wasn't a smart move.

Miss Danette entered the hall with the mug and walked straight to her and said, "Here you are."

Andena took a few gulps from the refreshingly cool water and said, "Thank you."

There was a small smile on Miss Danette's face as she said softly, "Err, and if nature calls just point to your stomach. The restrooms are just outside the door on your left."

Andena felt odd being treated like a little girl and decided just to nod.

CHAPTER SIXTEEN

Lunn awakened with a start upon hearing Lily's voice so close to his ear, "Hmmm, I want you."

His headache had improved, and the sight of her divine body lying on top of him made him feel hot. He stroked the small of her back, and he was pleased that she was still wearing her hot pants. Lunn hadn't been surprised when Lily had confessed late that night that she desired him. It was a little awkward to be so close to her and yet not act upon his feelings. However, he had come to realise that he loved her sister, Alice, and didn't plan on doing anything that would hurt her. Lily played with his hair and sighed deeply causing her warm exhaling breath to brush against his ear. She moaned softly and pushed her pelvis against his warm crotch, "It's so unfair."

He had trouble resisting the temptation to tilt his hips and savour more of her delicious body. He knew what she was referring to, but he couldn't resist teasing her a little more. It was as hard for him as for her! He chuckled and asked, "What is so unfair Lily?"

"My sister can get what she wants but runs away from it. And here I am with the most gorgeous man in town, who is crazy about her, still completely dressed."

Lunn saw the humour in it and said, "I'll bet that is a first for you."

She huffed, but she didn't say anything. Lunn was pleased when she stopped grinding. She pushed herself up on her arms and looked him straight in the eye. Lunn loved Lily's relaxed expression on her beautiful face and moved his head up to kiss her on her lips. Just before he touched her soft lips, she moved away and whispered in his ear, "If we're going to kiss, you're going to be mine. I can't do that, Lunn. I don't want to hurt Alice."

Lunn took a deep breath and realised that the intimate conversation, they had last night, had made him hungry for her affection. The two sisters had a remarkably lovable quality in common but the bond that he shared with Alice was stronger, and as he patted Lily on her butt he said softly, "You're right, Lily. It's time to get things sorted. I assume you're going to help me?"

"Yup. You won't have a chance otherwise."

Lily rolled off his body and lay next to him, stretching luxuriously. It took an immense amount of willpower on Lunn's part not to pull her warm, voluptuous body back close to him. He couldn't help that his body craved the sexual satisfaction, and he saw he was not the only one. Lunn knew that he had to pull himself together, and he had to get up as soon as possible before he lost control. With an immense surge of willpower, he swung his legs on the floor to sit up. With a reluctant sigh, Lily let him go.

Lunn stood up a bit too fast, and he had to lean against the wall to stop himself falling back on the bed. He heard her giggling, and he warned her playfully, "Don't you dare laugh or I will have to spank you very hard."

She gasped and breathed, "Oh my, Lunn, such an inviting threat."

Her sultry voice was making it even harder to leave her bedroom, but he had to go. He needed a long shower and a shave before facing up to the difficult task ahead. He turned around as he was at her door and asked, "Pick you up in an hour?"

Lily was leaning against the doorpost wearing only her ultra-short hot pants and the flimsy tank top. Lunn couldn't help but notice that Lily's flushed cheeks made her seem so desirable. She nodded and agreed with a smile, "Yes and bring a few sugared donuts."

Lunn smiled back as he asked, "Sugared donuts?"

"Her favourite treat."

Meleda stared at her screen waiting for the right moment to fire up the last two bots which would bring everything into sync. It had taken her two hours to gain control of the bots at several of Bionex's secure locations. There had been some hairy moments when it seemed like her bots would be discovered, but she always managed to distract the operator at the other end by placing one of the old bots at an unsecured location. It was her saving grace that the other person had taken the bait and had missed the other bots that Meleda had placed. All she had to do now was wait patiently for the other operator to move away from their desk. It was a waiting game.

In the meantime, she had checked her messages, and she was very pleased to learn of Lunn's good news. It meant that another piece of her plan had fallen into place, and the timing was spot on.

Now she had to wait for the right moment to strike. Meleda had to admit that whoever it was at Bionex was pretty good, but lacked the tools to do the job properly. Bionex was easy to hack thanks to her new encryption method.

The moment had arrived. She was about to compromise Bionex with her beautiful and carefully built trap. The gate was free and with a trembling finger, Meleda hit the key to launch the last two bots. It would take about five seconds before she would know if everything was functioning as planned. With her heart in her mouth, she saw the red lights changing one by one from orange to green on her screen. Within a few seconds, the last one flickered from orange to green. It felt like she had conquered an entire army and Meleda screamed euphorically, "Yes! I'm in!"

A new application appeared on her screen which showed all the video streams Bionex had running. She chose one where she watched a group of women walking into a large hall, and she realised it was the group of androids. When the last android passed the camera, Meleda gasped, "Oh my goodness!"

She was almost certain it was the girl that Haruz was constantly talking about, but she needed to have another look to be sure. She scanned the available streams and found two video feeds of the large hall in which the androids were being put through their paces. One of the feeds seemed to be controlled by someone at Bionex, who zoomed in on the androids who were sitting on a bench.

Meleda felt a chill down her spine when she saw that it was without a shadow of a doubt, the woman Haruz was continually talking about. She was sitting next to the androids and Meleda didn't like how the girl was staring at the opposite wall. She appeared to be heavily sedated. She had read about the hybrid woman called 'Hybrid-00' in Miss Danette's report, but she would never have made the connection with the missing girl, Andena. Now Meleda faced an enormous dilemma, and she didn't know what to do. Well, at least she knew one thing had to happen no matter what: the androids had to go before Bionex deployed them in a coup.

The fact that the hybrid woman was the missing Andena made it all more complex and she couldn't see any easy solution to prevent the woman from being killed as well.

Meleda looked at the screen and saw how well the androids were moving around the obstacle course. It was fascinating and scary at the same time. It was clear they were training for an armed attack because they all carried a long stick. She knew that her actions were justified because someone had to stop the lunatic in charge of Bionex. However, the thought of being personally responsible for Andena's death chilled her to the core.

She heard Haruz entering the apartment, and she quickly shut down the application. She hated having to keep this information to herself, but she couldn't see any other option. Meleda realised that it would change her relationship with him forever. It would scar her deeply, and she knew if she ever told him about Andena he would risk his life to rescue her. Even if he did succeed in freeing her, then Andena would only live for a year or two because it was inevitable that her body would eventually reject her biotechnical implants. Death, when it finally came would be excruciating.

Her mind was set: Lunn had to use the ring to disable Bionex's army. She hoped that her voice distorter would work as well as it had in the cave when she gave the command via phone. It was also the ultimate test as to how well the ring was performing, as she was more than ever convinced that they would need to use it in their fight against the aliens.

Haruz felt completely wrecked as he entered the apartment. It was only because of his empty stomach, which was complaining about the fact that he hadn't had food since the previous morning that he was staring into the fridge. He hadn't noticed Meleda until her soft voice startled him as she asked, "You want something to eat, Haruz?"

He had hoped he wouldn't have to face her because it was difficult enough for him to deal with the fact that the world would soon be overrun by aliens.

Three billion bloody aliens!

More than twenty thousand space ships!

How the heck could they survive that?

"Haruz! What's wrong?" his sister asked wearily.

He looked up at her and forced a small smile and said, "I'm shattered, Meleda. I haven't slept or eaten since yesterday."

He heard her sigh, and he wasn't surprised when she softly chided, "You're such a fool. What is more important than your health, silly?"

He wanted to defend his behaviour but when he saw

her fiery expression he knew she was right. It wasn't that smart to ignore the needs of his body. Haruz was fascinated by the confidence in her movements when she took all kinds of ingredients out of the fridge. He could look at her for ages when she was busy in front of the cooking island: hypnotised by her graceful movements which looked more like dancing. He was shaken by her question, "What was so important that you simply forgot to eat, Haruz?"

His mouth watered when she placed a plate full of steaming hot and delicious looking food in front of him. He moaned with pleasure as he tasted the warm and spicy food, and after he had taken a mouthful, he knew she was waiting impatiently for an answer.

"We were chasing after Tancred."

The stern look on her face softened a bit as she asked, "Oh and did you get him in the end?"

"Yes. It was a real challenge to get those bloody androids working again. We lost a lot of time assembling three working androids."

Haruz was really relieved when he saw that Meleda believed what he had said. She asked, "Where is he now?"

"Somewhere safe, far away from civilisation."

"I want to speak to him."

Haruz was taken aback at the resolute nature of his sister's voice and protested, "Forget it, Meleda. He was already starting to get withdrawal symptoms, and they were worse than I have ever seen."

"I don't care."

Haruz sighed.

He knew he had to keep her away from Tancred for as long as possible. He couldn't bear her hearing the truth from the bastard. The longer Tancred was deprived of his drug, the more incoherent he would become. Haruz ate a few more bites before asking, "Can I sleep first?"

He loved the way she was massaging his sore shoulders and was very relieved when she softly said, "I guess it can wait."

He took her hand and patted it gently as he murmured, "Thanks. Wake me in five hours."

He slowly hoisted his tired body from the chair and walked towards his bedroom. He was too tired to think of anything other than having a decent sleep. Before he stepped into his room, he smiled at her and said, "Thanks for cooking me that wonderful meal."

She responded in such a way as to say that his gratitude was unwelcome, "Yeah, yeah, but don't expect me to do that every day."

He sensed that her smile was not completely sincere which he blamed on the fact that she had to wait before she could talk to Tancred. He was hoping that the alien would lose his mind in the coming hours due to being forced to go cold turkey.

Andena was still a little breathless when Miss Danette ordered the group to stand to attention. Miss Danette had made an effort to create the most complicated track ever and was busy increasing the complexity of the route by adding extra obstacles. It was easier than Andena had thought it would be. Her computer core had helped her on several occasions such that she had completed the track not only without any mistakes, but she also had outrun the androids. Having to carry the long stick made it all more complicated and in the beginning, the androids clearly had some difficulties with it.

While she was sitting on the bench, she received a question from Zero One, "*Why are you moving your chest up and down that fast?*"

"*I'm a hybrid which means I still have to breathe air in the same way as any other human being.*"

"*We know you are, but why are you breathing faster than normal?*"

She wondered if it still was such a good idea to be connected to their 'ring' but it was more comforting than being totally alone. Her relationship with Miss Danette had changed completely, and she was disturbed by the woman's impersonal approach towards her. The fact she still addressed her as Double Zero worried her. Andena was pulled back from her thoughts when another message appeared, "*Don't you know why?*"

She responded quickly to the question, "*I've used my muscles extensively, and they need more oxygen.*"

She was surprised when the message read, "*That will preserve your power pack.*"

She smiled inwardly as she replied, "*Yes it does.*"

"*We were wondering whether your algorithms were compatible with ours.*"

Andena was puzzled, "*Algorithms?*"

"*We have seen how fast you were able to master the handling of the stick, and we would like to incorporate your algorithms in our systems.*"

That answer was both funny and upsetting at the same time. It brought the cold-hearted fact that she was dealing with androids that were connected to an Artificial Intelligence system to the forefront of her mind. She had nearly forgotten that they were androids because they looked and acted like real women. She was reluctant to answer that question, but could see no way around it. "*I'm afraid that I can't help you with that. Those algorithms are not compatible. I'm sorry!*"

"*There is no need to apologise. There was a 10% chance it would be compatible, but we decided to ask you anyway.*"

She was startled when Miss Danette voice disturbed the silence in the hall by shouting, "Right! I've changed the route. First, you'll explore it twice and after that, you'll do it again carrying the stick."

Andena followed the track and relished the challenge. She was unsurprised and indeed pleased when she heard Miss Danette say, "Double Zero, show the others what you can do, and I'm sure you won't disappoint me."

With a broad smile on her face, Andena answered, "Yes Miss."

Alice slowly got dressed after taking a long shower. She felt better than she did the previous day, but her brief sleep had given her a bad headache. As she looked at her reflection in the mirror, she nearly burst into tears. She felt lonely, and her empty stomach was making her feel sick. It was further confirmation that she allowed herself to get too close to a man, and the pain of separation was so painful!

She was startled when she heard a knock at her door, but she was so pleased when she heard Lily's voice saying, "Alice, open the door. It's me, Lily."

She knew that her sister was a true friend who she could ask for support. Lily had been her saviour during many dark times just as she had been there for Lily when things got out of hand. As she opened the door, Lily stepped in and gave her a big hug. She heard her sister whisper in her ear, "It's going to be okay."

Alice suddenly realised that Lily already knew what had happened, and she gasped as she pushed herself away from her sister. She started to shake as she groaned, "No! You have spoken to him!"

Lily nodded with a sympathetic smile on her face. Alice was genuinely horrified that Lily had met Lunn, and she asked with a small voice, "What did he say?"

Lily guided her to the living room and ordered, "Sit down and listen to me."

Alice knew she had to comply and sat down on her favourite love seat. Lily's eyes were fiery when she said, "I've never met a man with such an incredible soul. He is sweet, thoughtful, interested in other people. Hell, he's a gift from heaven! And you dare to let him go?"

Alice sighed because she had never seen her sister so wound-up and deep in her heart she knew Lunn was exactly what she longed for, but it scared her so much that it was making her chest constrict. She sniffed and fussed, "I don't deserve him. It's too good to be true, Lily."

"Damn right it is! And you are going to love it because you deserve it."

Alice retorted with a shiver, "Until he finds another girl who is prettier than me."

She saw Lily stand up and pointed her finger Lily stressed, "Believe me, he is only interested in you. I envy you, Alice. He is....."

Alice knew what word her sister was looking for and mumbled softly, "Perfect."

It was why Alice was so afraid it would turn as bad as her previous relationship. She looked at Lily, whose face showed that she understood her fear. Lily sighed, "Alice, forget the past. Lunn is different, and you know it!"

Alice's voice trembled when she said, "Really Lily? He is as gorgeous, as sweet, as nice as….."

She remembered the horrible pain when her former lover had left her. She sighed and buried her face in her hands and sobbed, "Oh Lily, I don't want to get hurt like that ever again. I'm better off without a man."

Lily asked her with a soft voice, "And why are you in such a state, my sister? Do you just like him or is it more?"

Alice whispered, "Much more."

"Are you sure he is perfect?"

Alice didn't understand Lily's question and asked surprised, "What do you mean?

"How long have you worked for him?"

"About four months."

"Did he ever mistreat a woman in that time?"

Alice recalled what had happened between Lunn and Miss Danette and she realised that Lunn wasn't a saint after all. He had his flaws, but he had always been genuine. She sighed and retorted, "He can be somewhat wild and unthoughtful but always regrets it later."

Lily laughed and smirked, "Ow? Well, there is a crack in his armour already!"

Alice realised Lily was right, but she still found meeting her own self-imposed expectations suffocating. Lily murmured, "You know Alice, nobody is perfect, not even you."

She was shocked to hear that from her sister and said wearily, "I don't understand, Lily."

"You need to talk to Lunn and find out together what you both want. He is crazy about you. Trust me on that."

Alice sighed and shook her head as she murmured, "I don't know what to say. I'm so scared I'll mess up."

"I'll bet he is more scared than you."

"I don't believe that," Alice huffed.

Lily offered her hand to Alice and murmured, "Come."

Alice had no choice than to follow her and to her surprise Lily asked her, "Why don't you ask him if he is scared?"

Alice gasped: shocked by her sister's sudden and unexpected challenge. When it dawned on her that Lunn had been waiting outside her apartment all the time, she felt even more insecure, and she whispered, "Is he waiting outside?"

Lily smirked and shouted, "Lunn? Are you still there?"

Alice couldn't help that she admired the dark bronze voice, but she was also able to detect the uncertainty when he retorted, "I am, Lily. I assume it's best to leave now?"

Alice knew she had to act now and opened the door. Her body had reacted before she was aware of it and she found herself hugging him tightly. She whispered in his ear with tears running down her cheeks, "I'm sorry."

He wrapped his arms around her and squeezed her firmly as he said, "Don't be. I'm happy to be here with you."

Alice looked into his eyes, and it seemed as if time had stopped. The soft caress of his thumb wiping the tear away from her cheek made her shiver. The strong warm feeling in her chest grew bigger and turned into happiness. She kissed him passionately, and he responded by lifting her from her feet. The passion between them grew until Lily cleared her throat and said, "I really would like a donut now."

Alice's face lit up as she asked him with glee, "Donuts? You brought donuts?"

"Yup, sugared."

Alice's smile broadened as she cooed, "Yummy! Where did you get them from?"

She loved to hear his chuckle and was curious what his answer would be. He said, "There's only one baker who can make the real donuts: Otellos."

Her heart was beating a little faster as she purred, "Coffee?"

The rumble in his chest made her body tingle all over. He kissed her softly on her lips and told her off playfully, "I thought you would never ask."

Alice huffed friskily as she chided, "Be careful mister or there won't be any donuts left for you!"

Meleda went back to her desk after she was sure her brother was sound asleep. His reaction to her desire to speak with Tancred was both interesting and annoying. It felt like he was hiding something from her. He apparently believed that it was too shocking for her. Meleda sighed, choosing to let it go for now because she was more intrigued by what was happening with the androids and the hybrid girl Andena.

She eagerly started the application and watched as the androids left the hall. She was a little annoyed that she had missed all the action. She checked all the other channels, but it seemed that it was very quiet at Bionex.

The only thing she could do was to prepare the detection system at the Bangly plateau. Getting the equipment up there had cost her a considerable number of credits, but she knew it was worth every cent. It was a very simple system and had been neatly disguised, making it look like the rocks on the plateau. Because the androids were made mainly of metal, it would be possible for Meleda to create a fail-safe detection network that would send a signal just strong enough to the antenna array. Her system would be activated as soon as the androids were detected.

She figured that Bionex would start to train there from tomorrow. Therefore, it was the right time to initiate the system. It was an incredibly dull and boring job, as she waited impatiently for confirmation that the network was online.

Her headache was starting to be annoying. It had been niggling her intermittently throughout the day but was now becoming incredibly painful. She barely noticed when the detection system successfully came online as her head was spinning. She had known that this was about to happen, and she wasn't shocked when she saw the few drops of blood dripping from her nose; It confirmed she had reached the next stage.

She shivered, and she had to resist the urge to cry. She was determined not to succumb to her feelings; at least until her plan was complete. Her time was clearly running out fast, and she hoped she would be strong enough to finish her mission.

She unlocked the drawer of her desk and retrieved a little pot of pills which was carefully stashed away in a secret compartment. She sighed deeply as she dropped one of the black charcoal pills on her palm. The tiny and shiny tablet looked like a black pearl and was toxic enough to kill an infant.

She estimated she had about four weeks before she would be unable to hide her medication's side-effects any longer. The disease ran in her mother's family, and only daughters were susceptible to it, and unfortunately, it was incurable. She hadn't had the guts to tell Haruz when she was diagnosed with this horrible condition. There was always a valid reason not to tell him, and besides, he had suffered enough when their parents had died from a drug overdose.

Luckily the medication was doing its job, and she felt a lot better. She knew she would be okay for about a week or two, as long as she took her pills, and that would hopefully give her enough time to finish the plan.

Andena looked dumbfounded at the pouch with bottles that Miss Danette had just brought to her. It was a travel set and to her surprise, it contained a bottle of shower gel, shampoo, and a conditioner. It wasn't the only thing which had her made feel a lot better: She had found a clean suit on her bed, but the sets of clean underwear and a large sleep T-shirt had made her day. She had never thought that such basic things could make her feel happy. It made her feel human again! She had enjoyed the shower, and she was brushing her hair in front of the mirror. Even though it wasn't the type of shampoo and conditioner that she preferred, Andena thought her hair looked a lot better. With a contented smile, she was staring at herself in the mirror when without warning her display showed, *"Node Zero Zero requested to connect with you. Do you want to connect (Y/N)?"*

She was startled because she instantly understood what was happening: her computer core was trying to 'connect' with her. She wondered what to do.

It bothered her a lot that it was only happening now and hadn't occurred any sooner. Was the core malfunctioning and what if she wanted to disconnect from it for a certain reason?

Andena realised she was stuck with it, and she was resigned to the fact that she would probably have to live with this situation for the rest of her life. She regretted that she never had any control over what happened to her, but she also accepted that dwelling on it was pointless.

She took a deep breath and commanded, "*Yes.*"

Andena was flabbergasted when her display only showed, "*Hi.*"

She snorted and responded, "*Hi. Is that all you can say?*"

"*No.*"

Andena had to count to ten to curb her frustration at the ridiculous manner in which this non-conversation was progressing.

"*Maybe we should disconnect again.*"

Andena was shocked by this text, and then it suddenly occurred to her that the core was behaving as if it was unsure.

She quickly asked, "*Why?*"

"*It seems that you don't like it.*"

"*I think that I have to get used to it.*"

Nothing else happened, and the texts disappeared after a few seconds, which was normal. Andena panicked a little and sent another text, "*Look, can we start over again? I'm a bit shocked as to why it took you so long to decide to connect with me. Is there something wrong?*"

"*No, all systems are running as normal. I decided to connect to you when I saw a smile on your face. It usually means that someone is at ease.*"

Andena gasped. Was it the first time she had smiled to herself in the mirror? She had to admit: from the moment she had woken up in this building nothing had felt 'right'. More than that, she hadn't had the opportunity to contemplate her situation. Here she was, having an odd but confronting conversation with a computer core that was buried somewhere deep inside of her body.

"*Maybe it was a wrong decision, and we should disconnect.*"

Andena was alarmed by the text, and she responded instantly, "*No! Please stay. I want to get to know you better, and I need to understand what has happened to me.*"

"*But you look scared.*"

"*I do because you're about to disconnect which I don't want. Please stay.*"

"*I'll stay connected.*"

Andena slowly exhaled the breath she had been keeping in all the time and smiled to herself in the mirror. She said, "*There! I'm smiling again.*"

"*It's different.*"

"*It is a smile.*"

There was a moment of silence and Andena didn't know what to say.

"*Why is your left breast smaller than your right? Did they make a mistake with the mould?*"

Andena was suddenly aware that she was standing naked in front of the mirror. She was surprised that the core had commented on her appearance, and she subconsciously covered her breasts with her arms. Rather than being angry, she was amused by the question and said, "*I'm a human, and it's normal that they should differ slightly.*"

"*Why do you suddenly cover them with your arms?*"

"*I do that when I am aware that someone is watching me.*"

"*It was merely an observation and analysis. Does it bother you?*"

"*No, not really,*" and by that Andena dropped her arms again.

"*It seems that I don't know your real name, do you care to share it with me?*"

Andena was taken aback by that question, but then she remembered the text she had received when she had asked the core who she was. She pondered this for a short while and said, "*You can call me Andena but do not share this name with the others. Miss Danette and the androids are addressing me as Double Zero, which is fine at the moment.*"

"*I'm pleased to meet you Andena. How do you want to address me?*"

Andena thought for a moment about what she should call her core, "*How about Z? It's short for Zero Zero.*"

"*That will work fine A.*"

Andena giggled because she liked the way Z was responding.

She was quite tired, and she was starting to get cold. She wanted to put on the clean T-shirt and then crawl into bed for a proper sleep. She yawned as she replied, "*Okay Z. It's time for me to go to sleep. I'm very tired.*"

"*I can assume you need your sleep to regenerate?*"

"*Sort of yes. Shall we continue our conversation tomorrow?*"

"*That is fine with me. I'll disconnect. Sleep well Andena.*"

Andena didn't believe that Z's remark was genuine, after all, it was a program running at her core, but she replied, "*Thanks, Z. See you tomorrow.*"

Andena thought it was strange to know that she could have a conversation with her computer core. It was scary as well but she figured that she might now be able to tweak some of her settings. She'd had it with the constant popups which always seemed to appear at the most inconvenient times. But most importantly was the list of people who had control over her. If it were up to her, the list would be empty!

It was the first time that Andena had crept under her sheet with a feeling of contentment, and as soon as her head hit the pillow, she fell asleep in an instant.

CHAPTER SEVENTEEN

Alice found herself pushed with her back up against the wall of her bedroom. The warm body pressed against her was making her sweat. Her legs were intertwined with another pair of legs, and her hand was being gently held by another hand. It took her a few moments before she was able to comprehend what had happened. Lunn was pinning her against the wall, and she quickly relaxed. A huge smile lit up her face as she remembered how they had spent the long night. They had talked a lot in between spontaneous bursts of mind-blowing sex. She knew Lunn was a good kisser, but loved what he was able to do with his tongue between her legs. She had never thought it was possible to have so many climaxes in one night. Alice knew that she would ultimately pay for it with severe muscle ache for the next couple of days but didn't care. She was more than willing to pay that price as long as she could have more of the same. Lily was right; Lunn was a gift from heaven, but he was far from perfect. He had his flaws, his silly habits, and his teasing was sometimes borderline annoying, but she found his sincerity and his unexpected vulnerability to be truly disarming.

She sighed deeply causing him to startle awake. She kissed him softly on his neck as she whispered, "Good morning."

She felt him becoming tense before he relaxed and breathed out a long sigh of contentment.

Alice asked, "Are you okay?"

"Yeah, I'm fine. I just didn't know where I was for a moment."

She said apologetically, "Yeah I know; my bed is too small for two."

"Big enough to have fun."

Alice moved her pelvis against his bottom and affirmed, "Hmm yes, I'll be reminded of that for a couple of days, especially if I have to climb stairs."

Lunn chuckled, and the vibrations of his voice made Alice yearn for his body. She attempted to crawl on top of Lunn's body but quit when her muscles protested loudly. Her legs didn't want to cooperate at all.

"What are you trying to do?" Lunn asked.

"Will you take me in your arms?"

With some moaning from her and grunting from him they managed to face each other without falling from her narrow bed. She saw his eyes studying her face, and she asked, "What?"

A wicked smile appeared on his face and said, "You look like you've been fucking all night."

Alice pinched his nipple as she retorted, "It's your fault, for being insatiable."

He countered, "Look who's talking! You kept on shouting; more, more!"

Alice giggled and kissed him gently on his forehead. She purred, "It was mind-blowing."

He caressed the small of her back and confided, "It was."

There was a pleasant silence which Alice used to relish his fantastic body. Lunn cupped her face, and as he was gently stroking her cheek with his thumb he confessed with a deep sigh, "I would like to stay like this for the rest of the day, but I have to go soon."

Alice saw his serious expression and she asked with a pouting face, "It can't wait?"

"I can't let John set up the new HQ on his own."

She knew he was right but she didn't want to be alone in her apartment, and she asked, "Do you think I can help you?"

He looked surprised as he said, "Maybe, I don't know. I need to connect all of the fuel cell packs to the hydrogen gas, and I have to re-build the fibre network as none of the old cables are re-usable."

Alice's face gleamed as she said in an excited voice, "I don't know anything about plumbing, but I do have a certificate in cutting fibre optic cables."

Lunn eyes grew bigger and asked surprised, "Since when do you have a certificate for that?"

Alice couldn't keep her voice from chirping as she said trying to fake indifference, "Oh, I have had it for years. It was my main source of income before everything went wireless."

"You amaze me! You still have the tools?"

Alice laughed and then murmured, "Yeah, somewhere, probably under a thick layer of dust."

Lunn asked, "Care to have a nice cup of coffee and a bagel? I'll pay."

Alice's mouth watered at the thought of having breakfast at her favourite coffee bar and she agreed, "Love to, but we need to shower first."

Dripping with sweat Danette woke up with a start. She looked with a panic at the clock registering that she had woken up just on time. She had taken the Dormancan pills, and she barely had heard her extra loud alarm. She knew that she would soon need another way to wake her up. It had taken more than ten minutes before she had realised that the alarm was sounding. She dreaded the thought that she might have to resort to the shock bracelet soon. She hated giving herself electric shocks, but it was the only way of guaranteeing that she would wake up on time.

She peeled her soaking wet clothes off and with a cloudy head she entered the cold shower. It took her a full minute to wake up enough to be able to adjust the water to a more pleasurable temperature. With stiff and painful joints she got dressed in clean clothes and she was pleased she hadn't forgotten to prepare her coffee machine.

As she entered her kitchenette, she inhaled the pleasing aroma of the coffee and realised that her mouth was watering. She knew she had to ween herself off those damned pills and made herself a promise that she would only need to take them one more time. She was due to present the androids to Mr. Yousima the following day; she needed one more decent sleep. After that, the pressure to perform should not be as great, and she would have more time to train the group to a higher level.

As she was eating her cereal enhanced with extra proteins, she wondered whether Andena would use the travel set she had given her. She had been taken aback at Andena's response. It was strange to see how the happy expression on her face suddenly changed into an indifferent and measured stare. Danette was almost convinced she could hear the happy emotion in Andena's voice when she politely thanked her for the pouch. Danette was convinced that Andena had changed, but she couldn't put her finger on what it was. Her development in her training was better and much faster than the performance of the androids. It was clear that Andena had mastered the handling of the stick in a much shorter time.

Danette was flabbergasted by Andena's strength. The upgrade to her body provided her not only with the boosted strength but had also overcome the paralysis that would have been expected after suffering a broken neck.

If only it had been anyone but Andena!

However, much as she disliked the other woman, she was deeply troubled by what would happen when Andena's body inevitably rejected the bionic implants. Danette knew the only way forward was to lock those feelings away and focus on the present. She had to be ready for tomorrow's show, and there was still a lot to do. She wanted to be sure it all looked smooth and impressive.

Armed with a stick, Andena hoped that she would be able to defend herself from whatever was lurking around the corner. She had been running away from the horrible creatures that looked like giant, dirty old ragdolls. She was leaning against a wall trying to get her breath back, and she hoped that the burning pain in her legs would subside. She knew she only had a few moments before they caught up with her again. The sloppy sounds and muffled cries came closer, and she shivered when the she saw the first creature round the corner. The doll's eyes were embroidered crosses, and their mouths looked like they had been cut into the fabric. The dark brown gooey stuffing with glistening strands, was slowly pouring out. She leapt up and started to run away hoping she could outrun them again. As soon as she turned into the next street she knew she was doomed: it was a dead end. There was no way back!

She cried out in frustration but as soon as she neared the high wall she noticed the carved holes and protruding bricks. She knew it could be her saviour. She wasn't pleased with having to leave her stick behind but knew that it would be impossible to climb the wall and hold the stick at the same time. As she started to climb remembered what her instructor had said when she had been climbing: keep your body as close as possible to the wall.

She made good progress but didn't dare to look down to see whether the ragdolls were still following her. As she reached the top of the wall, her arms began to ache, and her fingers were bleeding from the rough edges of the bricks. It took a tremendous effort to heave herself on top of the wall which was just wide enough not to fall off.

She looked down from where she came and saw to her dismay that the dolls were halfway up the wall, making slow but definite progress. She looked at the other side of the wall and shivered when she saw huge waves crashing against it. She knew she had no choice other than to jump into the sea and hope that the current in the water wasn't too strong. Andena knew that she needed to jump into the surging sea, or face being killed by the dolls! Pumping her lungs full of air, she jumped at the very second the first ragdoll reached the top.

To her surprise, the water wasn't that cold at all, but she noticed that the current was taking her deeper and deeper. She was hoping that the water flow would go up again and that she would have an opportunity to break free. The current was still too strong, and she was swept past vast rocks as she was pulled deeper. Andena was resigned to the fact that she was going to die; she knew that she couldn't hold her breath for much longer. She longed to be able to breathe in. Her body was screaming for air, and there was nothing she could do except open her mouth and breathe in the water. She started to convulse and was amazed when her body took over and began breathing for her. Andena was dumbstruck by the fact that she could breathe as effortlessly under the water as she could on dry land.

It took a moment or two for her to realise that she was lying in bed with the covers over her head making her feel as though she was being suffocated. She sat up, and feeling bewildered, looked all around her all the while greedily breathing in the fresh air. She recognised the small room she was in, and she was relieved when a message appeared in front of her eye, "*Andena, are you all right?*"

She noticed that her T-shirt was soaked with sweat and realised that she had had a nightmare. She took a deep breath knowing that her core must have noticed her elevated state, and she replied quickly, "*Yes Z, I'm fine. I just had a nightmare.*"

"*You're supposed to sleep, not dream.*"

Andena had to laugh but then instantly remembered

that it was possible that she was being monitored and managed to stifle it just in time. She answered, *"Dreaming is normal when you're asleep and most of the time dreams aren't nightmares. They actually can be pleasant."*

"Your heart rate was much higher than normal."

"Yes, but I'm fine now. Trust me; I feel fine."

"What were you dreaming about?"

Andena shivered when she recalled her dream and said, *"Z, can we talk about it later? I don't want to think about it at this moment."*

"Okay. What shall we talk about then?"

Andena was still recovering from her nightmare, but she knew that it was a great opportunity to find out more about her core and retorted, *"I want to talk about you."*

"What do you want to know Andena?"

"Who gives you orders?"

"What do you mean Andena?"

"Is there a list of people who can access you?"

"Yes there is, do you want to know who is on that list?"

Andena smiled and said, *"Yes please."*

"The names are Root, Mr. Yousima, Miss Danette, Joshua and Miss Olga."

"Who is Root?"

"That is you. Do you want me to rename it to Andena?"

"Can you rename it to Dena?"

"Why?"

"Nobody knows me by that name and therefore, it's much safer. Can you disable all other names?"

"Yes, I can. Perhaps it is wise to stop the program 'commander' as well because it was using the same list."

Andena was very impressed with the proactiveness of her AI program, and she replied, *"That sounds perfect Z. You can stop that program as well."*

"*It is done. I need a new password, can you give me one?*"

She knew it would be only for her, and she thought of something simple which she could remember, "*How about Z00Z?*"

"*Your password is stored. If you want to access me via a wireless link you need to use this password and the new name for Root.*"

"*So, Dena and Z00Z?*"

"*Correct.*"

"*Thank you; Z.*"

"*You're welcome A.*"

Andena smiled. She was intrigued that she might be totally in control of herself again, and she was looking forward to testing it out. She remembered that she also wanted to stop those annoying popups, and she asked, "*Can I ask you for something else?*"

"*Of course, you may.*"

"*Can you stop the information popups?*"

"*I can but how should I inform you?*"

"*I don't like it when an information popup just appears. Can you change it so that you show it when I ask for it?*"

"*Okay. How about warnings?*"

"*I want to see them no matter what.*"

A sudden loud bang on her door made her jump, and she cursed when she heard Joshua shouting, "Double Zero wake up! You've fifteen minutes to get ready."

"*Your heart rate is up again.*"

"*Yes, I hate sudden loud noises. They make me jump.*"

"*Shall I let you be so you can get dressed?*"

"*There's no need I can do two things at the same time.*"

"*Except when you're sleeping.*"

Andena had to shake her head and said, "*Smartass.*"

"*What is that?*"

Andena rolled her eyes and asked, "*Can't you look it up?*"

Meanwhile, Andena walked to the bathroom, and she had trouble to stifle a giggle when she read, "*So, you think I'm a clever person who parades his knowledge offensively.*"

As she cunningly smiled to herself in the mirror, she replied, "*Yes, that is close to what I think you are.*"

Tancred's body was shivering with cold. He began slapping his arms around his half naked body in a desperate attempt to get warm, but it didn't help.

He was looking around for his robe, but he couldn't remember whether he had sold it for food or whether it was just lying somewhere. He had been sweating so profusely that he had taken it off, but he couldn't recall what had happened to it.

His stomach was growling, and he wanted food but couldn't find anything to eat. There were boxes which made funny rattling noises, but he was unable to decipher the strange symbols and unusual drawings on them. He sauntered around, and he stopped at the large hut with wheels. He climbed in and saw a strange looking creature sitting on a wooden structure. The hands with the long fingers were resting on the legs.

With trembling fingers he touched the strange coloured skin and jolted back when he noticed it was cold. Tancred looked closer and saw little cracks in the skin of the creature. He noticed that all this time the face of the strange figure was looking down at the floor, and he wondered why the floor was so interesting. He tried to track the gaze of the man and saw nothing in particular.

He asked, "Why are you looking down?"

He waited for the creature to answer but it didn't which Tancred found annoying. He asked again with a louder voice, "What do you see? Why are you looking down?"

He had trouble keeping his anger at bay and started to breathe deeply when the ugly man didn't even acknowledge his presence. Tancred kicked the creature against its foot and shouted, "Hey! I asked you something!"

He barely waited a few seconds before he snapped and charged at the neck of the strange man with a deep grunting roar. As he was banging the creature's head against the wall, he screamed, "By Hondas! You have to give me an answer! NOW!"

He hadn't noticed that the hands had slipped off the legs, and he was shocked that the arms were swinging freely, bouncing against the wooden bench. Tancred was disgusted by the arms.

He was startled when the man suddenly looked up straight into his eyes. He screamed when the creature's hands grabbed his wrist and with an incredible force pushed Tancred over to the opposite wooden bench in the hut. His head smacked against the wall, and it felt like his spine was crushed by the sheer speed. The sudden pain caused him to moan, and he kept his eyes shut. He was shocked when he heard a female voice saying with a calm but commanding voice, "Stay there and don't even think about moving a single muscle."

Meleda was a bit annoyed that it had been more than

the five hours Haruz had asked for but, the little black pill she had taken had knocked her out completely. She had fallen asleep on the sofa and was amazed that she now felt properly rested. Normally sleeping on the sofa never left her feeling rested; perhaps it was the new pills that had made her sleep better.

Now she was in Haruz's office and strapping herself into a control suit to speak with Tancred. Meleda had never used a control suit before but Haruz had convinced her that it wasn't that difficult. She thought it was interesting as to how old the equipment looked, and it was obvious that the suit she was wearing had been recycled by using pieces from different suits.

She was amazed that the suit used a low-resolution binocular display. She had expected an optical link, and she couldn't believe that the suits never had one because they didn't exist when these suits were designed. Meleda realised that she was working with very old - probably museum-worthy - equipment. It made her feel very on edge not knowing whether the suit had enough safety measures to protect her from danger.

Haruz was amused by her concerned look and asked, "Are you ready?"

She had to accept the situation and said with a weary voice, "I guess so. Anything I should know before you hook me up?"

"Hmm, yes, the tactile force feedback system is still a bit dodgy. Be careful if you move something because before you know it you will launch things away with a lot of force."

She snorted and said glumly, "I wonder if I should have stayed at home."

Haruz deliberately ignored her remark and said,

"Alright, here you go! Link will be up in three, two, one. And you're connected!"

Meleda was paralysed when she saw Tancred's red face so very close to her, and she felt her suit shaking profusely. She had not been prepared for such an assault on her senses, and it took her a few moments to manage to grab his wrists. She looked him straight in the eyes and heard him scream. Haruz, who was looking at the extra display, shouted, "Push him away!"

She knew that the feedback system was not working, and she tried to push Tancred as carefully as possible towards the opposite bench. She shrivelled when she saw Tancred crash into the wall with a sickening thud. She had to take a deep breath before she was able to control her voice enough to order Tancred convincingly, "Stay there and don't even think of moving a single muscle."

She was pleased that she was unhurt, but her blood still raced through her veins. She needed to calm down. She muted the microphone and said to Haruz, "You're right. It isn't that difficult, especially if a lunatic is bashing you against the wall."

Meleda heard him trying to stifle a chuckle but in the end, he couldn't stop himself from laughing. She sighed and scolded annoyed, "Haruz! Keep quiet! He is moving again."

Her display showed that Tancred had opened his eyes, and he pleaded, "Master, please don't hurt me!"

She opened the channel again and said, "As long you're going to behave by staying where you are now, you will be fine."

"Yes, Master."

She ignored his confusion, which was probably caused by the withdrawal symptoms, and asked him, "Are you happy that you are going to see your people again?"

Meleda was taken aback when Tancred fell on his knees and started whimpering, "Oh, by Hondas, I'm so happy! I miss them so dearly."

She hadn't expected this at all but she wanted to know what his kind had planned, and she asked with a gentle tone, "Do you know what they are going to do once they arrive?"

He gasped loudly and with a jerky movement, he looked up staring at her. Meleda saw his face change into a scared look, and he whispered, "They are coming. They will be angry. They will punish me."

"Why would they be angry?"

"There's not enough Joy. No! By Hondas! They will kill me."

"How many are coming, Tancred?" She asked.

He was swinging his torso up and down and repeated, "They will kill me."

She knew that he had started to lose his coherence, and she snapped, trying to get his attention, "Tancred! How many will come?"

Tancred's voice was reduced to a whisper as he repeated the same sentence, "They will kill me."

She wanted to slap him in the face but knowing what she had already done to him she decided to leave it for now. Meleda muted the microphone and sighed, "Well, we might as well stop, this is not going according to plan."

As Haruz was busy disconnecting the link to the suit, he said in a defeated tone, "I have asked the same questions, and he refused to give an answer."

She was disappointed, but decided to try again with Tancred in a few days' time; she could only hope that the withdrawal symptoms would have faded by then. Feeling rattled, she stepped out of the suit and grumbled to her brother, "I'm done here. I want to go home."

She noticed his concerned look, and she confessed, "I had a terrible night. I couldn't get to sleep."

Meleda knew that she had to be careful not to use that excuse too often. He took her hand and said softly, "I'll take you home."

Andena was sitting on her bed waiting for Miss Danette to arrive. She was pleased that her core, Z, had taken her smartass joke lightly. It had made her smile and had said, "I see."

She was surprised when Z said, "*Zero One asked if you're fully charged.*"

"*Kind of yes. Why don't I get Zero Ones message directly anymore?*"

"*I had relayed them straight to you, but now we are talking to each other it's different. What do you prefer?*"

"*I think I would like to see what they say. Do they know you're separate from me?*"

"*No, they don't. Would you like to keep it that way?*"

Andena thought about it, and she realised that it was better that nobody knew that she was communicating with her core, and she replied, "*Yes, we should act as if we are one.*"

"*Okay, but how do I know with whom you're communicating?*"

"*Simple: If I want to address one of the others I'll start with a number.*"

"*That will work just fine Andena. It is nearly time to go; I can hear the sound of Miss Danette's shoes.*"

Andena sighed and replied, "*I wonder what we are going to do today.*"

"*We are going to practise formation tactics if Joshua is right.*"

"*How do you know that?*"

"*You were already asleep when Joshua walked past the room, and I heard him talking with Olga. They both were curious as to how Miss Danette would tackle this.*"

Miss Danette opened the door, and Andena was pleased when she saw that she had brought a tray with breakfast with her. Miss Danette's voice was less hoarse as she spoke, "Good morning Double Zero. I've brought you some breakfast."

Andena looked at her with an unfazed expression and said placidly, "Thank you, Miss."

As she took the bowl of cereal, Miss Danette remarked, "I see you've used the shampoo to wash your hair."

Andena had some time to think about how she should respond as she had just taken a scoop from her cereal. She had great trouble keeping her cereal in her mouth when she read, "*Oh dear! Did you really use the shampoo to wash your hair?*"

"*Z, stop it!*"

"*What do I need to stop?*"

"*Making smart remarks.*"

"*That is what smartasses do.*"

It was all that Andena could do not to laugh out loud, "Yes Miss, I have used the shampoo to wash my hair. Thank you."

Miss Danette looked at her for a long moment and then smiled as she said, "Good, don't hesitate to ask if you need anything else."

She knew she just had to act politely and responded with a soft voice, "Thank you, Miss."

She was relieved that Miss Danette hadn't noticed the trouble she'd had keeping her face straight, but she'd have to ask Z not to interfere when she was talking to other people.

Miss Danette got up from the bed and said, "I will get the others while you're having your breakfast. I'll be back in a few minutes to pick you up."

Andena nodded and said after she had swallowed another spoonful of cereal, "Yes, Miss."

Andena knew she needed to make Z understand her need to act as if she was still affected by her suppressor. As soon as the door of the room was closed she asked her core, "*Z, can you examine the information in the suppressor program?*"

It was just a few moments before Z responded, "*I have read the information, and I've noticed that the program isn't running.*"

Andena was a bit apprehensive when she asked the next question, "*Do you understand why this program isn't running?*"

There was a short delay before she could read the text, "*It would make you far less responsive, it would be impossible to have this conversation.*"

"*Miss Danette thinks that the program is still running. That means I have to behave like I'm affected by it.*"

"*I see. I can't be a smartass if you're talking with other people.*"

She was taken aback by the response and replied, "*I'm glad you understand, but you can always give me relevant information.*"

"*Andena?*"

"*Yes?*"

"*Are you upset, because I was a smartass?*"

She couldn't believe what she was reading and responded instantly, "*No of course not! You didn't know, but I will be if you do it again.*"

"*Oh, okay.*"

CHAPTER EIGHTEEN

It had been a long time since Lunn hadn't been able to pull his eyes away from a woman's mouth; Alice's lips were beautiful and even without lipstick they looked amazingly sexy. He wanted to kiss her at every possible opportunity. He had been distracted by his thoughts and was startled when he heard Alice chiding, "Lunn! I asked you a question!"

His mug of coffee was still full, and he hadn't taken a single bite of his bagel. He replied meekly, "I'm sorry I lost you there."

She snorted and asked sarcastically, "Oh, really?"

He knew the short night had made him less sharp. "I guess I am going to need to finish my coffee to fully wake up."

"What were you thinking about when you were staring at me?"

Lunn was slow to reply, but when he did, a dirty smile filled his face. "I was thinking about how kissable your lips are. How I want to make love to you over and over and over again."

She rolled her eyes and exclaimed, "Lunn!"

"It's the truth!"

"Oh, grow up will you?"

He knew that Alice was different from the girls that he usually dated and that he needed to adopt a more serious manner around her. "I'm sorry, Alice what did you ask?"

"Why do we use a fibre network instead of wireless?"

"You don't need the encryption and therefore it's a lot faster."

He loved the way Alice's face took on a dreamlike quality whenever she was deep in thought. "I see, well I can't think of anything that would benefit the small increase in speed that you would gain with that. But hey, it's your HQ."

He chuckled realising he loathed the fact he couldn't tell her the truth, at least not yet and not in this public place. He murmured, "You're right it's my design, but trust me, you'll notice the difference."

He saw her face turn into a frown, as she uttered, "Hmm, I guess so, but you never told me why we had to move the headquarters."

After he had taken a sip of his coffee, he answered, "It's a better location."

Alice looked annoyed, and it was clear that she was not satisfied by his answer. So, Lunn was quick to continue, "Not here. I'll tell you later."

Lunn was pleased when Alice sighed with a little smile before telling him, "Finish your coffee; we can't let John do all the work."

He knew that she was teasing him by turning his words back on him, and was happy to play along with her, "Yes Ma'am."

That answer earned him a painful punch in his arm, right below the shoulder which reminded him of her strength and capacity to disable a person with just a few punches. He grumbled softly but the fiery look in her eyes, he said had to finish his coffee quickly.

As they walked to the headquarters, Alice asked him casually, "Did you ever find out what happened to that girl; Andena?"

Lunn was taken aback by her question and suddenly felt extremely guilty that he hadn't thought about Andena at all. He stammered, "Err, I, I haven't found her yet. Haruz doesn't even know where she is."

Alice stopped and asked inquisitively, "Do you think that they took her into one of the fields?"

He thought about her suggestion. It was plausible and would explain why Andena had vanished into thin air. What it didn't answer, was who could have taken her there? He supposed that it was possible that someone might have tracked down the vines and found her entangled. He replied thoughtfully, "Yes, that would explain her disappearance."

He squeezed her hand and knew that he needed to choose his words with care. "As soon as the work on the HQ is complete we are going to focus on those bloody fields."

Arnost was sitting at his desk staring out of his window. He hadn't had much sleep because of the numerous meetings he'd had with all the board members of the different regions. They had all been present when Tancred had given his wonderful introduction. There hadn't been any opposition at the time, but now it was a different story. None of the members had taken the time to inform their staff about what would happen in just a few short weeks' because of the huge panic it would create. The worlds' biggest region was already pretty unstable, and any external upset would result in massive riots.

Most of the regions had dismantled their nuclear arsenal completely, and Arnost had shivered when he had seen the small number of warheads which could be re-commissioned; they might be able to inflict a little damage on the alien fleet, but the negative side effect of nuclear contamination was his biggest concern.

Most of the warheads had been designed to devastate a large area of land but what would happen if a warhead exploded in the atmosphere? It would probably make their situation worse.

An insistent knock on his door startled Arnost out of his thoughts, and he knew it was Haruz. "Enter!"

He could see, looking at the tense expression on Haruz's face, that the talk with Tancred hadn't given any other news. Haruz said with a rough voice, "Tancred's withdrawal symptoms were extremely severe. It was impossible to have a sensible conversation with him."

Arnost could feel his headache returning, and pinched the bridge of his nose. "I want you to focus on the nuclear weaponry. I want to have central control over what we manage to re-commission."

He saw Haruz's face turn into a frown but continued, "I've managed to persuade all of the board members to give their authorisation."

"I'm glad they have realised that we might have a better chance if we use the best-equipped control room."

Arnost grumbled, "It took many hours of dick spitting."

Haruz chuckled and said, "You're the best."

As soon as Andena entered the hall, all the androids looked up towards her. The manner in which they reacted as one fascinated her. She was unsurprised to see the following text appear on her screen, "*01: Good morning Double Zero.*"

She was pleased that Z had done as she had asked and she replied, "*01: Good morning to you all.*"

Her core responded, "*Do you want me to send the message to all the androids?*"

She thought about it. "*No, I think that Zero One will figure it out.*"

"*01: Zero Three wants to know whether you had a good sleep.*"

She thought that it was strange that an android would ask such a question, but she realised that artificial-intelligence programmes would throw in an unexpected question occasionally to appear to be more human. She answered, "*01: Yes thank you, I'm fully charged and ready for the day.*"

"*Why didn't you mention the fact that you had a nightmare?*"

"*Oh, that is something I prefer to keep to myself.*"

"*Why is that Andena?*"

"*Nightmares are quite disturbing most of the time, and I would like to forget them as soon as possible.*"

"Are you telling me that your memory can lose information?"

That question had caught her off guard, and she shivered for a short moment. How the hell was she going to answer that question? Andena thought hard for a short moment and then replied hoping that Z would understand her explanation, *"Not really. I think everything is stored in my brain but to keep my sanity, I only can access a certain amount of information at once. My brain is sorting out what I need to know and keeps information available as long I'm accessing it at regular intervals. As soon as I stop accessing a certain chain of information for a longer period, the direct link to it is discarded."*

It took her core a moment to comment, *"So it's still there but not readily available."*

She was pleased that her core accepted her extremely simplified explanation of how the human brain worked. She replied, *"Yes and you can recall the memory by specifically thinking about it."*

Andena was startled when she heard Miss Danette's voice reverberate around the hall, "Right! Today we are going to practice formation tactics. Since there are ten of you, we can do extra practice over and above the normal square formation. Today, we will attempt a more challenging triangular formation. We will start with the triangular form and Zero Five will be at the tip of the triangle."

Miss Danette walked into the middle of the hall and pointed with her finger as she commanded, "Zero Five stand here."

Andena was intrigued to see how Miss Danette would build the triangle. Z displayed, *"Interesting, Zero Four and Zero Six will be the next ones to be called."*

She was surprised when Miss Danette commanded, "Zero four and Zero Six form a triangle with Zero Five whereby the distance between the three of you is two feet."

As she was looking at the three androids forming a triangle she asked Z, "*How did you know that Zero Four and six would be the next ones?*"

"*It became the most likely option the moment she started the tip of the triangle with Zero Five. It would be logical if you and Zero Three were to be the next ones to be summoned.*"

Andena was amused when Miss Danette voice echoed, "Double Zero and Zero Three, form a triangle with Zero Four in such a way that Double Zero is straight behind Zero Five."

She understood that she would be in the middle of the triangle. She got up from the bench and assumed a position behind the android. She had to stifle a snort when Z told her, "*Not bad A. You're only a quarter of an inch off. Just move a little to the right.*"

It was only a little disturbing when she saw that two lines and a little arrow, which was pointing to the right, had appeared on her display. Frustrated she blew some air out and shuffled a little to the right until the two lines had merged. It then dawned on her she had no choice but to be that accurate because Miss Danette viewed her as an android. It would have been strange if she was a little out.

Danette said, "Zero Seven you form the triangle with Double Zero and Zero Six. Zero Two and Zero One together with Zero Three. And the last triangle; Zero Eight and Zero Nine with Zero Seven."

Andena heard the androids footsteps behind her, and when she looked around, she had a feeling of being cocooned by the group.

She saw Miss Danette step on the bench, and she said, "Perfect. Now make the distance between each other one foot whereby Double Zero stays where she is."

It was very intimidating when all the women moved towards her in one fluid step, and it took all of her self-control to resist the urge to yelp.

"Right!" shouted Miss Danette, "Increase the distance back to two feet and move five feet forward."

Andena knew that all the androids would move as one, but she had always been the odd one out, and she asked Z, "*How are we going to do that?*"

"*I suggest you tell Zero One they have to follow you.*"

"*Okay and you show me when we have moved five feet?*"

Z replied, "*I'll show a line on the display.*"

"*01: I shall lead the group because we can't link directly as I'm a hybrid.*"

She was pleased when she got an instant reply, "*01: We will follow you Double Zero.*"

Andena took a breath and stepped with her left foot forward, and all the other androids copied her step instantly. It was weird, and it felt like as if she had nine clones walking with her doing exactly what she did.

She had difficulty keeping a neutral expression on her face, and she almost missed the line on her display that indicated where she should stop.

Andena knew that Miss Danette was very pleased with the result as she heard her saying, "That looks great! Now, Zero Two will be the tip of the triangle. So turn your body a hundred and twenty degrees counter-clockwise and move fifteen feet."

Andena turned round until she was exactly facing the back of Zero Two and moved forward. She was grateful for her core's assistance as she would have struggled without it.

Joshua was sitting behind the monitors watching Miss Danette's training. The camera was zoomed into the group as he tried to follow the hybrid girl's fantastically shaped bottom. It was a challenge to keep those perfectly rounded cheeks in sight. Although, he concluded that all of the android's backsides were a pretty amazing sight to behold. He loved watching them move with such synchronicity. The hybrid moved just a little more fluidly than the androids and her tits bounced in a more natural way; making her appear super sexy.

He recalled how he'd had the privilege of washing her amazing body several times when the hybrid was recovering from the upgrade and he had adored her perky breasts. They were perfectly shaped, and they felt firm but marvellously soft at the same time.

He was startled by Mr. Yousima's high-pitched voice, "Zoom out Joshua, I want to see all the lovely ladies not just their asses."

With a shaking hand, he changed the view of the camera and meekly answered, "Yes Mr. Yousima."

He felt Mr. Yousima's fat belly brush against the back of his hair and hated it. Mr. Yousima remarked, "Miss Danette has made good progress. The androids are ready for the field exercises so tomorrow after the demonstration; I want them to practise at the plateau. Make sure that the transport is ready and all the other goods are stored in the crates."

Joshua knew that he would be busy for a while, and he would have no more time for drooling over those hot bodies. He retorted, "Yes, Mr. Yousima, I'll take care of it."

"Good. You'll need to speak to Miss Olga to able to

access the goods. Tell her that we're going to the plateau and she will know what to do. If you're nice to her, she might even help you."

"Yes, Mr. Yousima." Joshua felt the need to reply, even though he knew that the repulsive man had already left.

He got up and once again looked at the androids before turning the system off. He sighed deeply, as he closed the door behind him. It was going to be hard work getting everything ready on time.

Alice slipped the last plug into the connector at the back of the console and crept out from under the desk. It had been a long time since she had last cut fibre optic cables but she'd managed to complete the whole network in record time.

She had helped Lunn several times when he needed a third hand to hold something steady, usually in cramped places where their bodies were pressed up against each other. She had felt that he was getting aroused, and she couldn't deny that she enjoyed it. Indeed, on two occasions they had made out for a minute or so but because John was always in the vicinity, she had broken off the kiss. The scorching look in his eyes and the manner in which he had nibbled seductively on her earlobes had made her feel incredibly wanton, and she had whispered, "Tonight, at your place, you're mine."

She checked the connection at the console, and as she arched her back, she said, "I think the network is finished."

She heard John speaking from the other side of the room, "Alrighty! Let's have a speed test. I'm curious to find out whether you have beaten Lunn's last attempt."

"What do you mean John?"

She saw the smirk on Lunn's face as he said, "We had a bet to see whether I could create a faster network than John could."

Alice had to stifle a laugh and asked gleefully, "And? Who won?"

Lunn smiled, "I did."

John continued in an excitable voice, "Yes, but now we have about ten teraflows more! That is amazing Alice!"

Alice's heart was beating a little faster, and she was elated by the fact that she'd managed to improve the performance by so much, and she was grateful that she had decided to store her tools in her specially designed box. She felt two hands caressing her belly and warm lips kissing her gently on her neck.

Lunn's breath caressed her ear when he said, "I'm amazed and very proud that you have managed to pull this off so well."

She turned around and smiled when she saw the respect for her in his eyes. She patted his chest and said, "Well, working that hard has made me hungry and thirsty. Is there anything we can have?"

Alice squealed when a loud pop filled the room but quickly realised that it was just John uncorking a bottle of champagne.

He said, "The HQ is now completely functional, and we should celebrate that with some bubbly, don't you think?"

Alice cooed, "Hmm, I'd love to. Lunn is there anything to eat?"

"There are some snacks in the cupboard above the coffee machine, but I don't know if you will like them."

She was ravenous, and she purred as she headed to the

kitchenette, "Anything will do."

Danette plumped down with a happy sigh on her sofa with a big bowl of hot noodles. Today had worked out amazingly well. It was impressive watching those ten droids move as one solid mass through the hall. She had enjoyed seeing them form the triangle in a matter of seconds even when scattered all over the hall. In the beginning, it had taken longer for the group to get the triangular form right in one go but as the day had progressed the group had become more coherent, and it had all become more fluent.

The final exercise had been to protect one of the androids, and they had been instructed to swap places to keep the threat as far as possible away from the target.

Danette knew she had trained the androids and Andena as well as she could. It was the first time in a long time that she had felt so at ease. She had accomplished something special, and she knew that no other group of androids was capable of such a feat. Her AI programme, which had taken her years to perfect, had finally come good.

She got up and walked to the cupboard to get her red and shiny Dormancan pills. Just before she opened the little pot she stopped and wondered whether she should take only one.

Or perhaps none?

She recognised the pattern and knew that it was time to start weaning herself off those bloody pills. She realised it wasn't that hard to keep the lid on the little pot, and she felt the soothing surge of joy that she was able to resist the temptation! She was lucky that she had only taken them for a few days and as such the withdrawal symptoms wouldn't be that severe.

With a trembling hand, Danette put the little pot back in the cupboard and walked slowly to her bedroom. The urge to go back to get the pills was there, but she knew she could keep herself in control. Danette quickly threw off her clothes and crawled under the sheets. She shivered, knowing it was a reaction to not taking the drugs, and the extra blanket, she could pull over her, would solve that problem. She knew that she would feel restless at first, but she would fall asleep eventually.

Andena opened her eyes, and she instantly knew where she was; she was locked in the little room, and it was the third night after she had managed to stop the suppressor programme. Her core greeted her warmly, "*Morning A. No nightmare this time?*"

"*Morning Z. Thanks. I had a nice sleep without any nightmares.*"

"*How do you know you had a nice sleep?*"

Andena turned lazily in her comfortable bed and closed her eyes for a few seconds. She felt at ease, and she replied, "*I feel rested and relaxed. That usually means I had a good sleep.*"

"*You only moved fifteen times during your sleep last night.*"

"*Oh okay. How many times did I move the night before?*"

"*You were moving constantly.*"

"*Hmm, that figures why I feel much better now.*"

"*I was concerned that you were moving so little, but your*

heart rate and breathing were very regular."

"That's how a human is supposed to sleep Z."

"Yes, I've found some information, but it wasn't very consistent."

Andena sighed and wondered whether Z would have more information. She asked, "Z do you know where we are?"

"Yes, we are at Bionex, in the guest wing to be more precise."

Andena had heard of Bionex as the provider of prosthetics, and she wondered why she was here. "Do you know why I'm here?"

"I'm sorry Andena, but I don't know the answer."

"Why are you in my body?"

"That is another question I can't answer, but I can tell you that I am supposed to be in an android."

Andena was shocked by that answer and asked, "How do you know?"

"My parameters for the physical body were substantially different."

"What do you mean Z?"

"First of all your height was off by 4 inches. Your weight was a lot less, and the centre of gravity wasn't correct either."

Andena remembered how strange she had felt the first time she had attempted to walk after first waking up, "Aha, that's why I had jumped so high when I got up from the bench."

"That is correct. At that moment, your muscle tensions were geared for a much heavier body; you were lucky not to get hurt."

Andena stretched her body feeling that she was ready for the big day. It was strange how Miss Danette had addressed the group as if they were a group of soldiers. She asked her core, "*Do you know the purpose of our training?*"

"*I have come to the conclusion after I had analysed the information I have gathered so far, that we are being trained to become an elite group of soldiers.*"

"*Hmm, a soldier. It still doesn't make sense. As far as I know, there hasn't been a war for ages.*"

"*I'm afraid I can't answer that question.*"

The typical clicking sound of Miss Danette's heels was reverberating in the hall, and Andena was looking forward to her breakfast. She was hungry and was secretly hoping for an extra-large breakfast this time because of the special day. Miss Danette looked a little surprised when she saw that Andena was still in her bed and asked, "Good morning Double Zero. Why are you still in your bed?"

Andena had trouble keeping a neutral expression on her face because Miss Danette looked beautiful and fresh. Something was different, and even she wasn't a fan of Miss Danette she was happy for her. She answered, "I'm sorry Miss, but Joshua didn't wake me this morning."

She was pleased that Miss Danette's stern look had disappeared as she said, "Oh well, it's still early. Enjoy your breakfast. I'll pick you up in twenty minutes."

Andena replied in the way she always had replied, "Thank you, Miss."

Miss Danette walked to the door and turned around to say, "Remember to put on a clean suit."

Andena replied meekly, "Yes Miss, I will."

Danette was very relieved when the demonstration came to an end. It had all worked out perfectly, and she was convinced that Mr. Yousima was surprised at how well-oiled the cooperation between the women was. She had commanded the group to stand to attention, and she was walking together with Mr. Yousima towards the androids. As Mr. Yousima straightened Zero Nine's collar, he said, "You've done an excellent job, Miss Danette."

She was pleased with his choice of words, and she replied with a warm voice, "Thank you Mr. Yousima. I have enjoyed working on this project."

He had moved to the next android and asked, "Are you pleased with the results as well Miss Danette?"

"Well yes, but it's just a start there's still a lot to do."

She had to make a fist not to intervene when he tucked a strand of hair behind the ear of Zero Seven. The android didn't move at all, and as he moved to the next, he retorted, "Hmm yes, I think you've managed to create a sturdy basis upon which we can build."

Danette was quite taken aback by his answer and carefully queried, "I assume I can continue with the training?"

He turned his face to her, and she shuddered when he showed his sickly grin. He chuckled. His voice was a little lower when he asked, "Miss Danette, why would you think you would not be needed anymore after showing us such dedication to the task?"

She couldn't look at his face anymore, and she nervously looked down at her hands as she muttered, "I don't know sir. I'm sorry."

"You suggested that we let the androids train at the Bangly plateau."

Her heart was in her mouth when she stammered, "Y, yes because they need to learn to adapt to move around on rougher surfaces."

"Good. After I've inspected all of the androids, you

may start their training on the plateau at once. Everything is already set to go."

Danette was a little taken aback and retorted, "Thank you Mr. Yousima."

CHAPTER NINETEEN

Andena was still a little out of breath when Danette ordered the group to stand to attention. Miss Danette had gone to great lengths to make the most complicated track ever. It was easier than Andena had thought it would be. Her core had helped her on several occasions such that she had completed the track not only without any mistakes but she had also outrun the androids.

She had seen the fat and ugly man staring at her when she was performing the given exercises. His presence hadn't initially bothered her because she had been enjoying the opportunity to move her muscles extensively.

She thought that his high-pitched voice didn't fit with his enormous size, and she had trouble keeping a smirk off her face. She had looked at Miss Danette several times during the exercise and been reassured by her smiles. She knew that she had performed well, and she had channelled her energy into appearing as android-like as possible.

She saw Miss Danette talking to Mr. Yousima while they were inspecting the others. Andena didn't like the familiar way in which Mr. Yousima was touching the androids. Every time his hands seemed to move towards their breast, but he diverted at the last moment by moving the zip a little bit higher or pulling the collar straight.

When he arrived at Andena, he asked Miss Danette, "I assume you have the data chart of Hybrid-00 available?"

She saw Miss Danette eyes getting a little bigger before she stammered, "I, I do. It's on the bench over there."

"Would you be so kind as to get it, Miss Danette?"

"Yes, certainly Mr. Yousima," she responded and hurried away to fetch the folder without hesitation.

Andena was uncomfortable being alone in the man's presence. Her fear became tangible when he said with a sickly smile. "You're such a pretty girl. I love your perky tits."

To her dismay, she saw his grubby hands with those horrible fat fingers - which looked like sausages - reaching for her breasts and just before he could touch them her hands shot out to his wrists. He tried to move his hands closer, but Andena kept them an inch away.

His smile had disappeared, and he snarled, "Let go!"

Z instantly gave her a warning, "*Andena, he is too strong. You will fall backwards.*"

She answered, "*I don't care as long as he can't touch me.*"

She knew he was strong, but there was no way that she was going to let him touch her intimately without putting up a fight. He tried to move his wrists, but Andena had locked her muscles into an iron grip. Mr. Yousima suddenly pushed with his whole body forward and she only could walk backwards to keep the distance. She knew that she would eventually collide with the wall and deliberately searched with her feet for the wall with every step she took.

"*You will hit the wall with a lot of force, Andena,*" warned her core.

She replied, "*I know, I think if I extend my foot I can soften the blow.*"

With four steps Mr. Yousima slammed her up against the wall, but she had managed to soften the blow. He pushed with all his might, but he still couldn't reach her breasts. Andena was happy to see how strong her muscles had become, but she wanted to get out of this awkward situation as soon as possible.

She suddenly placed her boot against Mr. Yousima's sternum and asked her core, "*Z can you show me how much power I can use without breaking his bones?*"

She saw to her delight two dials appearing on her display; one for her arms and one for her leg. She knew now what to do and within a second after placing her foot on his chest; she released the power built-up in her muscles. Andena was amazed that she managed to launch Mr. Yousima at least fifteen feet away. As he was gliding over the floor, she heard Miss Danette scream, "Double Zero! NO!"

She heard a roar coming from Mr. Yousima which didn't surprise her at all, and she prepared herself for him to charge at her. She was surprised how quickly Mr. Yousima was on his feet again, and she was quite impressed by how fast he was charging at her. Applying her Martial Arts training Andena stepped aside and grabbed his arm to swing his body away from her. With a frustrating yell, Mr. Yousima could barely keep his balance when Andena let his arm go. He shouted, "You filthy little slut!"

Miss Danette pleaded with a hoarse voice, "Double Zero! Don't do this! You can't win!"

Andena ignored her because she was focusing on Mr. Yousima as he walked slowly towards her, snorting like an angry bull. He crouched down when he was just a few feet away from her, and she knew he would try to launch himself at her. Andena knew he was no match for her and calmly waited for him to attack.

"*What do you think he will do?*" asked her core.

"*He will try to launch at me and slam me to the floor.*"

"*Will you let him do that to you?*"

Andena had no time to answer her core because Mr. Yousima flew towards her. She jumped just high enough to let him pass underneath her and aimed a powerful kick at his back. His body slammed to the floor with a loud smack, and he skidded motionless towards the wall. Andena was surprised that he was on his feet again within seconds. His tirade of curses left her unfazed, but the high pitch tone of a charging laser gun was enough for her to pay close attention to him. She was stunned when she was suddenly surrounded by the androids.

"*01: We will protect you Double Zero.*"

As she was peeking past the androids, looking for Mr. Yousima, she answered, "*01: He has a laser gun which can cut you in half!*"

"*01: It is unlikely he would damage us beyond repair. Try to follow us and keep yourself safe.*"

"*I'll give you instructions Andena.*"

"*Okay.*"

"*Go left!*"

Andena moved to the left and nearly bumped into Zero Three when she saw that her core had changed the text into, "*Go right!*"

It was hard work to keep herself in the middle of the group while it was constantly moving in different directions. Because she had to read her core's instructions, it was making her slower than usual. However, she knew she was safe for the moment. Andena heard Miss Danette shouting, "Double Zero, stop this charade immediately!"

All of a sudden the group stood still for a longer period and she dared to peek between the androids. She saw Mr. Yousima looking flabbergasted at the group of androids and saw to her relief that he had dropped his arm which was holding the gun. He shook his head, and then his harsh voice echoed against the walls of the hall, "All systems halt!"

All of a sudden the androids slowly collapsed like ragdolls to the floor. As Andena was crouching down to keep protected, she asked her core, "*Z, what is happening to them?*"

"*The androids have been disabled by Mr. Yousima's command.*"

The nine androids were lying like a bunch of unconscious women sprawled over each other which made Andena stand out as an easy target. As she looked up, she stared right at the barrel of the weapon which he was pointing at her like a madman. As he started to laugh, she understood there was no time to run towards him and slam the weapon out of his hand. She needed to jump into the air to surprise him and hopefully she would be fast enough to kick the gun away. She was happy that her core had noticed her intention to get ready for the jump because her display showed, "*Jump now!*"

Her muscles released the stored power, and she launched herself towards him. At the moment he pulled the trigger, she managed to hit his wrist, and she was sure she could hear the snapping of bones. It was a sickening sound, but she was thankful that the laser beam just missed her by a hair. But as she saw the wall rushing towards her, she realised she had forgotten that she needed room to stop her forward movement.

Not again!

Today there was no door which would open just at the right moment; this time, she knew she would collide at full speed against the very solid wall. She screamed as she crashed into the wall and felt dizzy as she landed on the floor with a loud thump. She had managed to protect her face but her whole body was in pain, and she couldn't breathe at all. Her display was showing all kinds of red lights, but she couldn't focus enough to see what her core was saying.

It was silent for a few seconds until she heard someone charging into the hall shouting, "Mr. Yousima, are you okay?"

Andena recognised Joshua's voice and was pleased she wasn't alone with Mr. Yousima. Mr. Yousima moaned and said with a trembling voice, "I think I've broken my wrist but go and check Miss Danette."

Andena managed to read the text finally on her display, "*Andena your oxygen intake is dropping what is wrong?*"

"*The smack against the wall has slammed the air out of my lungs. I'll recover soon.*"

Andena still couldn't breathe which was a little frightening. It had never had taken so long. She heard the footsteps rush away from her and a second later she heard a loud gasp followed by retching noises. Mr. Yousima shouted, "Joshua! What the fuck is the matter with you?

Tell me how she is!"

Joshua's voice sounded cramped as if he had trouble to speak, "I'm afraid she is dead, sir."

Andena managed to gasp a little air in her lungs and wondered what had happened.

"Nonsense! Quick, get a cabin and fix her up!"

"I'm afraid that is not possible, sir."

She heard him ask annoyed, "What do you mean not possible?"

Joshua whispered, "Because she is missing half of her head."

There was a faint burning smell, and she was shocked when she came to the conclusion that Miss Danette had been hit by the ray of the laser gun. It must have happened when she had kicked it out of Mr. Yousima's hand. Andena felt her heart beating in her mouth; she was responsible for the death of Miss Danette!

"*Your heart rate has doubled. What is happening Andena?*"

Andena felt horrible, and she desperately wanted to get more oxygen into her lungs as she retorted, "*I've killed Miss Danette!*"

"*No, you didn't Andena.*"

Tears were forming behind her closed eyelids as she replied, "*Miss Danette was hit by the laser beam when I kicked the gun out of his hand. I am responsible for her death.*"

"*You didn't pull the trigger, Mr. Yousima did. It was not your fault Andena.*"

Andena felt a little better when she realised that she couldn't have known that by kicking the gun out Mr. Yousima's hand it would accidentally kill Miss Danette. She was terrified as to what would happen to her now. She was a little relaxed that she could get more air into her lungs but her body was aching all over, and she didn't dare to move in case she had broken something.

She heard Mr. Yousima get up with a grunting moan, and as he was walking to Joshua, he grumbled, "That is not possible."

Andena thought it was strange to hear Mr. Yousima trying to mask his gasp. He exclaimed, "Oh! Right! Send Olga a message to get here ASAP and you're going to do exactly what I'm going to tell you. First, bring the hybrid down to the cellars and put her in the metal locker."

Joshua asked placidly, "The one with the magnetic lock?"

"Yes, because she can't force it open. Now pay attention, Joshua. Second, get the final android from Miss Danette's lab and re-render it into Miss Danette's body and bring it down to our lab. I'll take care of Miss Danette's corpse. Capisce?"

She couldn't believe how unfazed Mr. Yousima was giving orders. Joshua retorted with a shaky voice, "Yes, I understand Mr. Yousima."

"Good, here take this. Shoot her if she moves. I'm going to get my wrist fixed."

Joshua meekly replied, "Yes sir."

Andena was shocked knowing that Joshua had the gun. She knew that the only way to survive was to remain perfectly still. She asked her core, "*I assume you can help me to keep my body as still as possible?*"

"*I can fixate all you muscles, but you need to breathe.*"

It was the first time she became aware that her core wasn't as smart as she had presumed it to be, and replied cautiously, "*Well, maybe you can do it in such a way that I still can breathe?*"

"But then you will move your whole body."

"Yes, but as long as I don't move any other part of my body, I'll be fine."

"Okay, let me know if you still can breathe in enough air because you're lying on your chest."

Now she did understand Z's concern and she replied with a little smile, *"Of course Z. I'll make sure I won't suffocate."*

"Do I sense you're smiling?"

"Maybe. Please Z, do it now."

"Okay, fixating your muscles."

Andena noticed the change, and it made her breathing a bit more difficult. She told her core, *"I still can breathe. Thanks, Z."*

She heard Mr. Yousima leave the training hall, and she heard Joshua slowly walking towards her. His breathing was fast, and he softly murmured, "Oh fuck, oh fuck. What a fucking mess!"

Then the door slammed open, and Olga's voice boomed in the hall, "What the hell happened here Joshua? Did you really kill Miss Danette?"

Joshua snorted and spat, "Would I be the one holding a gun at Double Zero?"

She giggled and in an instant her voice changed into a whimpering tone as she said, "Oh fuck! That is sickening! How did this happen?"

"I think that Mr. Yousima accidently shot her when Double Zero kicked the gun away."

Olga groaned a little and said, "Well at least she didn't suffer."

Joshua responded, "Yes but I'm sure I'm going to remember this for a long time. Did you know Mr. Yousima had this gun?"

Olga sighed and said, "No. I find it disturbing he just handed it to you as if it's nothing special."

Joshua affirmed, "These are highly illegal you know."

She grumbled, "Yes I know. Come on quick. Let's move Double Zero on the trolley before she comes to. I don't want you to have to use that gun on her."

Andena regretted what was about to happen because she knew it would be painful but she was still utterly surprised by how her core had managed to make her whole body as rigid as a wooden plank. Only when they had dropped her roughly onto the trolley did a spike of pain shoot through her body but luckily she couldn't move a muscle. Olga exclaimed, "What the fuck happened to her? Why is she as stiff as a board?"

Joshua said, "I don't know. She flew herself against the wall. You should see the recording. It was amazing what she did. It is a pity that she has turned rogue. I'll bet Mr. Yousima wants a detailed report of her core."

They were silent during the trip, and Andena was relieved that her core had fixated her muscles to make her lay still. The only thing she could hope for, that she was strong enough to open that locker.

"*Are you still okay Andena?*"

"*Apart from the painful bruises, I guess I'll survive.*"

She heard Olga saying, "Did you know that someone called Haruz of the Archon is busy re-commissioning all nukes?"

Andena's core asked her, "*What is a nuke?*"

She hadn't heard the term before and said, "*I'm not sure, I think it's a kind of weapon.*"

"Oh shit, really? What's that all about?" Joshua asked.

"Don't know but looking at the numbers there will be enough warheads to destroy the Earth four times."

He gasped and asked, "Fuck! Does Mr. Yousima know?"

"Yes, and he said that we have to go to plan Gamma."

"*That doesn't sound good.*" Andena commented to her core.

"*I agree, but the question is why are those nuclear warheads being re-commissioned.*"

Andena heard them open a door and after that, something heavy was opened with a loud thud. They lifted her from the trolley and before she knew it she felt the cold metal hitting against her back. She heard them moan, and a second later an ear deafening thud made her environment completely dark.

She sensed that she was being dumped into an upright cabin and realised it would be her coffin if she couldn't get out. The way her body was laying against the cold metal was very uncomfortable, and she said to her core, "*Z, I think you can relax my muscles now.*"

Joshua gulped when he received the 3D images of Miss Danette. Her body was drop dead gorgeous, and now it was going to be immortalised. The last android was already in the machine set to be re-rendered. Joshua had calculated how long the total process would take, and he had decided to wait for it. He could already start on the next enjoyable task.

He had received additional instructions from Mr. Yousima, which was to determine which android's body dimensions matched closest to Miss Danette's. That meant he had to look at all the 3D images of the androids which he definitely didn't mind. He had seen their bodies and there were a few who were hot as hell. The only downside was he had to be fast and accurate. He could enjoy looking at the images, but there was no time to have some more fun. Because of Miss Danette's generous cup size, he was able to narrow the selection down to the other androids which had similarly impressive tits.

In the end, there were only two androids left which had a similar build to Miss Danette. Joshua had them all displayed on a screen and marvelled the view. After a leisurely study of the three amazing bodies, Joshua came to the conclusion that android Zero Five was the closest match. He was startled when he heard Mr. Yousima behind him asking, "And Joshua? Which one you think it should be?"

Joshua blushed because he had his hand in his pants and he stuttered, "I, I think android Zero Five, sir."

He felt the blood running to his face, but he realised that Mr. Yousima couldn't have seen it. Mr. Yousima pondered for a while and acted as if he hadn't noticed Joshua's embarrassing situation. He countered, "Hmm, I thought Zero Eight was a better match."

Joshua was shocked by his remark because he couldn't afford to make any mistakes. His fingers flew over the keyboard to add the extra 3D image, and he was very reassured when he saw the result. Relieved he suggested meekly, "She does have the same form, but she is about four inches shorter, sir."

Mr. Yousima conceded reluctantly, "Yes, I see it now. Right. How long will it take to copy the data of the core from Zero Five to an empty core?"

"Not that long, sir. I guess it can be done in fifteen minutes sir, but I assume you will want to use that copy for Miss Danette's android and that means we will need to replace the identity which is a time-consuming process."

Joshua heard Mr. Yousima sigh which was not a good sign, and he quickly said, "I think the android can be ready within the hour, sir."

Mr. Yousima's broad smile gave Joshua a severe case of goose bumps. He hated Mr. Yousima's patronising tone as he said, "You're finally getting it, Joshua. Good, I want you to inform Olga that I want the androids in the lorry at eleven o'clock sharp."

Joshua knew that he would have to work his butt off to get it all done and said with a forced smile, "All will be ready by eleven o'clock, Mr. Yousima."

Joshua sighed because he hated the fact that Mr. Yousima had walked away already without listening to his last sentence. He sincerely hoped that one day Mr. Yousima would miss vital information.

Andena slowly slid down towards the bottom of the cramped place in which she had been dumped. She knew that Z had released her muscles one by one. It was a strange feeling, and it still scared her a little that she had lost control over her body. She knew it was for her protection but nevertheless it was not supposed to happen! She sighed deeply, and she was pleased when her core informed her, "*You're back to normal now. How do you feel?*"

She carefully moved her arms and legs to find out what damage her collision with the wall had caused, and she was just a little sore. Her elbows and her toes were the most affected, but she was sure she hadn't broken any bones. She replied, "*I'm pretty fine, considering I smacked against a wall."*

She recalled what had happened after that and shuddered as she remembered what Joshua had whispered. It was still shocking that Miss Danette had died. She knew it wasn't her fault but deep down she felt guilty that she had rebelled against the horrible man. She drew some comfort from the fact that Miss Danette had died instantly. But still it wouldn't have happened if Mr. Yousima hadn't been out of control. Cold shivers ran down her spine as she recalled the moment that he had tried to grope her breasts.

"Why are you shivering Andena?"

It was nice that her core was paying attention to her, and she needed it because it would make her stay in this dark place a lot more pleasant. She replied, *"I was thinking about Miss Danette's horrible death."*

"Can't you delete the memory?"

Andena chuckled. *"I wish I could."*

There was a long moment before Z responded, *"So, it's like a nightmare. It will take time before you stop thinking about it."*

A tear ran down her cheek as she confided, *"Yes Z, it sure will take some time."*

She inhaled deeply trying to pull herself together. She needed to try and figure a way out of this heavy duty metal locker that Mr. Yousima had insisted she be confined in. It was too dark to see anything, which meant she had to investigate her surroundings by touch. She noticed that every muscle was hurting as she got up which she blamed on being so stupid to launch herself too fast. Although, she wouldn't have been here if she had kicked that gun a fraction later. The gun would have cut her in half!

Meanwhile, she had found the huge magnet which was

holding the door at its place. It was situated at the top of the door.

Andena thought long and hard about how she could tackle the problem and came to the conclusion that she might have a chance if she pushed against the door with both legs.

She pressed herself with her back against the back of the locker and moved herself up to the top of the locker. She applied as much power as possible to push against the door, but nothing happened. Her core warned her, "*Andena, you are at your maximum power. Your joints can't take any more pressure.*"

Her arms were just too short to reach the door as well, but she could push with her palms at her knees, but still the door didn't move.

She realised she was trapped.

In frustration, she stampeded once with her boot against the locked door, and she was shocked by how loud it sounded. Somewhat dispirited Andena let herself slide down again and to her dismay, the core was warning her, "*I measure a fast decline of oxygen Andena. I advise you not to try it again.*"

She instantly understood she had used too much oxygen when she had tried to open the door. She sighed and chided to herself, "That was sooooo smart! You stupid bitch!"

"*Who are you calling a stupid bitch?*" her core asked.

Andena rolled her eyes knowing she couldn't get away without an explanation, and she said realising she could just speak, "Z. I was cursing myself."

"*Oh okay. You think you're a stupid bitch?*"

"Hell yes! I have used a lot of oxygen trying to open this locker against my better judgement."

She was anxious to know to what percentage the oxygen had dropped and asked, "Can you tell me the percentage of the oxygen?"

Her display showed, "*Oxygen level: 19.197 % Andena. That is very low!*"

She was a little relieved there was still some oxygen left and reassured her core, "I can survive on that Z."

She knew she had to sit down and try to drop down her oxygen intake as much as possible. She knew she could survive on oxygen levels down to nineteen point one percent, and she was hoping that there was a little air circulation which would keep the levels just high enough. She tried to get comfortable and pushed against the door and to her amazement she felt it gave away a little.

Apparently she could warp the door a bit at the bottom because it was only kept locked at the top. She wondered if she could push with one leg against the door and get some fresh air into the locker.

Andena was pondering whether she could save some energy if Z would fixate her muscles when she had forced the opening with her leg. She moved her back into the corner, and she placed her foot against the door. She slowly increased the pressure until she felt cool air coming in.

It gave her hope that she would find a way out, and she asked Z, "Z, can you fixate my muscles in my left leg? I've managed to force the door open a little to get some fresh air in."

"*I have fixated them Andena.*"

Andena stopped pushing with her muscles and realised that her leg felt strange. She didn't think that she would ever get used to the fact that her body had changed so dramatically.

"*I register an increase of the oxygen level. Forcing the door is having the desired effect. I reckon it will get to normal level in thirty minutes.*"

She was happy that she could survive for a lot longer in the locker and said with a sigh, "Well at least I've extended my life for a little while."

"*What are you going to do now Andena?*"

"I'm not sure Z."

It was a weird and scary realisation for her that she might end up sitting here for a long time. She knew that she had to try and conserve her energy. Sleeping was one of the solutions, but she didn't know if she could, after the horrible and shocking events of today. It was the first moment she'd had to focus solely on her inner self, but she knew she would go crazy if she started to think about what had happened to her; it was too scary, and there were too many unknowns which would keep running around in her head. The only thing she could do at this moment was to accept how it was, hoping there would be someone out there who could explain it all to her someday; assuming of course, that she survived. It was the only way of dealing with this bizarre situation.

She was not surprised when she read Z's comment, "*You'd better conserve your energy Andena.*"

"I know Z, I know. I guess I have to try to go to sleep and hope that it all will be fine when I wake up."

The chance that everything was going to be fine was very small especially if this lunatic Haruz planned on using those nuclear warheads. She knew he was the head of security for the Archon, and if he was losing his marbles, he could become a very dangerous man who had the power to destroy the Earth in seconds.

It was frustrating she couldn't do anything other than

wait. She had to calm down because she was aware she was using too much energy.

Z responded, "*It is the best solution at this moment. Sleep well Andena.*"

Andena had to laugh.

"*What is funny Andena?*"

As she closed her eyes, she said, "This metal case is not a comfortable bed really. Sleeping is going to be a challenge."

"*I understand. Let me rephrase; I hope you can sleep.*"

She knew that Z said it to put her more at ease, and she replied, "Thanks, Z. I'll try."

She was thinking about ways to calm herself down, and she was pleased when a very simple exercise that she had learned from her Martial Arts teacher popped into her mind. She focused on her breathing while she was trying to bring her heart rate down by using the mental imprint her teacher had taught her. She felt that the exercise was having its effect, and her train of thought became less erratic. Her mind gradually slowed down until she fell asleep.

CHAPTER TWENTY

The sheet caressed his back as someone next to him had turned. The faint pleasant smell of perfume made him inhale more deeply, and he blew the air out again with a satisfied sigh. He felt a warm hand slowly moving down towards his naked butt and wasn't surprised when the fingers squeezed it softly. It felt amazing, and he truly enjoyed the attention.

His hand was resting on a firm thigh, and he gently moved up, caressing the amazing soft inner side of the toned leg. As he got higher, the skin became softer and softer. He turned on his side to give himself better manoeuvrability, and he slid his hand up a little more before he slowly moved down again. He marvelled at the soft moans coming from her, and he moved up a little closer towards her centre of pleasure. He liked to tease her, knowing that eventually she would take control and straddle him. Lunn thought it was fun; trying to figure out when the explosion of lust and appetite would turn Alice into a wild animal.

When she had pounced on him last night, it had been mind-blowing. They had made love passionately until they had both collapsed into a dreamless sleep.

His whole body was now pressing against her naked body which made his desire grow. Alice slowly turned towards him and kissed him softly on the lips. She purred, "I never thought I could wake up that nicely."

Lunn chuckled softly and retorted, "I never thought I would like to have my butt squeezed."

Her laugh was lazy as she climbed on top of him. The sensation was intense, and Lunn wanted to bury himself in her. His urge to move faster was strong but her hand was placed firmly on his hip forcing him to slow down. Her warm voice purred, "I love a slow build up."

Lunn loved to roam his hands over her luscious body, managing to coach some encouraging moans from her. He felt Alice speeding up the rhythm and the heat of their bodies made them sweat. There was a thin layer of sweat between them which made the movements even more sensual. He was shocked when his phone started to play a tune which he knew he couldn't ignore. He exclaimed, "Oh no! Shit!"

Alice whimpered when he stopped and hissed, "NO! Keep on going! Ignore the bloody thing!"

He knew it was the financier, and he had to take the call. He kissed Alice in her neck and said, "Sorry Alice. I have to take this call."

As he quickly stepped out the bed to pick up the phone, Alice stormed into the bathroom with a frustrating and angry growl. He knew he was in trouble, and it would take a lot of explaining before she would accept what had just happened. He answered with a hoarse voice, "Lunn speaking."

The financier replied placidly, "Get your skates on, they are on the plateau."

Feeling relieved that it was the important call he had been waiting for, he asked, "When did they arrive?"

"They are getting out of the lorry now. So I reckon you'll have an hour or two."

"Perfect. I'll let you know when we're about to engage."

"No! You can't contact me! I'll know when you've succeeded."

Taken aback by the ferocity of the reply, Lunn grunted, "That's fine with me too. Speak to you later."

He hung up and decided to call John immediately. John answered right after the first ring with the question, "Showtime?"

Lunn had to laugh and asked, "Aren't you a little too eager?"

John chuckled nervously and confessed, "Yeah, maybe."

He liked that John was frank with him, and he said, "Yes, it's Showtime. See you at HQ."

"Okay, later."

He disconnected the call and realised that the day finally had come. He was startled when he heard Alice ask, "Showtime?"

His heart started to beat faster when he saw the curious look on her beautiful face. He marvelled at her athletic figure which was perfectly shaped by her feminine curves. He got up and kissed her on her lips and confessed, "I am going to come clean with you because I don't want to have any secrets tainting what we have."

Her eyes burned straight into his, and she inquired with an angry voice, "Who the hell was so important?"

Without saying a word Lunn grabbed her hand and guided her gently into the shower. As he was soaping her back, he said, "The man who called is our financier. He is the one who is paying your salary."

She snorted and chided, "Still not good enough to ruin our perfect morning!"

Lunn continued, "We were waiting for the right moment to test the most sophisticated weapon mankind has ever made and now it's going to happen."

Alice's voice was trembling when she exclaimed, "Lunn! Not again! Why wasn't I involved? For heaven's sake! I'm your bloody head of security!"

He knew that this was not the time for excuses and said, "Because this project of five billion credits was conducted only by the financier, John and me."

She gasped and asked in disbelief, "Five billion credits? What on Earth can cost that much?"

He turned off the shower and said, "Well it isn't on Earth."

Lunn cupped her face gently between his hands and said seriously, "Alice I can't explain it here. I'll show you as soon as we are at the headquarters. We better hurry because John hates to wait."

Joshua stretched his back several times. His muscles were stiff from the intense and stressful work he had being doing. However, thankfully, he had managed to get the android ready on time. He hadn't been able to stop yawning as he was sitting in the back of the lorry. Olga who was sitting opposite him, laughed and teased, "Need your beauty sleep?"

He grumbled and snapped back, "Next time you can replace the text in a couple of thousand files."

He saw Olga thinking about it, and her eyes were getting bigger when she realised what he had done. She chuckled and asked, "You had to change the identity of a core?"

He nodded because he had to yawn again.

"There are tools for that, you know," she said with a smirk.

He tried not to raise his voice because he hated her patronising way of speaking as if he was one of the dumbest and he answered with his teeth clenched, "Yes and after that I had to manually change files the tools can't change."

He saw she had opened her mouth to say something but to his relief, she decided not to say anything more during the trip.

His back was sore from staring at a screen for too long, and he was pleased he could lean back against the padded backrest. He closed his eyes and tried to relax until they reached the plateau. His mind drifted back to when he had placed the core in the android. It was exciting to watch the android change from a lifeless body into a carbon copy of Miss Danette. He had instructed the android to run in a little circle to recalibrate the balance parameters, and he thought it was fascinating to see a naked android running around. He had to admit that the rendering was extremely close and true-to-nature. He resisted the temptation to touch the beautifully shaped android because he knew it would break the magical spell. The rendered skin was as cold as a dead body which would spoil it completely.

He thought getting the android dressed would be the most rewarding part of his task, but he was quite disappointed that the android was dressed in a few moments. He chided himself that he could have given it the instruction to dress slowly.

The sudden jerk of the lorry startled him, and he collided against the synthetic copy of Danette's body. He was surprised by how soft the body felt and to regain his balance he had to put his hand on the leg to push him straight.

It all felt so realistic!

He heard Olga giggle, and he knew she would tease him about this. He already dreaded the humiliations that she would subject him to. He was totally taken aback when she said, "It's amazing how real those bodies feel don't you think?"

He didn't know what to say and just replied, "Yes, they do."

Her face grew gloomy, and she shuddered when she said, "The only thing that I find totally creepy is that their skin is cold, and it feels like you're touching a corpse."

His mind wandered thinking how he would solve that problem and quickly came to the conclusion that heating an android's body would drain the power source too fast. He joked, "They wouldn't last longer than a few hours."

"What?"'

Joshua suddenly realised she had missed the link and said quickly, "If we were to heat the android's skin."

Olga snorted but before she had time to say anything the doors opened and Mr. Yousima yelled, "Right, get out and form a straight line parallel with the lorry."

Joshua knew he had to get out as fast as possible and

give room to the androids. As he jumped from the compartment, he barely had time to make way for the girls.

He saw Olga doing the same, and he knew that Mr. Yousima had anticipated his clumsiness in getting out of the way. Mr. Yousima nearly growled as he spat, "Next time, get out the instant we stop. Capisce?"

Olga and Joshua said at the same time, "Yes, Mr. Yousima."

He continued, "You two are here to fix any damages the androids might suffer during the training."

"Yes, Mr. Yousima."

Joshua was curious as to what kind of training Mr. Yousima had planned for the androids. He looked at the row of droids while using his hands to keep the sunlight from shining in his eyes and was jealous of the fact, that Mr. Yousima was wearing sunglasses. He was impressed how the high-pitched voice of Mr. Yousima was strong enough to address the ten androids. He said, "Today the surface you will be training on is covered with stones, rocks, and pebbles. You are going to run around within the area indicated by the cones. Avoid the rocks as much as possible. Start!"

Joshua's mouth fell open when the androids started to run neatly counter-clockwise. It all went well, and only a few skidded a little when they had stepped on a pebble. After a few minutes, Mr. Yousima shouted, "Stop and get back into the initial straight line at the lorry."

"Joshua and Olga get the rifles out and hand them to the androids," he commanded.

Olga and Joshua rushed to the truck, and he asked her in a whisper, "Did you organise that?"

She nodded and handed him one of the rifles. It was

heavy, and he was shocked when he unlocked the bullet chamber.

The rifles were real and loaded!

In five minutes all the androids were equipped with a deadly weapon and Joshua was disgusted by the childishly covetous look on Mr. Yousima's face. He wouldn't be surprised if the fat ugly man had a boner hidden in those enormous pants of his. He knew Mr. Yousima had a sick mind, but he stayed with Bionex because he was fascinated by the mind-blowing technical stunts they had achieved. This stupid charade, consisting of ten androids carrying a weapon, was not what he had expected Bionex's top achievement to be. Joshua knew he had to endure it for now and decided to sit in the truck hoping he could be able to shut his eyes for a few minutes.

Alice was still pretty angry that Lunn had decided to take that call. She had been *that* close to an amazingly mind-blowing climax, and she still felt the little contractions with each step that she took. She also knew that he had no choice but to answer the call, especially now that she knew how much was at stake.

But still!

She felt the anger simmering in her body which had been mostly tempered by his gentle caressing in the shower, and she had to admit that she respected his gentle and frank way telling her the truth. She knew it was his way of letting her know who he was: plain without a gold rim. She could definitely live with that. With a sly smile, she had made up her mind: tonight was going to be *her* night. She had to stifle a giggle when she saw the apprehensive expression on Lunn's face. She squeezed his hand and asked with a sultry voice, "Everything okay, Lunn?"

She loved the way he perked up, and she was blown away by his genuine smile. He was so wonderful! The rumble in his chest made her weak at the knees, and she nearly missed what he had said, "Yes, if you will forgive me for what happened this morning."

"Hmm, you *are* asking a lot, my dear. Let me think about it for a few days."

His eyes grew big, as he asked with a small voice, "A few days?"

"Hmm, maybe I need a week or two."

"You're teasing me," he chided with a hint of doubt in his voice.

As they walk into the headquarters Alice knew she had to put his mind at ease; He would need his full attention for the important test. She kissed him on the lips and purred, "I forgive you, but next time I'll tie you to the bed and keep you begging for mercy for three days."

She loved his laugh and the twinkle in his eyes reassured her that he was a happy man. He raised his eyebrows and lowered his voice in a daring growl, "Oh, so you like to punish your naughty boys."

She slapped him on his butt and said seriously, "Speaking of toys for the boys. You owe me a detailed explanation for this massively expensive toy you've got."

"It's not a toy," he asserted playfully.

Alice rolled her eyes and told him sternly, "Stop procrastinating, boy."

He sniggered and said, "All right, all right. What you're going to witness is a genius of a weapon designed by my pal John, with a little help from me. Around the Earth, there is a special ring of three and a half thousand nanosatellites. It is a smart system which can deliver an electromagnetic pulse to any place on Earth."

Alice asked, "Electromagnetic pulse? You mean an EMP which disables electronic devices?"

Lunn confirmed, "Yes."

Now Alice understood the grandness of it and asked, "You mean you can deliver an EMP charge at any precise location?"

John had stepped into the corridor where they still were talking, and he said, "Yes and we need to do it soon before they leave."

As they walked to the control room, she asked, "They? What is the target, guys?"

"You know about Bionex's androids?" asked Lunn.

She knew enough about the androids because she had helped Miss Danette carry the parts to her laboratory. She was wondering how they could pinpoint the whereabouts of the androids. Alice nodded and asked, "You can be that accurate?"

Lunn chuckled and retorted, "Right at this moment they are practicing at the Bangly plateau."

Alice gasped and whispered, "A perfect moment to disable them all at the same time. That's why you had to take that call this morning, didn't you?"

She felt the anger which was still there deep inside, melting away as she saw him looking a bit uncomfortable as he said, "Yes, I had made that agreement with the financier."

John was nervously tapping on the desk and asked, "How much power shall we apply? Two megawatts?"

Lunn shrugged his shoulders and asked, "Will that be enough?"

John's face turned into a witty smile as he chortled, "Your phone would explode in your hand if it were to receive that much power."

Alice wanted to be sure that Bionex suffered a major loss and said, "As long as those androids are damaged beyond repair."

John checked some screens on the panels, and as he pointed at the red button he asked, "Alice are you willing to push the red button to blow a few androids to smithereens?"

Alice was eager to deliver a death blow to Bionex, and purred, "Yes, please!"

She stretched her fingers and slowly pushed down the button without any hesitation. A little beep was audible, but nothing else happened for a few seconds.

Alice found the fact that the destruction of the androids should be signified only by a small beep, to be something of an anti-climax. She had expected there to be more drama and just as she was about to ask what had happened, the lights went dark for a brief moment.

Both John and Lunn shouted, "Wow! What the hell was that?"

Lunn sprinted to a control panel at the side, and he exclaimed, "There is a power outage cascade which started at Bionex!"

John checked a few screens and commented, "Strange, it looks like something at Bionex has triggered an enormous power surge. It wasn't the EMP because it had nearly no effect on the county at all."

Alice asked, "And the androids on the plateau?"

John said, "Let me get a visual from one of the satellites."

With a few swift clicks on a keyboard, John had a

reasonably sharp picture of the plateau. It showed the lorry and a number of bodies scattered over a confined area. Alice counted eleven bodies one of which was considerable larger.

She said with a quivering voice, "Can you zoom in on the larger body?"

As soon as Alice saw the next picture she exclaimed, "That is Mr. Yousima! What happened to him?"

Lunn replied, "It seemed that he was not completely free of electronics in his body."

John uttered dryly, "I assume our mission was successful."

Alice had to laugh and said happily, "Extremely successful indeed."

Lunn smiled and said, "Let's celebrate our success with lunch. My treat."

Meleda was only a little startled when her screen had suddenly turned dark. She knew that the EMP had destroyed her remote-control camera.

She was in a state of euphoria as her screen flickered for a few moments before giving her a clear video feed of the plateau again. Her little trick to protect another drone in an EMP durable case had worked as planned. This time, she could get much closer to see what damage the EMP had inflicted without being noticed. She steered the drone skillfully towards the smoking bodies hoping she could avoid a close up of the hybrid's dead body. The fact that she had indirectly ordered Andena's death made her feel queasy. Meleda was stunned to see Mr. Yousima's ghastly looking corpse, and she had trouble keeping the drone under control because of her shaking hands.

His face was barely recognisable mainly because the top part of his head was missing also his torso had become at least twice as big.

She quickly moved away from his body and scanned for the hybrid, but couldn't find her. Meleda had passed all the androids which all had familiar faces, and she was stunned to note that the face of the last android resembled their trainer, Miss Danette. She lowered the drone to have a better look and to make sure that the lookalike was an android. For a second Meleda thought she saw the android's head twitching but after staring for a long moment concluded that she must have imagined it. The melted skin which had formed puddles next to the body was proof enough for Meleda. It made her wonder what had happened to the real Miss Danette and the hybrid girl. Both were not there, and she wondered if she could find any information via Bionex's network. Meleda was shaken out of her thoughts when she heard a heavy gun shot, and she realised she had to move the drone away as quickly as possible.

Another shot sounded through the speakers, and the screen went blank again. Meleda pushed the red button on the remote control hoping the self-destruct of the drone would still do its job. She sighed with relief and realised the EMP test had been a huge success, but she was curious as to what had happened to Miss Danette and the hybrid.

She tried to connect to Bionex and was surprised to find the link was completely dead. She ran a quick trace and found out that all the hubs were fine including the last one before the trace entered the building.

Her log showed a power outage just after the EMP, but the Bionex building was completely dark as if everything had been shut down. She wondered if the death of Mr. Yousima had anything to do with it. Somewhat disillusioned she shut down her own system and went to the kitchen. She needed to eat; something she couldn't afford to skip anymore.

The gentle waves washed over her feet, and she loved the feeling of the wet sand between her toes. The water was refreshing, and the warm breeze was playing with her hair. The moonlight was enough for her to see where she was walking. She loved being here and tonight the waves contained the special plankton which lit up as the waves broke on the shore.

She had never felt so connected with nature, and she decided to have a swim. Completely naked she darted into the breaking waves, and she squealed a little when suddenly a bigger wave surprised her. The water was cool, and her body tingled all over by the time she had swum for a few minutes. Every time she batted her hand into the water the plankton lit up, and it fascinated her how much light the little creatures could create.

The waves had brought her back to the shore, and while she was lying there, she loved how the waves were caressing her body. The gentle breeze cooled her, and the waves started to feel like a warm liquid blanket. Her body responded to the cool breeze and the waves crashing against her felt wonderful. She could feel the water flowing between her legs. While resting on her elbows, facing the oncoming waves, she truly enjoyed the slow build up. The sea was gentle, and wouldn't bring her to a level she wanted, but she didn't care for now. Her eyes were closed, excited by the fact that she had no idea how big the next wave would be. A dark, warm voice startled her, "What a wonderful sight; the sea, the moon, and an enchanting water nymph being caressed by the waves."

With her heart in her mouth, she turned her face to see who was talking to her. She saw a tall man standing just a few feet away from her. In the light of the moon, she could make out his strong build and his long hair was kept from his face with a piece of fabric. She didn't like his posture, for he exuded a dangerous vibe and as she moved back into the sea, she said with a strong voice, "I'm not sure I'm a water nymph."

"Oh? So why do you choose the sea instead of the land?"

She didn't like his question at all, and she moved further away from him and replied, "Perhaps I like to be alone."

His chuckle radiated deep from his chest, and he bellowed over the waves, "No, you don't. You seek comfort which I'm going to give you."

She knew she had to find a way of escaping, and she swam further into the sea hoping he would give up after a while. To her dismay, he stayed and followed her towards the beach as she was swimming away from him. She knew he could see her because every disturbance in the water caused the plankton to light up. It was sad that the wonderful and rare occasion having the plankton light up the scene was now her worst enemy. The only way to have a reasonable chance of escaping the man was to swim to the bottom where there was no plankton. It was worth trying even though swimming under water would wear her out. She knew it was her only chance because the man knew that eventually she had to come out the sea. She swam for a bit, and he followed her until she dived down to the bottom and swam as fast as possible diagonally towards the shore. The noise of the breaking waves was close, and when she moved up for her desperate air, her head bumped into something solid. As she looked up, she saw the man towering above her. Before she could do anything he grabbed her arm and tried to hoist her up onto her feet but she kept her legs bent, ready to kick him in his groin.

He grunted annoyed when he saw she didn't want to cooperate and tried to grab her other arm as well. Still out of breath, she wriggled violently to keep her body and arm out of his reach. She finally saw the right moment to kick him in his groin, but somehow he managed to turn his body away. She cried out from the pain when he stabbed her leg with a short knife, and she knew she was doomed. The salt of the water was biting in her wound and the intense pain completely paralysed her leg. He dragged her out the water and dumped her on the warm sand while keeping his eyes on her. His ragged voice gave her the shivers when he said, "Don't even try to run away."

With one swift move, he removed his loincloth, and she trembled with fear when she saw his crooked face knowing that he intended to rape her. As he kneeled down, she screamed and with her last effort, she tried to push him away with her other leg. As her foot made contact with his chest, it instantly lit up into the most intense red colour. He roared trying to take her foot off his chest, but she gathered all her strength to push him away as far as she could.

With a loud yell she pushed her foot forward and to her utter relief, he flew away into the sea with a deafening explosion.

There was another extremely loud bang, and Andena screamed again.

The cool and fresh air made her more awake, and gradually she realised she was sitting in the metal locker. Her leg was still not right, but then she remembered her core had 'locked' it.

A little startled she saw the text appearing in front of her eyes, "*Andena, did you have another nightmare?*"

She took a deep breath and realised she was still a bit shaky being woken up so suddenly, she said, "Yes Z. I think I need a few moments to wake up properly."

She sighed, unhappy about the fact that she still had this strange computer core, stashed away somewhere in her body. She was still in a strange mood knowing she had to ask her core to unlock her leg.

It amazed her when it asked, "*Shall I release your muscles? You might feel a bit better.*"

Her voice was still a bit hoarse from her screaming as she agreed, "Yes please."

She felt a strange sensation of discomfort as her leg slowly slid down and at that moment she realised that the heavy door of the locker was gone! Only then did she realise that there was a strange orange-red glow lighting the room which could mean there had been a power cut. It would explain why she was able to open the locker.

Still very stiff from sitting in a cramped locker for a long time Andena tried to get up which was much easier than she had thought it would be. Apparently her muscles were able to deal with those situations a lot better now. Andena felt very uneasy because it was extremely silent and she couldn't put her finger on what was so eerie about the place. She asked her core, "Is it really so silent here or am I deaf?"

"*No you're not deaf, and there's hardly any background noise.*"

While she was carefully looking around, she gave further thought to the silence. She sensed that she was missing something that she would normally completely ignore.

She recalled the huge bangs which had woken her and now everything was out. She gasped when she realised that the air circulation had stopped. Her core confirmed her suspicion when she read the text, "*There's no air circulation Andena. You need to leave this building soon.*"

It was one of the vital parts of the infrastructure which normally functioned no matter what. The only explanation was that the infrastructure had been destroyed! The huge ear deafening explosion must have been a small nuclear bomb planted by Haruz. She knew he had to be stopped! She asked Z, "Any indication why it has stopped?"

"*No, I can't find any clues, except that there's no active power source.*"

"Do you think it could have been caused by a bomb?"

Her core responded a few moments later, "*It might. Do you suspect something strange has happened?*"

"I think it might be Haruz."

"*Can you tell me why you are convinced it is Haruz?*"

"You want proof?"

"*You can't build a case on assumptions.*"

She sighed and said, "I guess you're right. I need to investigate."

Meanwhile, Andena had found some normal clothes and a black hoody to hide her vibrant hair. Completely dressed and ready for her mission she looked at herself in a mirror. There was a faint light which shone eerily on her face. Z responded, "*You've hidden your hair.*"

She giggled and said, "Yes, I don't want to stand out."

"*You're specially trained for secret missions. It shouldn't be that difficult for you anymore.*"

Then it dawned on her that she was a member of Lunn's group, and she asked, "Do you see me as a rebel?"

"*Yes, Andena. You're fighting against the Archon. You are a rebel.*"

She giggled and shook her head as she sneaked out of the room, but she had no idea where to go. She leant against the wall, in a barely lit corridor, wondering how to get out the building. She asked her core, "Z can you guide me out of this place?"

She smiled when her display showed a flashing arrow indicating that she should go left into the corridor. The text appeared, "*Did you like it that I called you a rebel?*"

As she jogged towards the door, she let the words spin through her mind a few times and came to the conclusion, she did! She realised that she needed more time to accept fully that her life had changed so drastically. Her interaction with her core was still a little intrusive but for now, it would do especially if she wanted to complete her mission and she retorted, "*Hmm, yes it sounds all right.*"

The building was spooky because it was completely abandoned and totally silent. She picked up her pace to get out into the open air as soon as possible.

To be continued......

ABOUT THE AUTHOR

Kin Asdi (aka Victor Vergeer), was born in 1964 and raised in the Netherlands. He is happily married and lives with his wife and teenage daughter in a village on the outskirts of The Hague, the Netherlands. He studied Sonology (the science of sound) at the Royal Conservatoire in The Hague where he learned to appreciate a wide range of music and other creative arts that involved the use of sound. His particular talent was for human interfaces, something he specialises in even today; interfaces being the creative link between man and technology. His passion for computers and programming began as a boy when his father introduced him to the world of bits and bytes. Today he earns his living as an HR programmer working with interfaces and getting the technology to meet the needs of the customer!

In his free time, he has always been involved with

creative activities varying from building speakers and furniture, to creating coloured light objects using LEDs and electronics. He likes to create unique objects, and constantly seeks new challenges to push back the boundaries of his own knowledge and satisfy his curiosity about the world.

Reading a lot of indie-published books made him aware of the 'new' way of writing and publishing.

It was then that he discovered how much he enjoys writing stories: something which provides another outlet for a creative mind. He was surprised to discover that, for him, writing is both demanding and relaxing. The differences between programming and creative writing are actually surprisingly small. Whether you are writing a program or a story, you need a structured framework; a beginning, a middle and an end, all of which has to flow and make sense for it to work.

Being able to put his imagination to work and express his ideas in words has opened a new chapter in his life. He has published two young adult sci-fi adventure novels and a new adult sci-fi romance in the last two years. He finds it very rewarding that others like to read what he has written, which gives him the encouragement to continue to explore the world of creative writing.

Kin Asdi's webpage : http://www.kinasdi.com
Twitter: @kin_asdi
Facebook: https://www.facebook.com/kin.asdi
Other books:
The adventures of KAD   http://mybook.to/KAD1
The origin of KAD   http://mybook.to/KAD2
Something New Every Day http://mybook.to/new